HYS
TER
ICAL

HYSTERICAL

A NOVEL

AMBER DEAN

ISBN (hardcover) 979-8-9940089-0-4
ISBN (paperback) 979-8-9940089-1-1

First paperback edition December 2025

Book design by Christian Storm | Stormhausen Design

To my husband, Nael.

Thank you for loving me through every meltdown, plot spiral, and caffeine binge — and for your remarkable ability to ignore the fact that I now know seventeen different ways to hide a body.

HYS TER ICAL

1

I'M LOADING MY NECESSARY belongings, my cat, diary and spider plant, into the Uber courtesy of my mother's credit card. I've had it with this guy. Fucking Ukrainian DJ I met at Camp Bisco three Summers ago who I couldn't shake. The air is crisp. That perfect Fall chill that makes you feel invigorated and excited for what comes next. This guy's biggest mistake was not giving me space. That, and he was a child who wanted to live in this suspended juvenile existence of cohabitational monogamy that even he admitted would never lead to marriage. Women need space. Women need real commitment, especially if monogamy is on the table. At least I do.

Man-children, though, can't give you that. They lack resilience and need constant reassurance, and it's not entirely their fault. Society raised them this way—weak, unstable little boys rewarded for never growing up. The longer they stay in this fuck-boy, prepubescent state, the higher the societal rewards they reap. As long as boys will be boys is an acceptable pass - boys will never become men.

He wasn't just afraid of commitment. He leeched off me. He humiliated me. He drained me. He tried to drive a wedge between me and the one person I actually love.

The story started with a bang. An upstate New York music festival hosted by The Disco Biscuits. Tinsel and I were inseparable that summer, sharing cheap tequila, inside jokes, and tangled limbs in borrowed sleeping bags. It was magic.

Then came the guys. They approached us near the main stage. Tinsel liked one, so I took the other. That's what good friends do. They entertain the side character so the lead can shine. We found out they had press passes, which got us backstage. We smoked a blunt near Wiz Khalifa, dropped MDMA, and ended the night in their tent. It was fun. Brief. Disposable.

By morning, it was back to me and Tinsel, the way it should be.

A few weeks later, I moved into a small apartment near Fordham in the Bronx. That's when the DJ texted to say he was moving to the city. Tinsel lit up.

"You're meant for each other," she said. "He's your soulmate."

She knows me better than anyone. So I believed her.

He moved his turntables into my living room. Then his clothes. Then his toothbrush. We never talked about him living there, it just… happened. He told me he'd never marry me, so I wasn't sure why he was acting like we were building a life. But I didn't question it. I didn't want to disappoint Tinsel. She was so sure. So excited. I wanted her to be proud of me.

He taught me to DJ. Called me his muse. Said we'd perform together, like a team. I fell for it. For him. For the fantasy of being seen.

We moved into a Bushwick loft, started performing at clubs, raves, warehouse parties. But then he began sending me on "emergency" errands mid-set—fetching chargers, running messages, retrieving USBs. Photos from our gigs never had me in them. Then he said people complained about my transitions. Said I was dragging him down.

He asked me to stick to making pre-recorded mixes, said that's where I really shined. When I said no, I caught him stealing files off my laptop. When I confronted him, he exploded. Accused me of being ungrateful. Said I owed him everything—my taste in music, my style, my stage presence.

Tinsel didn't think it was a big deal.

"That's the price of dating an artist," she said. "You should be flattered to be someone's muse."

He loved that I was still on my parents' health insurance. Taught me how to game the system. Told me what to say to doctors to score prescriptions. I filled them. He sold them. Said it was the least I could do since he paid the rent. As if he hadn't already bled me dry.

One day, I found him flipping through my journal, tearing up my Polaroids. The ones I take of my friends. They're just candid pictures, artsy. Nothing weird. He completely misunderstood them, like everything else about me. "You're a batshit crazy lesbo," he spat. "Sick in the head."

The next day, I walked into the apartment and found him alone with Tinsel. She said she'd come to see me. He told her I was home. Then he started planting ideas. Said I was obsessed with her.

Tinsel didn't buy it. She knew he was jealous. He couldn't handle how close we were. How I always chose her. That's when I knew I had to leave.

Now, I sit in the back of a rattling Uber, my cat in her carrier on my lap, watching the city smear past the window as we cross the Williamsburg Bridge. For the past month, I've been quietly plotting my exit from the DJ. I posted a Craigslist ad that read: *Twenty-something girl and her cat in need of housing. Fine art model. Quiet, clean, loves to cook, and DTF. Can pay $500/month cash.*

I got a lot of responses, most of them useless. But I landed on a Wall Street guy. Shockingly respectful, predictably addicted to cocaine. He has an empty apartment in the Montrose building in Midtown. Apparently, he broke up with his girlfriend and moved in with his mistress in Bumblefuck Brooklyn. A bit messy, sure, but lucky for me, he's still paying rent on the empty apartment and is happy to offset the cost.

I figure he's got a savior complex. Loves the fantasy of rescuing me from a messy breakup—playing white knight to the poor, broken girl. Maybe he reads dark romance and sees himself as the morally gray hero of his own story. Most men like the idea of keeping me tucked away in their apartment, ready to fuck whenever the mood hits. One thing's for sure: Wall Street guys hoard three things—money, pussy, and coke.

2

NEW YORKERS LOVE TO say the city's cleaned up since the '80s, when the Queens-Midtown Tunnel greeted you with "Abandon All Hope Ye Who Enter Here" smeared in blood-red graffiti, and it felt like prophecy. Sure, Times Square's now a cartoon hellscape of Elmos and LED billboards, and Bushwick is filled with almond-milk cafés and vegan art collectives run by hipsters who sneak off on weekends to shame-eat Ramen Burgers at Smorgasburg.

But the cleanup was cosmetic, not curative, like trying to scrub out a bloodstain with organic cleaner. The stain's still there; it just reeks of lavender and vinegar now, a distraction from the deeper rot.

Beneath the gloss, the city still pulses with sex, drugs, and filth. If you want it, it's not hard to find. There's a sex club under a Ridgewood laundromat where girls in pleated skirts let finance bros choke them out while trance music pulses overhead. There's a white guy in head-to-toe Alexander Wang and Supreme sneakers loitering near Grand Street, selling baggies of something he calls "Fairy Dust". Snort it and you might see your dead exes.

The filth never left. We just filtered it through a tasteful Instagram preset to make it palatable.

I came here in 2010 to study psychology at Fordham University in the Bronx. If you want to relive the 80s in NYC, the Bronx can make that happen. It's the borough time forgot, and by time, I mean white politicians and racist city planners actively chose to create segregation when designing the subway system and boroughs. Like look at the glaring absence of a subway connecting the Bronx directly to Queens, despite their proximity. Traveling between them takes an hour, compared to the 27 minutes it takes to cross Manhattan. Cutting off transit cuts off opportunity, and the streets tell the story: broken car windows, gaunt faces outside the AIDS clinic, and teenagers throwing threats like knives. It's all so fucking bleak. Fordham was no escape. I transferred there expecting intellectual rigor—visionary professors, lively debates on ethics and the collapse of modern civilization. Instead, it was underpaid grad students and ancient, sexist faculty clinging to tenure. College has been the most expensive disappointment of my life.

My Uber pulls up to The Montrose, a sleek, dark-gray building with polished double doors. The driver helps unload my bags, mostly black trash bags stuffed with clothes, while the doorman appears with a hotel-style trolley. It's been half an hour since I left the DJ, and already my life feels lighter. Inside, the lobby is warm and plush, with velvet couches circling an electric fireplace. I show the doorman my key and tell him I'm staying with Mr. Wall Street in apartment 736.

When I first met up with Mr. Wall Street, we agreed to go to the Apple Store in Grand Central Station. He needed a new MacBook charger. I liked that it was public, neutral territory. Safe. And choosing somewhere *he* needed to go made me seem easygoing, thoughtful. The kind of girl worth keeping around. I wanted him to want me. To see me.

I was wearing tight grey skinny pants from Uniqlo, 3-inch black and brown suede stilettos, and a grey vintage 90s blouse. My dark hair was done as it usually is - in this purposely messy updo that suggests to men I just had sex, but women assume I spent hours shaping it. I had black liquid eyeliner on my upper lid in a 50s cat eye style, highlighting my big green eyes. He replied to my Craigslist ad with a photo of himself in front of some tacky faux-medieval castle upstate. I joked about his apparent love of castles; he volleyed back with wit, and we agreed to meet. I arrived early, positioned at the top of the grand staircase, phone out, looking bored. When he arrived, I was pleasantly surprised. He was better-looking in person—thick, salt-and-pepper hair, heroin-chic skinny, and impeccably Iranian. It's true what they say, the suit really does make the man. And god, I felt my G-string dampen as I greeted him with a hug and ran my hands over that Berluti masterpiece.

"Shall we see the place?" he asked. I said yes.

The apartment was sparse: a bare air mattress in the center of the room, a smudged glass coffee table shoved against the wall. No art, no couch, no signs of a life lived—just echo and dust. I was surprised it was so empty, but for $500 a month in Mid-Town Manhattan, I wasn't about to complain.

He perched on the edge of the mattress, pulled out an iPad, a bag of coke, and a credit card, and started cutting lines with the focus of a surgeon. His sleeves were too crisp for someone casually doing coke on a Tuesday. He looked important, or wanted to. I clocked the watch: vintage Rolex, probably real. His nails were clean, too clean. The kind of man who gets manicures but won't admit it.

When I sat beside him, the plastic mattress dipped and bounced. I laughed. He didn't even look up. I adjusted my shirt, smoothing out the wrinkles in silence. I wasn't used to silence meaning disinterest. Most men stared—hungry, expectant. This one didn't. It made me want to try harder.

"So, you work in finance," I say, turning on the interest like a switch. "What exactly do you do?"

"I was in investment banking at Goldman Sachs," he replied hesitantly.

"Oooh," I leaned in. "And what does an investment banker do?"

He leaned down, snorted a line through a rolled-up hundred, then passed it to me. Chivalrous. "Mergers and acquisitions, capital structure, activist defense," he said. "Managed analysts, I maintained client relationships, executed deals."

I bent down, inhaled my line, and passed the bill back. "You're speaking in past tense."

"Yeah. I'm on a hiatus," he admitted. "I've been there nearly ten years. It was... everything. High-rise apartment, office till midnight, endless competition. It burned me out. I've made enough to take a break, so I figured, why not?"

"Admirable," I said, leaning closer. "Self-care is so important. I can't imagine Wall Street makes that easy."

Men like him always rebrand collapse as reinvention. He wasn't burned out. He was bored. Too rich to be hungry, too cowardly to disappear completely. He didn't want a break from power. He wanted a softer version of it. Someone like me.

Someone to flatter his ego, to stay in her place. Someone who knows how to play the role—cool, grateful, effortlessly fuckable. Easy to be around. Easy to control.

"They said I can come back anytime. I probably will," he shrugged. "So, in your ad, you said you're an art model?"

"Mhm." I bent down, inhaled my line, and passed the bill back, careful to avoid touching his hand. I was conscious of every interaction, every signal I sent. Within the first minute of meeting Mr. Wall Street,

I'd decided I wanted to sleep with him. There was no way I'd let him know that yet.

"You can do more you know." He says motioning to the coke.

I laugh. "Oh, thank you. I just didn't want you to think I was one of those people who snorts all your drugs and peaces out or gives nothing in return."

Smirking again "I really appreciate that about you. But please, take as much as you like."

I did a second line. "So, yeah I'm an art model "Mostly for photographers. Some private fetish sessions—foot worship, spanking. Sometimes foot parties. It pays better and I feel more respected than any internship I've had. I also have my real estate license, but that hasn't taken off."

"Are you happy doing that?"

"For now." I paused. "Long-term, I just want to be someone's wife and a mother. I'm done pouring energy into careers that underpay and discard you the second you have a baby." I could feel his surprise, maybe even interest. Men like to believe they're rescuing you from something feral. It makes them feel bigger, useful. I let him see exactly what I wanted him to see—me, soft-edged and safe, full of domestic potential and need. A fantasy he could project onto.

"Huh. I don't meet many women who feel that way."

I licked my lips, letting my tongue linger before biting my lower lip. "Neither do I."

People think manipulation is some big, dramatic thing. It's not. It's a tone shift. A planted doubt. It's making someone think your idea was theirs. I'm not even sure I'd call myself manipulative. I just need people to see me a certain way. To react a certain way. So I can stay safe. So they'll want to stay.

He did three more lines, then raised his head. "What do you think? Want to live here?"

I smiled. "Yes, I'd like that very much."

"You don't have to sleep with me. No pressure. Whatever you decide won't affect your ability to stay."

"Thank you," I said, my voice honeyed. "I appreciate that."

Of course, I didn't believe him. They always say it doesn't matter— that they're kind, evolved. But the moment you stop being what they want, the tone shifts.

I already knew I'd sleep with him. I wanted to. But that didn't mean I trusted him. I was still filing away exit strategies, just in case he got bored, or worse, entitled.

3

THE NEXT TIME WE meet is a week later at a Holiday Inn Express in the Garment District with the purpose of handing over the keys to the Montrose apartment. He arrives before me. I walk into the lobby and go up the elevator without hassle. I knock on the door, and he opens it without looking at me, speaking into his phone in another language. I think it's Farsi. There's a plate of coke on the nightstand. It's 2:00 in the afternoon, and I'm thinking, *Wow. This guy never stops. He'll probably have a heart attack before 50 at this rate.*

I quietly sit on the bed, waiting for him to finish. Like most hotel rooms in the city, it's pretty tiny. A king-sized bed dominates the room, with a small sofa against one wall and a desk opposite it.

The pale chartreuse wallpaper was stomach-turning, like bile splashed on the walls. Who gets paid to make choices like this?

He hangs up the phone and turns to me, a self-satisfied grin spreading across his face. I twist my body around to face him, sitting up straighter. I give a small, sweet smile back.

"Hey there," I say softly, looking up at him from the bed.

He laughs. "Hey."

My grin widens as I let out a short giggle. "Sooo... Why are we meeting at a hotel rather than the apartment?" I ask, keeping my smile light and playful. No 35-year-old man wants to fuck on an air mattress.

"Well, as a member, I get free nights here. Sometimes it's easier than going back to Brooklyn or across town to the apartment," he replies casually, like living in hotel rooms is a perfectly normal habit for someone leasing two places in the city.

He passes me the plate of coke with a rolled-up bill. I take it, setting the plate on the bed. When I glance down, the bill catches my eye. It's a $20. My brow furrows slightly as I take an exaggerated second look before glancing up at him, deadpan.

"Did you lose big in the stock market this morning or what?" I say, straight-faced.

He stares back, studying my expression.

I break into a wide grin and quip, "I thought we only snorted coke with $100s. And what's this? You give me a *twenty?*"

We both burst into laughter. Still chuckling, he reaches into his wallet and hands me a $100 bill.

"You get comfortable quickly," he says with a smirk.

I smile, giggling again as I roll the bill up and take a line. He moves to sit in the desk chair, rolling it closer to the bed. I slide onto my stomach, arching my back just enough to draw attention but not so much that it's obvious. His eyes drop, exactly where I want them to, before slowly climbing back to meet mine.

Perfect.

His gaze lingers, and I know the energy between us has shifted. The night he showed me the apartment, he barely touched me, playing the gentleman. But here, in this claustrophobic hotel room, that façade is cracking.

"Do you still want to break up with your boyfriend?" he asks.

"I do," I respond, sitting back on my knees.

"And you want to live in my apartment?"

"Yes," I say, meeting his gaze.

The pause hangs between us. His eyes linger too long.

He wasn't her. He wasn't Tinsel. He never would be. But he looked at me like I was the center of the room, and right now that was enough. I was tired of sleeping next to a man who used me. Who told me my love language was sickening. Who wouldn't commit to me forever but take what he wanted for now.

I was tired of checking my phone a hundred times and finding nothing, or worse, a photo of her with someone else. The DJ can't love me the way I want. Tinsel refuses to give me the attention I crave. I don't want love from Wall Street, I just want noise. Something to drown out the quiet that settles in when Tinsel stops answering my texts.

I smiled sweetly, holding eye contact just long enough to make sure he kept looking.

He stands, taking a slow step toward me. "Should we seal the deal, then?"

My turn to smirk. "I thought you said I didn't have to sleep with you to live there."

He takes a step back, his hand reaching behind his neck. "You absolutely don't… I just thought…"

I let him hang on the edge a second longer before I reach out, my fingers brushing the soft cotton of his dress shirt. Armani, probably. *Of course, Armani.*

"But I really want to," I say softly, tilting my chin up and biting my bottom lip, letting my eyes do the pleading.

The tension snaps as he leans in.

His hands slid over my waist, up my spine, and I arched into him like I meant it. Maybe I did. Maybe I just didn't want to be alone. His mouth was hot, insistent, the kiss more transactional than passionate, but I closed my eyes anyway. Imagined someone else. Someone with sticky lip gloss and long painted nails. Someone who used to share my clothes without asking.

His hands moved lower, rougher now. He said my name like he was claiming it. I moaned, soft, practiced, perfect.

I know how to make men feel like they matter. It's my one real skill.

He whispered that I was beautiful. That he wanted to taste me. That he'd been craving me since he first saw me on the steps of the Apple Store.

I didn't say anything back. I just held on tighter. Pretended it meant something. Pretended maybe I really was the girl he wanted me to be.

October 7, 2013

I fucked him. For the 2nd time. Right after moving my stuff in. I let him taste me like a trophy he'd earned and pretended it didn't feel like a small death. I curled around him on that bare plastic mattress in Apartment 736 like I was some grateful stray, purring just to be let inside. The sound of the heater kicking on feels like applause. A new beginning. A new address. A new lie.

Mr. Wall Street smells like Tom Ford and risk aversion. He moans like he's in love and breathes like he's got secrets. I let him think he won something. I even let myself believe it for a minute. That I could be normal. That this could be something. But I couldn't stop thinking about her.

Tinsel.

Even with his hands on my waist, it was her fingers I felt. Her laugh echoing in the silence between our moans. Her name in my mouth, bitter and sweet, even as I kissed his throat and whispered things I didn't mean. I don't think I've had sex in the past five years without imagining her somewhere inside the act. Not watching. Not participating. Just... in the walls. In the skin I peel off after.

This apartment smells like potential.

The floor creaks in places that feel unfamiliar to my body. The air mattress is a joke, but it's mine, for now. I unpacked only what matters: lingerie, my red lipstick, my cat. My spider plant is already reaching toward the window like it believes in a future here. Stupid, hopeful thing.

I want to believe this is the start of something better. I want to believe that if I make enough lists and drink enough warm tea and take enough cocks with a smile, I'll stop wanting things I shouldn't want.

I didn't dip my fingers into raw meat tonight. I didn't crack an egg yolk open and swirl it in my palm pretending it was the slick warmth of her intestines. I didn't rock myself into sleep fantasizing about what it would feel like to slide my hand inside her body, past the skin, past the ribcage, into the part of her no one else gets to touch.

Progress.

Tinsel texted me while he was in the shower: Three sparkle emojis. Always three. No words. Just something to let me know I'm on her mind. I stared at the message until the screen dimmed.

She's everything I ever wanted and everything I was never allowed to have.

And still, she calls me Razor. Like I'm a tool. Like I'm her favorite little weapon.

I keep telling myself I can let go. That I can have this new life and still keep her. That I can smile when she posts pictures with other girls and not feel my throat tighten like a belt.

But what if that's the lie?

Mr. Wall Street likes me. He's stable. Wealthy. Predictable. There's no chaos in his hands. That should be a good thing. So why do I already want to scream?

He doesn't know I think of her when he touches me. That I swallow his moans and spit them out like poison. That all I want is to unzip her skin and crawl inside. He would throw me out quicker than yesterday's trash if he knew.

Who wouldn't? I'm sick.

Maybe this apartment is the beginning of my recovery.

Maybe I don't have to lose her to save myself.

Maybe I can have both.

Maybe.

4

I'M LYING ON THE air mattress with my cat, Pochemu. My phone buzzes, and I glance at the screen. It's Tinsel: *"RAZ!! Is he hot?? How's the place?! I need DETAILS"*

Tinsel has been my best friend since sophomore year of high school. She gives everyone these little nicknames. Her name isn't Tinsel, it's Stephanie. The seventh most popular girl's name in the USA the year she was born. She made up Tinsel because she couldn't stand the dreary reality of her given name. She calls me Razor or Raz because in high school I had these shaggy layers and emo kid choppy bangs cut with a straight razor. No one else calls me that.

Tinsel likes to do shitty things to me. Not only me, but most of the people she seduces into her surrealist vortex she calls reality. Sometimes I feel like the nicknames are just a way to dehumanize people so when she fucks with their lives she doesn't feel guilty.

The summer before college, she called me crying about how her parents were physically abusive like throwing her against walls, trying to shave her head. Horrific stuff. Naturally, I invited her to stay in my parents' spare bedroom. Two weeks later, she was staying in my brother's room and fucking him, acting like no one knew.

That's always been her thing—getting away with it. Senior year, we were inseparable. We'd spend hours lying around in my bed, shoulder to shoulder, whispering secrets like we were building a private language.

One night, watching *Black Swan* on my laptop, she turned to me and said, "Let's pretend we're together. Just for tonight." Then she kissed me, slow, careful, deliberate. It wasn't a joke. Not the way her mouth moved. Not the way she moaned when she pressed her hips into mine and said my name like it was her lifeline. We didn't have sex. We just came in our underwear, tangled in sheets, breathless. I thought it meant everything.

The next weekend, we went to a house party. She dared me to kiss her in front of a group of guys. I hesitated, and she grabbed my face, kissed me again. This time fast, messy, public. The guys cheered. She winked at them and said, "She's obsessed with me," like I wasn't right there, like I hadn't already memorized the taste of her breath.

She blew one of them in the bathroom an hour later. I waited outside on the curb, mascara running, pretending I was just waiting for my ride. That was the night something cracked. That was the night I started imagining her asleep, silent, still. Mine.

It's maddening being best friends with someone who knows they hold your heart in their hands, and squeezes just to feel something. I couldn't imagine life without her, yet I fantasize about roofieing her, fucking her unconscious body, then suffocating her. Gently, at first. Like coaxing her to sleep. Her lips trembling. Her chest rising and falling in shallow gasps, until finally, silence. For once, silence.

I'd lay her down carefully, smoothing the lines of her face, her arms, her legs.

I'd take my time with her. I'd start with her hair. That dark, thick, naturally curly hair she burns to death with a 450°F straightener every morning. I'd wash it with the good shampoo, the kind she never buys because she spends all her money on bullshit like Forever-21 mini skirts and overpriced fat-free milk lattes. I'd deep condition it with Olaplex No. 3, running my fingers through the silky strands, marveling at how beautiful it could be without her ruining it. I'd comb it out until it gleamed, then dry it carefully and store it in a hand-carved mahogany box I'd commission off Etsy—lined with velvet, of course.

Her lips, those perfect full lips, wouldn't spew endless words anymore. No more monologues about which hipster bar is hosting a secret show, no more whining about her raver boyfriend or some starving artist who's too obsessed with her. They'd finally be still. I'd press my fingers to them, memorizing their shape, then trace their edges with mine.

Her body would be mine to admire in peace. Her soft breasts, her flat belly, the curve of her thin waist. Silent and perfect, for once not trying to use them to seduce someone else. I'd feel her without the resentment, without the ache of knowing she gives nothing back. Finally, she would have given me something.

And when I'd had my fill, I'd lay her to rest in the river. Carefully, deliberately. I'd weigh her body down with precision, ensuring the Hudson swallowed her whole, drawing her into its cold, dark embrace until she disappeared entirely, leaving nothing behind but the memory.

The thought brings a kind of peace I've never known. For once, I'd feel full. I'd feel satisfied. She would be mine, fully, wholly, and eternally mine.

I think about that experience a lot. How one night she was able to be so intimate with me. Make me feel so accepted, seen, loved. Then how a week later she took the same intimate emotions she used to make me feel loved and weaponized them to publicly mock me and elevate herself. How can the empowering lover co-exist in the same body as the succubus? When she was laughing at me I wanted nothing more that to rip that repulsive mask off her face and dig behind her eyes until I could pull out the real her. The one from my bed. The one who knew me. Who loved me.

I glance back to my phone and text back:

Heyyy! It's soo amazing. And Mr. Wall Street… OMG. What are you doing tonight??

I scroll through myopenbar.com and find an art opening in SoHo. Tinsel and I agree to meet halfway between Montrose and FIT, at Madison and 30th. I get there first. Leaning against the beige brick of Miss K's Italian Eatery and Cafe, I watch the crowds stream past.

In New York, people either act like you're invisible, glancing through you like cellophane, or they demand your attention with a force that feels invasive. Me? I notice everyone, the ones ahead of me, the ones behind, and the ones standing too close. In a city like this, you have to.

I once saw a woman in a full ballgown eating Cheetos with chopsticks at 8 a.m. on the G train. A guy in Union Square stood shirtless on a milk crate, screaming the lyrics to *Wicked* like it was a war cry. A woman on 6th Avenue laughed into her phone, then started sobbing mid-sentence, like a wire snapped in her brain. In a crowded coffee shop, a man stared into space for a full hour, only to suddenly whisper, "She said I was too intense… I showed her intense," and start laughing to himself.

You never know who's a prophet, who's a predator, who's having a breakdown, or who just forgot they were visible. And I like to watch the cracks form.

"I Icy Razzz!" I hear in my left ear. I snap out of my thoughts.

I turn and see her, perfect as always - white crochet shorts with a matching crop top and completing it with a red and gold vintage embellished boho silk jacket. She has legs for days, grinning with the knowledge the world revolves around her.

"Hey." I smile, trying not to look too eager. "Let's go. We need the 6 train to Spring Street."

We squeeze into one of the older cars—flickering lights, peeling posters, that burnt-metal subway smell. Tinsel flops into the orange seat like she owns it. I stay standing.

"So?" she nudges me. "Tell me about this Wall Street blutty."

I blink. "Oh. Um… he's nice. We've been spending a lot of time together. But who knows, right?"

She gives me that look. The one that says *try harder*. "Nice is boring. Come on. Aren't we ride or die? Spill it."

I giggle. A beat too long. "Okay, okay. We're sleeping together. We do coke. A lot. He's weirdly good at listening, and bad at texting. Like… bad. But he's sweet. Easygoing."

I pause. I shouldn't say the next part. But I do.

"He lives with this girl in deep Brooklyn. Total headcase. I don't get it. He talks about her like she's a burden, but he won't leave her."

Tinsel makes a face. "Oof. Baggage, babe." She sticks out her tongue, already bored.

I want to say: *He gave me an apartment for next to nothing.*

I want to say: *He tells me he feels calm with me.*

I want to say: *He doesn't make me feel like an afterthought.*

But I don't. Because I can already see her pulling away. And if I tell her too much, she'll roll her eyes and call me *wifey* in that tone she uses right before she ignores me for three days.

The train screeches. We arrive.

As we walk into the gallery it's already pretty packed. Tinsel and I push our way through the crowds of Brooklyn hipsters and middle-aged men in trendy leather jackets to the open bar. A bored bartender pours us white wine into cheap plastic cups. The artwork is bright and punchy. Very hip. Very now.

Basquiat was really the beginning of the end of street art. Leave it to the 1980s to commercialize and capitalize on street art. Is it even street art if it hangs in a gallery? Street art by definition should be on the street and the real achievement behind it is how it interacts with a fixed space. In a gallery space, it either looks like tacky pop art or straight scribbles. But fuck it, if you can hustle crusty white people who are desperately trying to look cool for their 20-something sugar babies to pay 30 grand for your scribbles, more power to you. I turn to tell Tinsel my insightful observation but she's already inching toward some tall, homeless-chic guy in a thrifted blazer.

I take a sip of my wine and watch her work. She needs constant validation, like she's trying to fill some endless void. Isn't she already dating that raver from Connecticut?

I trail behind her, watching her laugh too loudly, toss her hair just so. My stomach tightens. I remind myself I have a system for these moments now. I read somewhere, maybe in a self-help book, maybe on Reddit, that the key to managing emotional spirals is action. Do something. Change the dynamic. Reclaim the narrative. Early sparks like these are easy to smother—a glance, a well-timed comment, a tiny splinter of doubt slipped into the right place. Most people don't even notice it until the rot sets in.

They're talking now, heads bowed toward each other like conspirators. I drift closer, hovering by the wall like I'm studying a piece, a bright red canvas with the word *FEED* scrawled in thick black paint. It looks like ketchup and depression.

I nudge Tinsel. "Hey, remember that guy you dated last year that was obsessed with spoon-feeding you Pinkberry while watching reruns of 90s cartoons? This would be perfect for him!" I giggle at our inside joke.

She glances at me, smiles vaguely, then says to the guy, "Razor always has something to say."

Not *funny*, not *insightful*, just… something.

The guy chuckles. He doesn't even look at me.

I feel my body go cold. I step closer, wedge myself between them a little.

"Didn't we see this guy at that warehouse party in Bed-Stuy?" I say, loud enough for both of them. "The one where you got blackout and thought that girl's pet snake was her massive cock?"

Tinsel's eyes flick up toward the ceiling like she's bored, or deciding whether to engage. "Mmm… no idea. Maybe."

She turns her smile back to him. I don't exist. And just like that, I'm out of the conversation again. They keep talking. He shows her something on his phone. She laughs and touches his wrist. I stand there smiling like I'm part of the joke. Someone bumps into me from behind, hard. I spill half my wine down the front of my coat. No one notices. Outside, it smells like forgotten garbage and wet leaves. October in New York, everything sharp and dying.

Tinsel links arms with the guy, her head on his shoulder like they've been together for years.

I follow them toward the subway, still pretending I'm part of this. We're heading to a party in Bushwick. Some loft he says his friend is spinning at.

Apparently, I'm sharing our night now.

5

WE STEP OUT OF the Morgan Ave L train. It's cold. I wish I had
worn thicker stockings rather than the sheer black with embroidered
roses I chose instead. Earlier, I was being facetious when I called Tinsel's new guy homeless chic. However, now I'm pretty sure this guy is
a total drifter. He's from Durham, England, has been here 14 months
with no clear employment. He doesn't smell bad, but he does not look
clean. Absolutely Tinsel's dream man - *a free spirit, a starving artist, a
gypsy god*. I don't think I've ever felt such a deep burning hatred for another human. Luckily he'll either be deported or dead of an Oxy overdose by the end of the year. I remind myself, *he too shall pass*. We seem
to have reached our destination as we stop outside a black steal door on
Bogart. The Durham Drifter is texting somebody. Is that a BlackBerry?
Is the duct tape on the back really holding anything together? The door
opens, and a bulky frizzy-haired hipster is standing there with a crooked smile and wreaking of pot. They do their little one-armed hug, pat
on the back, man-greeting before introducing us. Tinsel and I follow
behind up a steep flight of stairs. The walls and stairs are heavily graffi-
tied. Tinsel gives my hand a squeeze, smiling, raising her eyebrows and
widening her eyes, as if we're about to enter Valhalla. I return a sarcastic
imitation of her expression. She playfully shoves me. Giggling, we stop
short on a platform in front of a painted pale gray steel door. The loft
is warm. You can tell the wooden floors and beams are all original and

around 100 years old. They have that worn softness only age can create. The lights are dimmed, string lights and battery-powered candles create the mood. The loft is set up more as an event space than a home. There's a bar someone woodworked themselves to the left of a stage about a foot off the ground. Whoever lives here is in a band. Scanning the room, my eyes go past the typical hipsters that occupy the Morgan Ave L stop. White, privileged, dumpster dived for their outfit. I bet I could wallpaper this loft with the number of Pratt and New School degrees that litter these kids' rooms. A perfectly petite woman with dirty blonde hair, blue eyes and pouty lips lounges on the sofa. She looks like she was transported here from the golden age of Hollywood - but then her body is absolutely covered in tattoos. She's like a breathing illustration. I could never tire of looking at her. I smile casually and nod in her direction. I'm sure I look effortlessly calm, cool, and collected. But something about being in the same room as Tinsel always turns my insides into a pressure cooker. Like I'm trying to pass as human while she's out there being worshipped. I can't breathe right when she's not looking at me. The portly - *I'm gonna go with bass player* - introduces Tinsel and I to the group. Her name is Emma, like my favorite Spice Girl - Emma Bunton AKA Baby Spice. Out of the corner of my eye I see Tinsel settling down with The Drifter on something that looks like an armchair and a bean bag had a child. I stand next to Emma at the bar. I wonder if Tinsel is watching me. I begin angling myself to try and monitor her sightline.

"So are you from Brooklyn?" I ask, rather lamely, but hey you have to start somewhere.

"Gainesville, Florida — you?" Fuck, she's not perfect. At least I found out quickly.

"Carmel, New York — it's like an hour upstate. I guess you hate Less Than Jake, then?"

She laughs. I smile.

"No, no…I can't say hate — it's better to be known for a band than like a Florida Man News headline right?"

"Right" I say smirking. "Are you like an artist or something?"

"Burlesque dancer, mainly private events and some indie acting, model gigs." Emma responds, now looking past me, while she leans over her breasts are right in my face. Before I'm able to fully process she's sitting back down, blunt in hand. She takes a drag and passes it to me. Moving closer so our knees touch, I inhale, release upwards, and hand it over to the guy on my left. The blunt circles, small talk droning in the background like static, until it comes back to Emma. This time, she leans in and shotguns the smoke into my mouth. It's warm and slow, like she's feeding me. My hand drifts up her thigh, fingertips grazing the edge of her tights. Her mouth is so close I can taste the spiced rum on her breath.

Then, like clockwork, Tinsel appears. Suddenly she's beside me, eyes wide and desperate, whispering urgently into my ear, "Come with me?" I freeze. Emma's hand is still on my wrist. The mood is right there—alive, pulsing—and now it's slipping. I shoot Tinsel a look, something between *seriously?* and *what now?* But she's already tugging my arm, dragging me away like it's an emergency.

Reluctantly, I'm dragged into a side room - exposed brick, floor-to-ceiling racks of clothes, and discarded records littering the surfaces in the most High-Fidelity fanboy way. In my mind, I start listing my top 5 cockblocked moments, and unsurprisingly, Tinsel seems to be lingering throughout the entire list.

Top 5 Cockblocked Moments, starring Tinsel:

1. The time I was making out with that bartender from Library Bar and she suddenly "blacked out"

and needed me to walk her home—even though she'd just posted a selfie on Instagram 30 seconds earlier, demurely sipping her French 75.

2. The night I finally got invited to that exclusive after-party in Greenpoint, and she showed up uninvited wearing my shirt and told everyone I "get weird on drugs."

3. The party in Bushwick where I was vibing with a hot musician, and she pulled me into the bathroom, crying about how she felt like no one saw her anymore.

4. The night she cried on my fire escape for three hours because her ex liked one of my Instagram posts. I had an art model I met at a photoshoot in my bed, waiting for me.

5. Tonight.

She's the recurring theme. Always pulling focus. Always inserting herself at the exact moment someone else starts looking at me the way *I* look at her. I fold my arms, ready to tell her off—but I never do. I never can. We've never really been apart. Not for long. I don't know what I'd do if she actually stayed gone. Even a few hours without her and I start to unravel—like a wire pulled too tight. It's not loneliness. It's withdrawal. I tell myself I'd be fine, but even a few hours of silence can feel like a slow death.

Then she spins around with that manic sparkle in her eye, like Christmas morning. She pulls out a plastic baggie. Two hot pink pills inside.

"Double stacks," she says, like it's a gift. Like she didn't just drag me away from the only person in the room who wasn't looking straight through me.

My face splits into a smile before I can stop it. That high-pitched giggle escapes my mouth like a reflex.

I hate how easily she flips the switch in me. One minute I'm furious, halfway to calling her out, the next I'm her obedient little Raz, grinning like she didn't just take something from me and call it love. And just like that, the frustration curdles into affection. Not gone, exactly. It just sinks lower, like sediment, waiting to be stirred up again.

"Should we do half or a whole?!" I ask, my eyes shimmering with the same Christmas morning magic as Tinsel's.

"I want to do the whole."

"Me too!"

We laugh, and each puts a pill in our mouths and wash it down with PBR. Now it's the waiting game, though I already think I can feel the tingle in my toes from the ecstasy.

"Raz, who was that girl you were talking to? Her tattoos looked so trash." Tinsel says.

"Uh. I don't know. I thought they were hot. Her name is Emma"

Tinsel looks down at me and releases a biting laugh. "Oh, Raz. What will you come up with next."

I feel my face darken. I want to stab her in the neck with a screwdriver.

When we leave the room, Emma is gone, and people seem to be shifting, getting ready to make moves. The Durham Drifter glides over, angling his 6'3" body to talk to us.

"Grabbing a taxi to Glasslands - you in?"

We put on our jackets and follow the group out. I close the taxi door behind Tinsel, who's already giggling in the back seat with the bass player. The car fills up quickly, leaving the Drifter and me to catch another cab together. Perfect. The ride is short, but I don't need much time to plant a seed. A casual conversation. A stray comment. That's all it takes to start dismantling something fragile.

I settle into the seat beside him, angling my body slightly so our knees touch. He doesn't move away. "So," I begin, flashing a shy smile. "You like Tinsel?"

"Oh, sure," he says, his accent smoothing out the words like butter. "She's mint. She's brill."

"Yeah," I say, dragging the word out just enough to sound uncertain. "She's a lot of fun. You both seem like such free spirits."

"Oh oh yeah. Totally. Nothin' holding me down."

"Mhm. You guys are perfect for each other. It's just too bad she doesn't have proper health insurance. It can make connecting with men so hard for her. But you know, I guess that comes with the whole nomad hippie free thing. I'm sure you'll understand."

"Errr… what do you mean?" He asks with a sideways look.

"Oh, well I thought she talked to you about it already. You guys looked so cozy. I probably shouldn't say anything. It's no big deal." I shrug.

"What is it?" he nervously asks.

"Well, you know. It's just that she has this little chlamydia thing she can't afford to get treated. In women, there are virtually no symptoms, but sometimes the guys she fucks start pissing blood after a few days. But it's no biggie. Just wear a condom or whatever."

Silence.

He laughs once—awkward, unsure. Like he's hoping it's a joke but can't quite ask.

"You're serious?"

I give him the smallest shrug.

He looks out the window. He shifts in his seat, suddenly cagey. Like his skin doesn't fit right. Like her name left a bad taste in his mouth. I watch his jaw tighten just a little.

The car slows to a stop outside Glasslands. The Drifter pulls out cash and hands it to the driver, he's quieter now. He steps out, walks up to Tinsel, and gives her a long hug. Too long. Like it might be a good-bye. Then he disappears into the night.

Tinsel catches up to me just outside the entrance to Glasslands, her breath puffing little clouds in the cold night air. Her eyes are wide, confused, and, if I'm being generous, maybe a little hurt.

"What the fuck was that, Raz?" she asks, crossing her arms. Her voice is tinged with frustration, but there's a lightness to it, as if she's already decided she doesn't care enough to dig deep.

"What was what?" I reply, feigning innocence and pulling my jacket tighter against the chill.

"My English Gypsy. He just… left. Like, out of nowhere. Did you say something to him?" Her tone is accusatory, but not serious. She's too self-absorbed to imagine I'd actually meddle. That's her blind spot. She always assumes I'm here to serve her, not complicate her life.

"Tinsel," I say, tilting my head and letting out a soft laugh. "Why would I do that? He probably just realized he couldn't keep up with you. You know how men get when they feel out of their depth."

She narrows her eyes at me, a flicker of doubt passing over her face. "Out of his depth? What's that supposed to mean?"

I shrug, leaning casually against the wall. "I mean, look at you. You're a lot, Tinsel. You're gorgeous, you're intense, you're… well, everything. Not every guy can handle that."

She looks at me for a long moment, her lips pressing together as she tries to process my words. I can see the gears turning, but I know her well enough to predict where this will land. It won't stick. Not really.

Finally, she sighs, brushing a strand of hair behind her ear. "Yeah, I guess you're right. His loss."

"Exactly," I say, offering her a supportive smile. Inside, something twists, but not in the way it should. She doesn't see it. She never does.

"You're such a good friend, Raz," she says, slipping her arm through mine as we head inside. Her voice is light again, the tension gone as quickly as it came. I let her words wash over me, warm and hollow all at once. I smile. I don't feel like a good friend. I don't feel anything at all.

Glasslands looms like a brick cathedral, two stories tall and hollow inside. "289" bleeds white over rust-red brick. The sidewalk out front splits and weeps weeds, everything clawing toward the light, trying so hard to be seen.

Last time I was here, I was DJing with my ex. The crowd was as sweet as can be expected, no one tried to request a song, and a few gave compliments afterward. Being the DJ is weird. You're the most popular person in the room, but nobody actually sees you. They smile to your face, give you drugs, dance to your set and then shit-talk your music the second your back is turned. The worst people in the DJ scene are the other DJs. They wear these curated personas: cool, chill, inclusive, but it's all branding. They're petty, jealous and exhausting. Everyone's pretending to be easygoing while sharpening knives behind their backs. I hate phonies. I hate how everyone thinks performance is authenticity. No one says what they mean. They just build masks they hope get them invited back.

As we step inside, a wave of hypersensitivity crashes over me. My face feels flushed, like invisible tears are streaming down, but I remind myself to hold it together. *I'm not some lunatic crying in public.* I'm about to feel amazing, just ten more minutes. The lack of a cover charge or ID check barely registers as we walk into Glasslands. My focus is drawn to the LED cloud installation, shimmering overhead like a pulsing sky. With the right cocktail of chemicals in your system, it looks alive, closing in, ready to swallow you whole if you don't keep moving.

The music hits hard—psychedelic, primal. The tribal chanting builds, melting into a beat that syncs with the rhythm of my pounding heart. *I feel it all rising—everything I swallowed tonight. That flick of her eyes when she pretended not to know me. The cab door closing. The silence after the lie I told. That emptiness she carved out of me just by looking away.* Then the bass hits. And just like that, it all starts to dissolve. Anger, anxiety—whatever cocktail of feeling I've been choking on—bleeds out into the floor. Rainbow-colored fractals smear the edges of my vision. Light swims. For a moment, I'm weightless. Connected. Every breath and vibration binds me to the strangers around me, their energy glowing in waves that threaten to blind me.

And then she's there.

Tinsel presses into me from behind, her warmth spilling over my skin. She lifts my arms, wrapping them around her neck, her breasts soft against my back. Her pulse, her heat synchronizes with mine. I let myself melt into her. Let her pull me into her orbit, where everything makes sense.

Snapshots flicker through my mind like a reel of home movies. The first time we met in AP Art History, when she saw me in a way no one ever had. Shopping at the Danbury Mall, flirting with the guys at Zumiez, her laugh lighting up the dull fluorescents. Sitting on subway steps, her voice low and confident as she taught me how to hold eye contact, how to draw men in. Dropping acid together at the Poughkeepsie waterfalls, staring at the universe as it unraveled before us.

She's everything. The only one who's ever made me feel seen. Whole.

Even the idea of losing her feels like annihilation. We've never gone more than a few days without talking. I wouldn't know how to exist without her orbiting around me. Her rejection is a black hole, sucking me into a void of anger, violence, and despair. I can't imagine breathing in a world where she doesn't exist at my center. I need her. I need her to need me, the way lungs need air. And if she ever left me? I would burn the whole goddamned world to ash. As the thought crosses my mind, an icy wave floods through me. I glance over my shoulder. She's gone. My chest tightens as I spot her further down the dance floor, her body pressed against some malnourished hipster, her hands roaming his chest like I don't exist. My heartbeat slams in my ears, and my vision starts to blur, edges fading into a dark, encroaching fog. If I keep watching this, I might black out.

I stumble toward the bathroom, shoving through the crowd. The thrum of the music follows me, relentless, like it's burrowing into my skull. In the bathroom, fluorescent light exposes everything. It's too harsh, too surgical. My pupils are blown wide, the pale green of my irises nearly gone. The beat outside loops in my brain like a warped record, thudding against the bone. A girl at the sink beside me is adjusting her eyeliner. We make eye contact.

"What?" I snap. I didn't mean to. Or maybe I did.

She blinks, startled. "Nothing. I like your…"

But I'm already turning away. I grip the edge of the sink. My reflection smiles at me, all teeth and sweat and empty eyes. I tug at the roots of my hair. The smile won't stop spreading—grotesque, wrong, like my face is trying to mock me. God, if I could just take a shard of glass and drag it along the edge of my scalp I'd tuck my fingers under the flap and pull down. Then you'd see the real me. Everyone would see the real me. No one could look away. The urge to smash the mirror flares hot and fast. I want to see if it cracks before I do. And then: a flicker of motion. A shift behind me. Emma steps out of a stall, her reflection catching mine in the glass. She waves, casual, like nothing's unraveling. I wave back. Of course I do. She crosses the tile floor slowly and deliberately. Her gaze pins me in place—hot and unblinking, like she sees too much.

"I love your eyes," she murmurs, voice low and purring.

"I love absolutely everything about you," I say, too fast, too true.

She smiles, wicked, knowing, and then her mouth is on mine. Tongue, teeth, heat. And just like that, the static goes quiet. Emma laughs, then leans in again. This time slower. Hungrier.

I follow her lead, matching breath for breath, fingers tracing the hem of her crop top. She doesn't stop me. She grabs my hand and presses it to her ribs like she wants me to feel her heartbeat. Maybe I imagine that part. We find the darkest corner of the warehouse, and she straddles my thigh, grinding into me like it means something. Like I mean something. Her lips on my neck. Her fingers under my skirt, inching into my tights. She moans once, softly, I bow into her lap and I eat it like communion. Then she pauses, pulls something from her wrist. A thin gold-beaded chain. She takes my ankle and clasps it around me, slow and careful, like a secret.

"You're mine now," she murmurs, grinning like it's a joke. I smile like it is, too. But inside I'm glowing. Branded. Seen. When it's over she straightens her skirt and winks like we've shared a secret. I stay frozen for a beat too long.

"Catch you later," she says, already walking away.

I sit there for a while, legs still shaking. Trying to memorize the moment so I can replay it again and again in my memory.

Maybe this is how it starts. Maybe this time it'll be different. Maybe she'll call me.

6

I WAKE UP TO the soft, rhythmic purring of Pochemu curled over my left arm. Her warmth anchors me for a moment before the weight of last night seeps in. My eyes are dry, my brain sluggish, like it's been wrung out. In the kitchen, I fill the kettle and set it on the stove. The morning ritual bringing me slowly back to reality. As I reach for the bag of Dunkin' Donuts blueberry coffee, I grab my phone, thumbing through the emails that piled up overnight. I post in the various Craigslist forums offering fetish sessions instructing the interested parties to use the subject line 'Room for Rent'. The post describes how I'm a terribly naughty girl who needs a strong hand and a sturdy lap to teach me a much needed lesson. I get a steady flow of three to five sessions a week.

Subject: Room for Rent

From: <2808dc952b063bcf8bd0b63e6c26b1b8@reply.craigslist.org>

Older man 57 would like to spank you for being bad. Please send more details and your picture. I'm available now.

I hit reply and paste in my usual response for first time clients

Hey, thanks for responding! It's 200/hr. I come to you. I can be free whenever with a little notice. No BJ no sex. Attached are some photos. Let me know!

Xxox

J

I attach a selfie and a professional nude I took last month on the Upper East Side by this photographer who likes posing women in front of erased chalkboards. He claims the photos look 'ethereal' after applying certain filters. New York artists have a knack for dressing up simple techniques, like using a plain background in photography, with pretentious jargon.

I move on to the next email .

Subject: Room for Rent

From: <17710db02e813617827367edd9a1a4d6@reply.craigslist.org>

Hey,

Scheduled to fly into NY this afternoon. If you are still interested in being spanked this evening, I would love to take you over my knee for a bare bottom spanking. MWM, age 38. Discreet. Can host at upscale midtown hotel.

I hit reply and paste the same message in. He replies almost instantly. That works for me. No expectation of sex. Spanking only. I will email when I get there and will give a couple of hours notice at least.

Will be at the Doubletree at Lex and 51.

Hitting reply I paste in my google number and say "Text me when you're ready. Have a safe flight ttys!"

That feels like a sure thing tonight.

The kettle starts screeching. I set my phone down and pour the boiling water into the French press, watching as the rich aroma of coffee and sweet blueberries fills the air, easing the tension in my chest.

Subject: Room 4 Rent

From: <59930mk80d261450177919baa4e2e2b4@reply.craigslist.org>

Pay for something YOU want? WHORE

Huh, that's rude. Delete, next.

Subject: Room 4 Rent

From: <86d84697f70c35cf84b5b22710808a4b@reply.craigslist.org>

Hi,

I just saw your ad and I would love to meet.

If it matters,Im white, 39, 6,2", in great shape, strong, dd free, good manners, strong hands and open minded

let me know what I can do for you !

best,

Kent

I respond, same message.

He replies right away. Most of the people who are actually going to meet up with you typically respond within 15 minutes of your response.

Sounds and looks great !

When can we meet ? Are you in the city?

I would like to meet soon....

Eager. That's not necessarily bad, but it's something to watch. When meeting strangers off the internet, you take your time. You look for panic, mood swings, or disrespect when they don't get what they want on their timeline. His rapid replies scream desperation, so I decide to wait an hour before responding.

Coffee in hand, I retreat to bed, my laptop open to freetvproject. org. Season 3 of *Dexter* loads as Pochemu curls up beside me. I fiddle absentmindedly with the gold-beaded anklet Emma clasped on me last night.

Emma.

The memory doesn't feel real. It's like a half-developed photo—edges too soft, light too bright, the center smudged. Her hands on me, her lips tasting like rum and citrus. The way she said, *"You're mine now,"* as she wrapped the chain around my ankle like a promise.

Or maybe I imagined that part.

I close my eyes, trying to replay it, but the timeline blurs. I remember skin, teeth, the sharp pull of hair, but then it fades. Did she kiss me first? Did I cry? Was it her?

Or someone else?

Three texts. No response. Just silence.

I start scrolling her Instagram. Looking for signs. Maybe she lost her phone. Maybe she's just bad at texting. Maybe it meant more to her than she wants to admit.

Then I see it. A flood of pics posted in real time from last night.

Emma and Tinsel.

Tinsel and Emma.

On the dance floor, beaming like they invented each other. In the bathroom mirror: Tinsel kissing Emma's cheek as Emma holds up her phone, smirking like she knows exactly what she's doing. Outside Glasslands, hand in fucking hand, skipping down the street like they're starring in some Sundance coming-of-age bullshit.

Did they skip all the way home together?

I feel it in my chest first. A kind of static hum, tight, rising, burning hotter with every breath. My fingers wrap around the anklet. My vision blurs. I rip it off and hurl it against the wall. It clinks to the floor in a useless little heap. Tears begin to pour down my face. I can't help it.

She probably just wanted an easy fuck. Something to laugh about with her friends. Some fun New York story to tell the girls back in Florida.

Or maybe not even them. Maybe my *friends*.

Maybe Tinsel.

I stare at the screen, jaw locked. The two of them glowing together, like I was never there. Like I never mattered. Where was I in any of this? I danced with Tinsel. I fucked Emma. But I'm not in a single photo. Not one.

Not even a tag.

No one wanted me in their story. Not even Tinsel?

Girls are all the same: they use you, pretend to care, then ghost you when they're done. Like I'm nothing but an empty Starbucks cup they toss away the minute they're finished with it.

I text Tinsel: "You were right. That tattooed girl was trash."

Immediately, I see Tinsel is typing something back. Then she stops. My grip on the phone tightens. What bullshit is she going to feed me? Will she act like she didn't spend the whole night with her? She starts typing again.

Ding!

Tinsel: "Oh..idk sweetbum. After you got weird last night me and her actually hung out. I think she's pretty major."

After I got weird last night? What the hell is she even talking about? I bite my lip and start rocking back and forth a bit. This isn't the first time she's said something like this to me. Reframes things to make it seem like I'm the problem. Creates stories like I'm the one who's too much or acting off.

I reply: "Weird?"

She starts typing. Stops. Starts again. Another long pause. *Ding!*

Tinsel: "Yeah. I mean not like weird weird. After the dance floor I went looking for you and just saw you sitting alone in a corner of the warehouse. I figured you were having your alone time. It's fine babe IK you get like that sometimes. No worries, should we brunch today?"

I roll my eyes. She's so full of shit.

"Can't. Client soon. I Iappy hour drinks at Library Bar."

Tinsel: "Maybe. Let u know?"

"Sure..."

I put the phone down. I stare at the wall where I threw the anklet. It's blank. Bare. No gold, no glint. I check the floor. Under the bed. Between the sheets and pillows. The sink drain. I even run my fingers along the baseboards like maybe it slithered away.

Nothing.

My breath slows. Thickens. My skin prickles like it's shrinking away from my bones.

I remember her fastening it around my ankle. Emma's fingers brushing my skin, the clasp catching slightly, her whisper: *You're mine now.* Her tongue tasted like citrus and sugar. No. It was citrus and vodka. No. Rum. I said citrus and rum. Her breath hit the hollow of my throat and I *felt* it—felt her press herself into me like she was branding me.

So where the fuck is it?

I open my messages again. Still nothing. No read receipt. No new post. No proof she exists.

What if I made her up?

Not the Emma part. She's real. Quickly, I slide back into Instagram to double-check the pictures. Sure enough her and Tinsel, still there, in all their phony filtered glory. The night though. The intimacy. Her hands. Her mouth. The gold anklet. What if I stitched it together out of stray touches and lust and loneliness? What if the sex never happened? What if I touched myself in the dark and gave it her face?

I blink. The room has a smear to it, like Vaseline over glass.

I go to the mirror.

My reflection looks normal. Not quite *me*, but close. My lips are swollen. My pupils blown. I run my fingers over my thighs. No bruises. No scratches. No evidence.

My skin is clean.

Too clean.

I press a finger against the soft skin inside my arm. Hard. Just to see the blood rise.

I think of Emma bent over me, whispering filthy things I can't quite remember. I think of her moaning my name. But the voice changes.

Fades into Tinsel's cadence. Then back again. It glitches, Emma's face, then Tinsel's. Lips, eyes, neck. One body, two ghosts.

I don't know whose breath I'm remembering anymore.

I stagger back from the mirror. My knees lock. I imagine Emma's mouth sewn shut, her jaw wired closed. I imagine cutting her open to see whose voice lives inside her throat. I want to find out if Tinsel's heart beats beneath her ribs.

I want to reach in and pull the lie out by its spine.

My cunt pulses.

I close my eyes and the scene replays, but it's flickering now. Her face changes. The gold anklet shatters into teeth biting into my flesh. Her fingers are scalpels, slashing my breasts into red, wet ribbons.

My body is soaked, and I don't know if it's sweat or arousal or memory leaking out of me.

I collapse onto the bed and lie very still.

Maybe I dreamed it.

Or maybe I stole it.

Either way, I don't think she was ever mine.

7

MY PHONE JINGLES. My eyes snap open.

I don't know where the last forty-five minutes went. My mouth tastes like metal. My thighs are sore. There's a smear of something on my inner leg—maybe lube, maybe yolk. My brain tries to make sense of the time warp, but I shove the questions down. That's not today's problem.

Thank god I set timers for everything. I always come back when I hear a sound.

I need to get ready for my client. Normal. Normal is good.

I boil a pot of water, waiting for it to reach a rolling boil before turning off the stove. I position my face over the pot, draping a towel over my head. The steam burns a little, but I need that. I let it open my pores for five minutes before applying First Aid Beauty Skin Rescue Purifying Mask with Red Clay. The red clay and rosemary oil pull the dirt to the surface, purging everything hidden under the skin.

It's not about skincare. It's about control. About peeling off the last mask and putting on a prettier one. While the mask dries, I unroll my purple yoga mat and load my 20-minute 'Buns and Thighs' workout from the laptop. As I move into chair and goddess poses, my mind drifts. I focus on my breath, in and out, and visualize the meeting ahead. It will go smoothly. I will be safe, and prosperity will follow.

In savasana, lying still, my thoughts turn to the day I dropped out of college. They had cut my financial aid —said my father's raise disqualified me. Never mind he hadn't saved a dime for school. Spent more on cars and Bluetooth speakers than on helping me. I returned to my one-bedroom apartment after another grueling day at an unpaid marketing internship. I'd gone to lunch with one of the women from the office and learned she made $30,000 less than her male counterparts. That was the moment I understood—I was trapped. A cog in a machine.

First, the desperate scramble to get into college. Then, the competition for the most prestigious internship, followed by a job that paid barely enough to cover the student debt I'd accumulated to earn a degree that only granted me the privilege of working for peanuts. So, I quit. I quit the machine. I quit society. I found a subculture where I get paid for what I'd do for free. I set my own schedule. I only deal in cash.

I finish the yoga routine, rolling up my mat with mindfulness, and head to the bathroom. The clay mask peels away in one smooth sheet. Next, I apply Fresh Crème Ancienne Ultimate Nourishing Honey Mask, the thick formula counteracting the drying effects of the clay, saturating my skin in honey and shea butter. The mask leaves me with a rosy afterglow and a dewy complexion.

As the honey mask sinks into my skin, I sit on the toilet, preparing to soften my feet with a callus remover—a tool that looks like a giant cheese grater. I scrape it along the ball of my foot and my heel, wiping away the dead skin with a dry towel. Satisfied with the texture, I coat my feet with thick foot cream and slip on microfiber socks.

I wash the honey mask off my face and spritz a homemade tea tree toner, made with Fiji water and organic tea tree oil. I pat my face dry with a black cotton towel, then smooth on Elizabeth Arden Flawless Future Powered by Ceramide Moisture Cream with SPF 30. I follow it with Dr. Brandt Glow Revitalizing Retinol Eye Cream. My dark circles are a permanent feature, the result of visible blood vessels beneath my skin. This cream, a combination of retinol and microscopic ruby particles, diffuses the light, masking both the circles and the lines. Some might think my routine is obsessive, but I believe it's important to look and feel your best. It's about presenting yourself as someone who is cared for, whether that's through your own self-care or the support of others. The unfortunate truth is that women who are perceived as disposable often end up dead. When society sees a woman as expendable, her value can diminish in the eyes of others.

I know this is an uncomfortable and unpopular truth, and it may not align with politically correct opinions, but that doesn't make it any less real. The reality is that women who are caught in cycles of abuse often continue to face it, and without intervention, they end up skinned alive and thrown in the Hudson River. We live in a world shaped by patriarchy, where men are often visual beings. By presenting yourself in a way that feels empowered and secure, you can influence how others perceive and treat you.

This isn't about playing a role or conforming to unrealistic standards, it's about navigating a world that, for better or worse, often judges a woman based on her appearance and demeanor. There's a difference between being valued and being dismissed. The stories we see in true crime are often of women who were overlooked or dehumanized, and we need to recognize that these dynamics are not just statistics, they're part of a larger, harmful cycle. As someone working in the sex industry, I'm determined not to become just another tragic headline in the true crime stories that dominate the media. So I will persevere to look as cute and delicate as a daisy. To give off an energy that says 'love me' 'protect me' not grind up my meat in your back-alley butcher shop. This is my mask.

I take a moment for the creams to absorb before slipping off my socks and running my fingers over my perfectly arched size 6 soles. I grab a bottle of Sally Hansen "Red My Lips" nail polish and carefully apply it to my toenails, finishing with a clear top coat. Once my pedicure dries, I apply under-eye concealer, liquid foundation, and black eyeliner in a 50s cat-eye style, finishing with mascara and a hint of blush. All drugstore brands, nothing worth mentioning.

I dip my finger into classic Vaseline, gently dabbing it onto my lips to soften and shine them without the sticky mess. Then, I moisturize my entire body, every inch, until I'm soft, smooth, and lightly scented. I rub vanilla and lavender essential oils on my pressure points. The vanilla draws men in like baked goods, and the lavender soothes, setting a calming atmosphere. Essential oils are stronger and less expensive than perfume.

I slip into black lace lingerie and dark skinny jeans, pulling on a purple and orange argyle V-neck sweater from H&M. I turn on my hair straightener, setting it to 280°F, then reach under the sink for a brown Trader Joe's bag filled with prescription drugs. All legally acquired. The DJ taught me how to work the system. He told me exactly what to say, which symptoms to mimic, how to flirt just enough to soften a psychiatrist's skepticism. As a white woman with health insurance and access to WebMD, it's practically a superpower. I have over a hundred Oxycodone pills from my dentist, 90mg Adderall prescribed three times a day by my psychiatrist in Bed-Stuy, Xanax, Prozac, Trazodone, Gabapentin (from my vet), Zoloft, Lexapro, and that's only the top half of the bag.

I take four Oxy pills and two Prozacs, placing them in my white marble mortar. Slowly, I crush them into a fine powder. Using my New York City Public Library card, I carefully push the powder into two clear pill capsules, ones I bought at a new-age health store in Greenpoint. They look just like Molly, but unlike Molly, these pills won't flood my brain with serotonin. They're a combination that could incapacitate someone, maybe even kill them, should they prove troublesome. I tuck them into the padding of my bra. Along with the pills, I keep a copy of *Murder on the Orient Express* in my tote bag that I hollowed out in the center. Inside, you'll find a folding blade, a travel-sized can of bear spray, and a tampon soaked in ammonia.

The blade and the bear spray are obvious. The tampon? That one's for a surprise attack, shove it in someone's face, the ammonia hits fast. Eye-stinging, breath-stealing. Just enough to knock them off their game long enough for me to get out the door and back onto the street.

It's not that I don't trust my clients. But you can never be too careful. I want to think the best of this man. But strangers can be dangerous. Men can be dangerous.

8

THE CLIENT WANTS TO meet in Duane Reade before heading to the hotel across the street. It's not uncommon. They always want to confirm I'm real. That I'm not a druggy or some old guy catfishing them. They think three minutes in a brightly lit pharmacy will tell them everything they need to know.

He texted me that he'd be by the beverage fridge in the back. As I walk through the aisles of junk snacks, the scratchy blue-and-gray carpet beneath my feet, I spot him. He's holding a 32-ounce bottle of Smart Water, wearing a navy-blue wool suit and a red patterned tie, just as he described. Dark brown hair, slightly receding, thick-rimmed glasses, and the faded tan of someone who hasn't quite let go of summer.

He straightens up, turning to meet my eyes. I smile, and he approaches.

"J?"

"Yes."

Relief washes over his face. New clients always expect the worst.

"I like you more than the pictures." He gives a small, cool guy smile. I'm guessing he's about 47 and was super hip in high school. "Do you want anything?" He gestures to the fridge.

"I'm fine, thanks so much tho!"

He pays for his water bottle and we walk across the street to the Double Tree hotel. The tall, silver building looms above us, its 1960s façade a relic of another era. Inside, the lobby's sand-hued marble floors gleam under the artificial lights, faintly scented with jasmine and clean cotton.

He swipes his keycard in the elevator, pressing the number four.

The room is exactly what you'd expect: small, functional, forgettable. White geometric wallpaper lines the walls, the orange wood headboard matching the nightstands. Beige curtains block out the daylight. His navy-blue suitcase is in the corner, next to a pair of worn white Reebok sneakers.

He's behind me as we move toward the center of the room. I step closer to the bed and turn to face him, offering a sweet smile.

"How would you like this to begin?"

"How does it usually begin?" His eyes flicker around the room, as if he's a guest here himself.

"Well," I say, keeping my tone light, "most guys like to get the money thing out of the way first."

He pulls two crisp hundred-dollar bills from his wallet and hands them to me.

"Thank you," I say, tucking them into the zippered pocket of my purse. "After that, they usually like to talk for a bit, get comfortable. Some like to make out before things start. Others get straight into it, lay me face down on the bed and spank me with their belt or hand, others like to scold me like a naughty little girl and say things like 'If you're going to behave like a child I'm going to treat you like one' before demanding I pull down my pants and panties and bend over their knee. I'm very open-minded."

"Let's talk for a bit." He pulls the rolling desk chair closer to the bed.

I slip off my ballet flats, revealing my red-polished toenails, and settle on the bed. Sliding my feet into his lap, I ask, "Is this okay?"

"Absolutely." His hands begin exploring the back of my calves.

"Do you like being spanked?" he asks.

"Yes," I say simply.

"Why?"

"I find the lack of control relaxing. The vulnerability turns me on."

"Were you spanked as a child?"

"No."

"That's good." His hands move higher, brushing against my thighs. I study his face as he begins to feel up my legs. I wish he, or any one of them, clients that is, would pause. Just once. Ask me something real. Not why I like being spanked, but what I dream about when I'm not being watched. I wouldn't tell them. But still, I wish they'd ask. Their questions always hint at wanting to understand me, but they never dig deeper than the surface.

He squeezed my knee and offers a firm but affectionate look as he says "Take off your clothes and lie on the bed, spread-eagled. I'm going to spank you with my belt. After each strike, I want you to say, 'Thank you daddy. I deserve this.' When I tell you we're done, you'll get dressed, say, 'Thank you, daddy,' and leave. Understood?"

"Yes, daddy."

I slide out of my pants, deliberately slow, before peeling off my top. I lie back on the bed, naked, positioning myself just so—my back slightly arched, my body at its most appealing angle. This is true relaxation. In this hotel room, in this interaction there are rules. Lines to repeat. Roles to play. I know how to deliver the scene, when to moan, when to thank him. There's a beginning, middle, and end. Everything was agreed on beforehand: our language, the actions, the rules of engagement. It's not like love. Love has no safe word. No script. It's messy, improvised, and always ends in tears. The first slap of the belt stings. I repeat the line he's told me to, my voice steady. The strikes continue in rhythm. My body moves on autopilot, repeating "Thank you, daddy. I deserve this." like it's choreography. I wonder if he can tell how empty I sound. How practiced. I used to get nervous. Flushed, even. The first few sessions, my breath would catch right before I spoke. Now I could say anything in this voice. I could recite a grocery list and make it sound like a confession. The pain dulls, my focus narrowing to the white light behind my closed eyes. The belt lands on the nightstand with a soft thud. His hand grazes my skin, gentle now, bringing me back to the room. I feel the heat of his body as he leans in, his sandalwood aftershave faint but grounding.

"Get dressed. You're done."

I sit up, meeting his gaze. I give him a lingering kiss, deep and slow, before whispering, "Thank you, daddy."

Then I pull on my clothes, slide on my flats, and leave without looking back.

9

I WALK FIVE BLOCKS from the hotel, shedding the sweet little girl who needs a spanking with each step. The mask crumbles. My real face returns, no blush, no giggle, no thanks for the tip. Just me. Or the version of me that's left. I walk into a bodega to get a bottle of water and check my phone.

I text Tinsel "How about those drinks tonight? Missing you xx"

I drift to the back fridge, leaning against the cold glass door, I just retrieved a bottle of Voss from. I stare at the screen willing the response to come through. The right response. Something that will glue us back together. A brush of warmth against my shin. I glance down. An orange cat is circling my ankles, purring like it knows I need a witness. I let out a sigh and sink to the floor, cross-legged, petting his ears while balancing my phone on my knee. Instagram opens itself like a wound. I scroll. First picture to appear on my feed: Tinsel and Emma, a pitcher of mimosas, smiling, of course, and clinking their champagne glasses together with the Brooklyn Bridge in the background. My brow furrows. It's like they're using Instagram as a scrapbook to curate some perfect life neither of them has. My fingers pause. My bottom lip trembles. I bite it and keep petting the cat. Are they trying to make people think they're honeymooners? I breath deeply. Close Instagram.

Then I text Mr. Wall Street: You around tonight? Thinking of you.

Tinsel won't want to go out. She's probably back at FIT, passed out in her duvet like a drunk baby deer. Meanwhile, I'm out here. A half-predator, half-abandoned house pet, waiting for someone to remember I exist.

Since moving into his extra apartment, I've been seeing Mr. Wall Street almost every night. We eat. We fuck. He falls asleep during the documentaries he picks for us. I wash his dishes. He tastes my food and moans like it's sex.

I like playing house. I like how simple it is to be wanted by someone who isn't trying to win.

But even when he's inside me, I'm somewhere else. He thinks I'm healing. From the DJ. From the breakup. But what I'm really doing is hiding. He's a warm place to go when I can't face the frostbite in my head. He never asks why I check my phone like I'm waiting on a call from the hospital. I think he knows better than to ask. I haven't told him about Emma. Or about Tinsel, not really. Maybe tonight I will.

I don't think he'd judge me.

But that's not the point.

The point is: no one keeps all of me. They take a piece, a pulse, a pretty lie, then flinch when it starts to rot. I want someone who won't look away when I'm bleeding. Someone who'll press their lips to mine even after I've gone cold. Who'll love the version of me that's quiet, still, and finally enough.

I take one final look into the orange cat's round golden eyes before pushing myself up and handing the man at the counter a crumpled five for the water. I don't remember leaving. Don't remember crossing Delancey. Just the motion of my legs and the glassy smear of sunset across the buildings. The street signs blur. I could be anywhere.

I could be no one.

By the time I blink back into my body, I'm on Broome Street, hands shoved in my coat pockets, wind chapping my lips, heartbeat mechanical. And then—there she is.

Emma.

Walking toward me like it's a rom-com meet-cute. Like she didn't clasp a bracelet on my ankle and tell me I was hers. Like she didn't spend the whole night kissing Tinsel and posting about it like I was never there.

Three texts. No answer.

A kiss. A fuck. A souvenir.

And then nothing.

She threw me away like trash.

Flashes of Tinsel on the dance floor flood my mind. Her hands sliding over my waist, then that guy's, then Emma's. Her grin wide, her body gold-lit and untouchable. The humiliation burns through me like acid.

Emma comes closer. Cheerful. Oblivious.

"Jennifer, right?" she chirps.

I blink.

Jennifer.

Like none of it happened.

Like I didn't exist between her thighs.

"Jessie," I say, voice tight enough to draw blood.

"Oh my god, right! Jessie Anne, I'm so sorry! I'm such a space case sometimes." She gives a weak laugh, like this is nothing. Like *I'm* nothing.

I fantasized about holding your heart like wet fruit in my hand. You don't even remember my name.

"I've actually got to drop off some paperwork at The Box... but if you want to walk with me?"

56

I nod, dead-eyed. She's babbling now, all apologies and fake concern. Phony.

On the way to The Box she talks endlessly about herself—her show, her career, her life. I can't believe I was ever attracted to her.

Inside The Box, the silence is jarring. Emma tells me to wait by the bar as she disappears into a side office. I learned on the walk here that Emma produces a weekly burlesque show called *"Show Me Your Noobs"*—her way of "giving back to the community," she said.

As if she's some benevolent queen of the downtown sex scene. I roll my eyes, but part of me still aches watching her disappear through that velvet curtain—like I'm missing something important. Like I still want her to pull me in. I tell myself she's fake. Self-absorbed. Probably rehearses those little giggles in the mirror. But then I remember the way she kissed me. The anklet. The way her voice dropped when she said "You're mine now."

I want to hate her. I do. But the thing about girls like Emma—like Tinsel—is they make you feel special *just long enough* to believe it.

And I did.

There's something eerie about being in a place like this when it's empty. When the usual chaos and energy have been stripped away, leaving only silence. The Box has a history, a soul soaked into its walls. It started in the 1970s as a secret refuge for gay men, a place hidden from the world's judgment. Even now, it stays true to its roots: no security cameras, a strict dress code: flamboyant, eccentric. The more over the top you are, the better your chances of getting through the door.

I run my hand along the slick black bar top, pouring myself a gin and tonic. My fingers curl around a long silver ice pick resting beside a bucket. I pick it up, feeling the weight, the cool metal in my hand.

"Hey lady - make me one too?" Emma's voice startles me. She's smiling across the bar, oblivious. I hand her my drink instead of making another. She takes it without complaint.

"Come I want to show you something." Her voice grates against my skull. I follow her up to the stage, her hips swaying as she skips ahead. She's beaming, breathless as she spreads her arms. "Stand here. Look out. Imagine the crowd, the energy. It's electric." Her smile is wide, joyous, and so self-serving. I see through her act. She's just like Tinsel—selfish, manipulative. Pretending I'm special, letting me into her world like it's some intimate, exclusive experience.

And yet.

I need people like her. That's the sick part. I gravitate toward the ones who take up all the air in the room and then act like they're the ones suffocating. The spotlight girls. The ones who make you feel lucky just to orbit them. I need them to see me. I need to believe, even for a second, that I could be part of whatever magic makes them so undeniable. And when they pull away, I tell myself it's temporary. That they'll come back. They always do. *But what if they don't?* And why go away at all? Why can't they just stay still? And if they have to leave—why does it always feel so personal?

I bet she's done this before. To everyone she fucks and then throws away. Takes them on stage, makes them the center of the universe. I wonder how many little gold chains she's given away. How many others are clinging to some worthless little trinket? I look out into the empty audience and see Tinsel. I see her abandoning me on the dance floor. I see her hands on that skinny, malnourished hipster.

A high-pitched ringing starts in my ears. The spotlight above us flickers once.

I blink. The cat. The orange one. I see its golden eyes in the dark. No. That's not right. Focus. Emma's still talking. Her mouth keeps moving, but it's like someone turned the volume down.

I turn back to Emma. The ice pick is still in my hand.

It goes in easier than I thought—just under her jaw, angled upward. Her mouth opens in a soft, wet gasp, but no scream comes out. She blinks once, as if surprised. I don't give her time to register anything else. I yank the pick free and drive it into her left eye. The bone makes a gristly crunch, dull and final. Her knees buckle. The gin glass slips from her hand and shatters across the stage. For a second, she just stands there—shaking. Then she crumples, a marionette with its strings cut. Her blonde curls pool in the blood spreading beneath her cheek like stage lighting warming up. One last performance. I stand over her, breathing hard but not out of breath. My chest feels hot. My fingers are sticky. I pull the ice pick free. It comes out with a soft pop, slick with blood and something thicker. My ears are ringing. I think I hear applause. I stare at her. If it weren't for the blood, she might be sleeping. I bend closer. No—she couldn't be. Her eyes are open. Wide open. But she's still.

She won't go anywhere now. She can't. I wish I could keep her. Suddenly, the front door of the club slams shut. Keys rattle. *Jingle. Jangle.* My heart leaps into my throat. I drop the pick into my purse, smooth my coat, and exit stage left, out the same alley we entered less than an hour ago.

The cold air hits my face like a bucket of water. I check my reflection in a darkened shop window. Surprisingly clean. No blood on my clothes. Just my hands. Red, shiny, glistening under the streetlights like they've been lacquered. I shove them into my coat pockets and start walking. Something in me has shifted. Not gone. Not burned out.

Just... quiet. Like the moment after a fire's been put out, and all you can smell is steam and smoke and wet wood. My mind replays the keys jingling. The door slamming. Did they see me? How long until they found the body? Not long, I'm sure. I walk fast, New York late-for-a-9:00-AM-meeting fast. I'm at least four blocks away by now. That wasn't the plan. Killing her.

I was surprised when the pick went in. Surprised when it went through her skull.

But the surprise wasn't entirely unpleasant.

Actually, it felt good.

She looked more beautiful than she ever had in motion. So still. Like a porcelain doll. No need for the makeup, the bravado. I gave that to her. I gave her stillness. And I gave it to her in her favorite place in the world. And it was electric.

I feel light, loose, like I just walked out of a deep-tissue massage, or a trance. When I open the door, Mr. Wall Street is sprawled across my bed, scrolling through his phone. He looks up, his face softening when he sees me. His eyes sweep over my body—instinctive, appreciative.

"Your energy looks different," he says.

"Yeah, I just came from a client," I shrug, setting my bag down.

"How was it?"

"Good."

"That's great! I want to take you out to dinner. Are you hungry?"

"Yeah," I smile. "Just give me a second to freshen up. Did you have a place in mind?"

I head into the bathroom, twisting the faucet on. The light flickers overhead. I hear the buzzing sound again, but quieter, a white noise. My hands, coated in syrupy red, go under the water. Pink swirls down the drain, slow and pretty. I scrub harder than I need to. The blood lifts easily. No sirens. No helicopters. Just the memory of the door slamming behind me and the sound of my own breath.

I left Emma on that stage, surrounded by silence. So still. So quiet.

We barely had a relationship. It was quick. Easy. Killing her felt natural.

Leaving her there was hard. I didn't want to. I look in the mirror, letting out a hard sigh. I wanted to...I wanted to lay down next to her. Just for a little while. I feel my eyes begin to tear. My hands are clean now. I look at them. I flex my fingers. I bite my lip, glance up again.

A small giggle bubbles up and escapes before I can stop it.

"Have you been to Sakagura?" Mr. Wall Street calls from the bed, his voice pulling me back.

"No, what kind of Japanese is it?" I grab my black leather skinny pants, a black blazer, a tank top, and the black patent leather Lanvin wedge boots I shoplifted from Bloomingdale's last year.

"It's this very hip sushi spot on 43rd. Underground, where all the Japanese businessmen eat. You said you're pescatarian, right? You have to try their uni. Most places serve it rancid, but Sakagura's is fantastic."

He has this way of making even his enthusiasm sound effortless, like he rules the world. There's something magnetic about it, something I don't want to admit I enjoy. I catch myself smiling as I step out of my jeans and pull on the leather pants, feeling the soft slide of the material against my skin.

"I can't wait, it sounds amazing. Thank you for inviting me, and I love that you remembered I'm pescatarian!" He looks pleased with himself as he lines up some white powder on his iPad with surgical precision.

Glancing up from his work, he hands me a $100 bill. "I also remember you only use hundreds."

I laugh, taking the bill. "Good memory." I lean down to do a line, his gaze lingering just a second longer than necessary.

"So," I say, straightening up, "do you need to make a reservation?"

"Oh, I made one earlier today. It's in 45 minutes."

I smirk tilting my head. "How did you know I'd want to go out?"

"With me? How could you not?" He grins. "But really, I just had a feeling."

"Hmm… Okay." I go back into the bathroom, my heels clicking softly against the tile.

As I reapply my under-eye concealer, the muffled voices of the couple upstairs drift down. He thinks brunch at Sarabeth's is overrated; she insists it's the only place to be on a Sunday morning. Their bickering sounds more like a dance than a fight, predictable, almost comforting. He'll cave. They always do.

"Ready?" Wall Street calls. "We can walk there."

I glance at myself in the mirror, brushing a stray hair back into place and studying my reflection. A quick, satisfied smile flickers across my lips.

10

WE TURN THE CORNER and stop in front of a dated office building. He opens the door for me. We walk in with his hand on my lower back leading me forward. The walls inside are white-painted cinderblock, the kind you'd find in a high school hallway, and the floor is covered in ugly gray tile that hasn't been updated in decades. At the end of the hall, a backlit sign directs us to a steep staircase. My excitement mounts as we descend, my heels clicking against the stairs.

The restaurant greets us with warm bamboo-colored wood and black-painted cement floors. It's intimate but lively, buzzing with quiet energy. We're seated at a small table near the sushi bar. Mr. Wall Street picks up the menu first, immediately delving into a discussion about food options. He's asking me questions, getting a feel for my palate, slipping in polite inquiries about my views on sharing. People who ask if you like to share always want to share. I put my preference aside—of course I do. For him, I don't mind. It's easier this way: let him lead, smile like no one's ever asked before.

Last year, 1950s marriage advice was making the rounds on Pinterest, stuff like *Be a good listener, Cater to his comfort, Don't forget the bedroom, Don't nag. Nagging ruins a man's appetite and sours his mood.* None of it leads to a happy marriage, but it's excellent for bait. Just be his agreeable little sex doll and you'll be taken care of.

"We'd like to start with the uni and clementine, the toro tartare, and the maguro yamakake," he tells the waiter. Then, turning to me: "Do you prefer warm or cold sake?"

"Warm," I reply, brushing a loose strand of hair behind my ear.

"And a bottle of Kenbishi for the table, please," he adds, handing back the menu.

As the waiter leaves, Mr. Wall Street leans back in his chair, studying me. "Tell me something," he says, pausing for effect. "First, I hope you didn't mind that I ordered for us."

"No," I say with a smile, letting a small giggle creep into my voice. "You were very diplomatic in analyzing my tastes beforehand. It was caring."

I've learned how to say the right things. Just enough to make men feel generous. Safe. Like they've found someone easy. Low maintenance. Low threat. Someone who doesn't take up space. Who doesn't ask. Who won't hope for more.

He smiles at my answer, pleased with what he thinks he sees.

"So, tell me," he says. "Do you fall in love easily?"

I meet his gaze, coy. "No, not at all. Why do you ask?"

"Well…" He leans forward slightly. "How we had sex the other night. My style is… very intimate. Some women misinterpret that, and I just wanted to make sure you're not getting too attached."

Smiling at his blatant narcissism, I say, "You know, I hadn't been overthinking it. But yes, I can see how your style could be confusing for some. I'll be sure not to fall in love with you."

"Good," he replies, smirking just as the sake arrives. We tap our glasses together and sip.

"Speaking of love, how's your Brooklyn side piece?" I ask casually, leaning back in my chair.

His expression shifts, his face sinking for the first time. "She's a train wreck."

"Oh? How so?"

"Yesterday I tried breaking up with her for the third time. She calmly unplugged my record player, smashed my Ornette Coleman vinyl, and started choking herself with the cord. She stared me straight in the eye while she did it. When I pried her hands loose, she spat in my face, pissed on the bath mat, and said she'd see me in hell."

He watches me, waiting for judgment. I trace my fingers along my chopsticks.

"She sounds intense." I smile like I'm impressed.

I can't flinch. Not now. He's being vulnerable, opening up, letting me peek into his dysfunction. I need to meet him there. Embrace all of it. All of him.

My mouth doesn't move. I just watch him.

He leans back, gaze drifting up to the black industrial ceiling. "I didn't call anyone. Didn't seem worth it. A hospital would keep her for 48 hours and send her right back. I told her I'd stay. Helped her bandage the cuts. Superficial, mostly, and just... stayed."

I nod slowly, studying the tension in his jaw. "She's keeping you in it. That's what people like that do." I soften my voice, just a little. "You know that's emotional blackmail, right?"

"I get that, but I don't think she means it like that," he says, shaking his head. "She's in a dark place. But it's not calculated, it's just... raw. Like everything hurts more for her. She once told me that loving someone feels like being flayed alive, and she still does it anyway. That kind of vulnerability — it's rare."

I study his face. So that's his type. Not calm. Not stable. But broken in a way that bleeds beautiful. The kind of woman who turns pain into poetry, who leaves scars like love letters.

He thinks that's brave. Romantic. Maybe it is. Maybe I am.

"Why are you so loyal to her?" It comes out too fast, too raw. But I don't take it back.

He exhales, slow and careful, like he's thinking through landmines. "I don't know. Maybe because she never pretended to be anything she's not. Even when she's spiraling, it's all on the table. And I think... some part of me respects that."

I nod, but something ugly curls in my chest. She spirals, screams, pisses on the floor, and he *stays*. He sees the mess and thinks: *I could fix that*. I've tried everything with Tinsel. Been good, been bad, made myself small, made myself essential. But no matter how I bend, she slips right through. Maybe the secret isn't being lovable. Maybe it's being impossible to walk away from.

He pauses, watching me now. "She'll say the worst shit you've ever heard and then text me an hour later asking if I ate lunch. That kind of contradiction, once you get used to it, it starts to feel honest. It's all right there—rage, need, fear. She doesn't make you guess. And she always comes back. No matter what she says or does, she always comes back."

He says it like it's a gift. That's what it takes? Not being lovable, but being relentless? I've spent so long trying to be easy. Clean. Manageable. The kind of girl who fits neatly into someone's life without making a mess. And Tinsel? She loves mess. Lives in it. Wears it like perfume. No wonder she keeps pulling away. I've been trying to keep the water still, and she only wants to drown.

"I have this friend. Tinsel. She's kind of like... everything."

I swirl the last of my sake, eyes fixed on the warm milky liquid. "I let her sleep in my bed. I cooked for her, gave her money when she needed it. I listen to her talk for hours about people who treated her like shit. And then she'd leave me on read for days. She says I'm her best friend, that we're forever. But, like, I feel disposable. I always seem to be *too much* or *not enough*. Never quite right." He's quiet now, watching me differently. "I tried being patient. Being strong. Being her safe place." I look up and hold his gaze. "But maybe that was the mistake. Maybe I should've let her see the wreckage, not just the cleanup. I just want her to stay with me. To see what I'm trying to offer her."

I let the silence stretch between us. He doesn't fill it right away. Just watches me, eyes sharp but softened at the edges. Like he's seeing something he hadn't expected. Something bruised and private that he wants to get closer to without scaring it off.

Finally, he speaks. "You're not disposable." His voice is low. Not performative. Not pitying. Just sure. "It sounds like you're giving a lot more to this relationship than she is. I don't think she pulls away because of anything you did wrong. She does it because some people only know how to chase what runs from them. And when someone stands still, offering real things, they don't know what to do with it." He leans in slightly, fingertips grazing the edge of his glass, but his focus is still locked on me.

"She should stay," he says. "I would."

I look down at the table, at the scattered drops of sake and the chopsticks I haven't touched.

He sees me. Not all of me. Not the worst parts. But enough. I give him a small smile, careful not to overplay it. "Thank you," I say. Just that.

He nods. The silence that follows isn't heavy. It feels... held.

The waiter arrives with a tray of glistening fish, small towers of rice and roe. Mr. Wall Street straightens up, offering a quiet "thank you" as the plates are set down.

I reach for the uni first.

Biting my lower lip and revealing a small grin "This looks amazing. Show me how to eat it."

He picks up his chopsticks, holding them about a third of the way down, perfectly supported with his ring finger and pinky; he carefully picks up the wide orange stripe of uni, lightly grazes it over the sauce, then devours it, swallowing, as I watch his Adam's apple bob up and then down.

"Now it's your turn." He says, having never broken eye contact.

I pick up my chopsticks and place the uni on my tongue closing my mouth. With a very subtle undertone of fresh salt water, the rich, buttery, sweet flavor and slight tinge of citrus ignite my taste buds. The orange sliver of uni melts in my mouth like a thick mousse before making its way down my throat. It is absolutely delectable.

"So….?" He waits for my review.

"It's *sooo* thick and creamy, I love it."

After dinner, Mr. Wall Street and I go home. I snort coke off his cock; he snorts it off my nipples. We fuck like animals—fast, sweaty, feral. When I finally cum, I start crying. Not a few pretty tears, full-body sobs. Inconsolable. He doesn't flinch. Just holds me like it's not the first time he's seen someone come undone.

The high from killing Emma is gone. I thought it would stay longer. I thought I'd feel powerful. Changed. Instead, I feel… cracked. Open in a way I didn't ask for. Her death didn't bring me any closer to Tinsel. It didn't change anything. It didn't fix the ache. I keep seeing her, Emma, collapsed on that stage. Her body slack. Her face frozen in that last surprised expression. It's the stillness that haunts me. Not the blood. Not the weapon. Just the quiet. Something in me broke, and I don't know if it was the part that makes you good or the part that makes you careful.

What's worse?

I want to do it again. I want to chase that high. Not because it felt good. Not even because it felt bad. Because it *felt*.

Mr. Wall Street doesn't ask questions. He just keeps his arm around me, thumb brushing the edge of my shoulder until I stop shaking. I fall asleep wondering if he can smell the blood beneath my perfume.

October 14, 2013

I tore her open like a gift.

Emma.

Still warm when I laid her out. Still twitching when the second puncture slid behind her eye and made that sweet little pop. I felt it in my spine like a kiss. The way her mouth moved after the sound, like she was still trying to say something. Like her body was arguing with death.

But I won.

The ice pick wasn't sharp enough. That's what made it perfect. I had to push. Twist. Crack. There was resistance. She made me work for it.

I've been replaying that night over and over in my head since sitting across from Mr. Wall Street at the dinner table. Each time the memory changes. Each time I seem to edit it bringing it closer to perfection.

Mr. Wall Street bought me uni and sake and called me sweetheart. And I smiled, and I crossed my legs like I wasn't soaking through my panties thinking about disemboweling a girl I barely knew.

I skipped dessert.

Because I had Emma waiting. Emma who has achieved immortality carved on the inside of my skull just underneath my pre-frontal cortex, like my own designer lobotomy. Giving me comfort and stability.

Did you know there's a procedure called the "ice pick lobotomy"?

Ha! Fitting.

If I hadn't been interrupted, regrettably, I would've staged it like performance art. Her legs bent back, toes pointed, arms draped across the stage like she was mid-routine. I'd sit her up and play with her hair. I imagine her scalp making a wet suction noise when I peeled it back to check the bone beneath. Pink. Fractured. Beautiful.

I suck blood from her eye socket. Just to taste it. Just to feel the heat of her last moment on my tongue. I swear I could still feel her thoughts in it. The flavor of panic. The spice of recognition.

She knew it was me.

She knew she was lucky.

I'd take her apart slowly. Slit her belly button open and run my fingers through the fat. Scoop it like frosting. Pry her ribs open just to hear the crack, crack, crack of surrender. Her liver steaming in the cold air. I press it to my cheek. It smells like copper and citrus and need.

I dip my hand in and press deeper, up through the diaphragm, into the hollow space where breath once lived. I want to wear her. To hollow her out like a fucking puppet and crawl inside. My fingers curl around her heart, still twitching. Like she misses me.

I would've fucked her if I had more time.

If the door hadn't opened, if the jingle jangle of keys wasn't closing in on me. Reminding me the world outside was still spinning.

I walked home with blood under my nails and cum in my underwear and a smile that split my face like a split peach. I let Mr. Wall Street hold me while my hair still smelled like the girl I killed.

He asked me how dinner was.

I said: Satisfying.

And it was.

God, it was.

I want to go back. I want to make her move again. I want to wear her face like a mask and finger myself in front of a mirror. I want to fill her like a piñata and let my fists do the rest.

She was so soft.

She was everything I needed in that moment. Not alive. Not noisy. Not laughing at me. Just mine.

Tinsel would've loved the show.

Tomorrow, I'll tell her I ran into Emma and she was rude.

Tomorrow, I'll make her feel like it was her idea to cut Emma off.

Tonight, I smell my hands as they work through a bowl of chicken livers and red Jell-O. I close my eyes.

And I cum thinking of the way Emma's spine gave in.

Delicate.

Sugared.

Snapping just for me.

11

I'M LYING IN BED still scrolling through Apple News articles on my phone. It's 11:07 AM. Mr. Wall Street left around 7:00 AM. I woke up for only a moment to kiss him goodbye.

> **"A Year After the Miami Face-Eating Attack, the City Still Struggles With the Memory."**
>
> *On May 26, 2012, a man named Rudy Eugene brutally attacked Ronald Poppo, a homeless man, on the MacArthur Causeway. The assault lasted nearly twenty minutes and was captured on video, drawing international attention. Eugene was later shot and killed by police. Poppo survived but was left permanently disfigured and blind. The press dubbed the case "The Causeway Cannibal," a phrase that stuck long after the headlines faded.*

I skim the rest, wondering how many times a man has to eat a face before society admits there's something fundamentally wrong with us. The headlines roll on:

> **"U.S. Weighs Iran's Nuclear Enrichment"**
>
> **"When a Pretend Friend Can Help"**
>
> **"NYPD arrests man in "Baby Hope" killing"**

"Two Dead, Two Injured in Nevada School Shooting"
Blah Blah Blah... middle-school student shoots and kills a math teacher. The student then shoots himself in front of other students....Thoughts and Prayers...

"Children's Internet use survey offers warning to parents"

"Photo of blonde girl found in Greece triggers thousands of inquiries"

"JP Morgan close to agreeing $13bn settlement with US authorities"

My thumb lazily swipes through the deluge of human misery and meaningless fluff, then I see it:

"Tragedy at The Box: Renowned Burlesque Star Emma Heard Found Murdered on Lower East Side"
Emma Heard, a beloved fixture of New York City's vibrant burlesque scene, was discovered dead on the evening of October 13th at The Box, a famed Lower East Side nightclub known for its avant-garde performances.

Details surrounding the incident remain scarce, with the NYPD withholding information as the investigation unfolds. Heard, celebrated for her magnetic stage presence and provocative artistry, had been a regular performer at the club and was widely regarded as a rising star in the city's nightlife culture.

The shocking discovery has left the burlesque community reeling, with friends and fans mourning the loss of an artist who brought glamour and grit to the New York stage. Authorities have yet to announce any leads or suspects, and they are urging anyone with information to come forward.

For a second, just a flicker, I think about it. Framing someone. It wouldn't be hard. Emma had orbiters. Obsessives. She was hot. Twenty thousand followers on Instagram. Most of them men. Almost-nude, seductive photos. The kind that invites attention, the kind no one ever takes responsibility for. I could find a name. Build a narrative.

The loner who flirted too long after her show.

The girl in fishnets who never left the green room.

Or... Tinsel. Emma's new friend. Recently appeared in her photos. Liked old ones too—going back months. As if I wouldn't notice. Framing her wouldn't be punishment. It would be proactive, preservation. Put her somewhere I could always find her. She'd be so grateful when I came to visit. She'd spend her days waiting for me.

I could make it poetic. An anonymous letter. A staged prop. A breadcrumb trail for the cops. If this were a movie, that's what I'd do.

But it's not. And honestly? Too much work.

I'm not paranoid. I'm not unraveling.

I'm just... managing the aftermath.

I barely knew her.

There's nothing that links us in any meaningful way. No calls. No photos. No clear motive.

I have the murder weapon. Still.

It's lying at the bottom of my big black purse, under my makeup bag, a mess of loose napkins from various cafés, my current book, notebooks, pens, and tampons. Just another piece of clutter. I thought about taking it out. Hiding it somewhere in the apartment. Or maybe throwing it over the Brooklyn Bridge, letting it drop into the dark water and disappear into the abyss. But I like knowing it's close. No one will find it unless I want them to.

It's mine. It brings me more comfort than anything else I own. Nothing else ties back to me.

It's fine.

You're fine. I'm fine.

My phone buzzes, slicing through my thoughts. I jump.

Tinsel: *Brunch? Feel like being trash with you.*

I stare at the screen for a full minute before responding. Wasn't she just brunching yesterday with Emma? *Emma. Emma. Emma.* How much avocado toast and cheap prosecco can this girl consume? Not to mention it's like totally a Monday.

I reply: *Sure. xo.*

We meet at some café in the East Village. Tinsel arrives 37 minutes late, hungover, fake Chanel sunglasses swallowing half her face.

"Ugh," she groans, sliding into the booth. "If I don't get a Bloody Mary in my system in the next thirty seconds, I'm going to combust."

She talks nonstop. About the party last night. Her roommate's new boyfriend. How she accidentally microdosed before her wax appointment.

Not one word about Emma. No mention of why she didn't reply to our plan for Happy Hour drinks. I thought she was too tired from brunch with Emma, but she was out partying with total randoms.

"You okay?" she asks finally, when the drinks arrive.

"Yeah." I sip mine. "Just tired."

"Same. Anyway. Okay, so this guy last night, total dick, literally asked if I was on birth control *mid-thrust.* Like what the actual fuck?"

I nod. Smile in the right places.

I don't say: *Emma's dead.*

I don't say: *I did it for you.*

I don't say: *Why aren't you different now? Why hasn't this changed anything?*

She eats off my plate. Tells me she missed me. Then it hits me. Of course nothing's changed. She doesn't know.

"Did you see this?" I pull the article up on my phone, cutting off her story about shoplifting underwear from a SoHo boutique where the Olsen twins were seen shopping.

I angle the screen toward her.

"*Tragedy at The Box: Renowned Burlesque Star Emma Heard Found Murdered on Lower East Side*"

Her eyes flick to the headline. She squints.

"Oh my god. Emma?"

"Yeah." I feign a blink of surprise.

Tinsel sets her drink down too hard. "Jesus. That's... insane. I mean, wow. We like just met her at that loft party before Glasslands."

I nod, watching her face. Waiting for something deeper.

Then she says, "You really liked her that night at the loft. I remember you two getting pretty cozy with that blunt."

I scoff. She's really going to play it like that? Like there aren't *dozens* of photos of her and Emma all over Instagram?

"Yeah, I guess but like you and her looked pretty cozy all over Instagram at brunch yesterday. You know, right before she was murdered."

She shoots me a look. A quiet, cutting one. Death glare. Takes a long sip, eyes aimed at the ceiling like she's searching for an exit sign.

"It really is a tragedy," she says finally. "Anyway, shall we get the bill?"

I pretend to get a phone call and walk away without a goodbye hug. Just a wave.

Then I power-walk down Second Avenue before she sees the tears start to fall.

The air outside feels heavy, like it's pressing against my skin. I take the long way back, through Tompkins, past the dog park, trying to slow my pulse.

I keep replaying it.

The way she acted like Emma wasn't in line to be her new BFF. Like she hadn't obsessively posted photos of the two of them together. Like I hadn't seen her tagged, smiling, draped across Emma's lap like they were old friends.

She looked me dead in the face and pretended she barely knew her. Glared at me for pointing out what's public for the world to see. That's the part that sucks.

Not that she lied. But that she didn't bother to confess. Even now. Even when the girl is literally dead. I just can't understand why she won't confide in me. What is she so afraid I'll do?

I wanted that conversation to go differently. I expected it to. All morning, leading up to seeing Tinsel, I've been having this recurring daydream. I imagine it. Tinsel shows up at my door, soaked from the rain, mascara smudged, voice small. She doesn't ask if I'm busy. She doesn't make a joke to soften the air.

She just says, "It was you, wasn't it?"

And I don't answer. I don't have to.

She steps inside. Closes the door behind her. Her eyes are wide, glassy—not scared. Reverent. Like she's looking at a saint. "No one's ever done something like that for me," she whispers. "No one's ever loved me like that."

She touches my face like it's sacred. Like she's blessing me for my devotion.

"Thank you," she says.

Not like I'm dangerous. Not like I'm fucked up. Like I'm hers.

We don't speak after that. I take her to bed. She undresses slowly, like it's a ceremony.

Her body pressed to mine, her breath on my neck, she says, "You're the only one who sees me."

And in the morning, she doesn't leave.

She makes coffee. Sits cross-legged on the bed in my oversized hoodie. I watch her laugh at something dumb on TV, skin soft with sleep. And I know she'll never run again. Because now she understands what I'm capable of. What I'm willing to do.

For her.

To preserve us.

Suddenly, I feel a vibration in my right hand.

A text: *Are you going to the penthouse party Friday?*

It's Jenny Hak. Jenny is one of those women who just exists in your orbit without explanation. I don't know how we met, and I don't know why I still talk to her. One day she was just there, and one day she won't be. She's currently dating the guy throwing Friday's party.

Jenny fancies herself a strong, independent woman, a role model for other women and her daughter. Once, she was a hotshot lawyer in Miami, sipping champagne by pools and attending polo matches in Palm Springs. But five years ago, she had unprotected sex on a tall Italian guy's yacht, decided to keep the baby, and threw her entire career in the trash. Literally. She shredded client files, tossed evidence, and left the state without a word. Her law license was suspended for a decade, but she blames pregnancy hormones.

Now, she lives in a dingy co-op on the Upper West Side clinging to an expensive white leather couch, a remnant of her past life. Most nights with Jenny end with her crying over Veuve Clicquot about the career she lost and the youth she wasted. I tolerate her because she knows people and buys good champagne.

I reply.

Jessie: *I'm seriously thinking about it. You?*

Jenny: *Hey Mama, Can you do me a HUGE favor?*

Curiosity piques. Jenny has never asked me for anything.

Jessie: *What is it?*

Jenny: *My friend flew in from LA for the penthouse party Friday.*

Jenny: *It's couples only and he doesn't have a date.*

Jenny: *Would you go with him?*

Each text comes in separately, like she's still stuck in the AOL Instant Messenger era. My internal groan is loud enough to reach Jersey. Jenny's boyfriend owns the penthouse and is throwing the party. So there's no reason why she shouldn't be able to manage this problem internally.

Jessie: *Can't your boyfriend just let him in?*

Jenny: *He says no single guys allowed.*

Jenny: *He's a nice Jewish boy. Tall, successful, good looking.*

Jenny: *He flew across the country! He has to come, or I'll look like such a crazy bitch.*

There it is. The magical New York phrase: nice Jewish boy. Never mind that he hasn't set foot in a temple in 15 years; his tangential connection to Judaism automatically makes him a prize. And let's be real, no nice boy flies across the country for a sex party.

I start typing *No, I honestly don't want to babysit some random guy who can't find his own date,* but erase it. Too direct. Too aggressive.

Jenny knows I'll say yes. That's the worst part.

I stew in my own manufactured compliance, feeling the edge of something sharp press against the back of my teeth.

My cuticle has split. I rub the jagged edge with my thumb. Then scrape at it with what's left of my nails.

When that fails, I bring my finger to my mouth and start tearing at it with my teeth. First biting down, then pulling. Slow and deliberate.

The skin rips. Blood wells over the nail, inching down toward my knuckle. The tip of my finger throbs, raw and sensitive.

I clench it in my fist, not to protect it, but to *hold it*. To *own it*.

There's something about the wound that feels honest. Something I can control.

With my other hand, I grab my phone and text Jenny:

Ok, I'll do it. Let me know where we're meeting.

Jenny: *THANK YOU! Owe you one!*

Jenny: *He'll meet outside the building at 10 Friday*

Jenny: *See ya then yaya!*

I read the three back-to-back texts as a sullen fog engulfs me.

October 17, 2013

Tomorrow, I have to go to the penthouse party.

With a man I have no interest in being near.

I can't keep his name in my head. It slides off like grease. Jenny sent me at least five photos. I can't recall his face. He looks like no one. He looks like everyone. He's a tech bro who "knows a guy" but always needs more: more financing, more favors, more time. Now he needs me. Complimentary arm candy.

She told me: "You just have to walk him through. They won't let him in alone."

Lead him in like a house pet pretending to be human. Like I'm not the one who deserves the entrance.

I'd rather be home with Pochemu.

I'd rather be anywhere with Tinsel.

But she's not coming.

She's out there somewhere, probably laughing over espresso martinis, wearing that perfect little mask she wore at brunch.

I keep thinking about it. The way she barely reacted to Emma's name in the headline: Tragedy at The Box: Renowned Burlesque Star Emma Heard Found Murdered on Lower East Side

Stir. Sip. Blink.

"That's sad."

Like Emma wasn't pressed against her at Glasslands last week.

Like she hadn't kissed her cheek in the bathroom mirror.

Like they weren't even friends. Probably more.

That mask is seamless. A perfect porcelain face, gleaming under café lights. But I saw it, the hairline fracture, the twitch behind her eyes. She felt it. She just didn't want to ask.

And maybe that's love for her:

Not asking.

Not looking.

Pretending blood is lipstick. Rot is perfume. Hunger is motivation.

I envy her mask sometimes. Mine slips too easily. I keep trying to hold my face in place, to smile and nod and play the good girl at sushi dinners and rooftop parties. But under the skin, the real me is wet. Shining. Starving.

I can still feel Emma's heat in my hands.

The way she jerked, once, twice, and stilled.

The little pop when the ice pick slid behind her eye and the shiver that followed. Mine, not hers.

Sometimes I press my fingers into raw meat in my kitchen, pale chicken breast, cold ground beef, and imagine it's her. Imagine I'm arranging her body. Imagine the stage lights are back on, and I get to finish the performance without interruption. I wanted to kiss her tongue, just to taste the last words she never said.

Tomorrow, I'll wear the mask. I'll let myself be wound up and spin around like a sweet little play thing. And in my head, I'll still be peeling Emma open like a gift.

Imagining her ribs giving way, her organs steaming against the October air.

Imagining how easy it would be to unzip her skin and climb inside, warm and red and real.

No one at the party will know.

They'll see the mask.

They'll clap for the mask.

And I'll be smiling under it, thinking of the girl who finally stopped laughing at me.

12

I'M WEARING ONE OF my favorite cocktail dresses—a black, spaghetti-strapped Kensie with a crisscross back. Short, sleek, and reminiscent of a ballet costume. Blue suede stilettos with dainty ankle straps and black Cuban-heeled thigh-highs complete the look. The stockings' seam matches the blue of my shoes, held up by a black satin garter belt—a gift from a client, partial to worshiping my stocking clad feet. Beneath it, a matching satin thong. No bra; it wouldn't work with the dress, and being an A cup makes that optional anyway.

I roll a body glitter stick over my cleavage. Subtle, strawberry-flavored, and just enough shimmer to feel like I tried. Tinsel swore in high school that it made your boobs look bigger. I'm not sure it's fooling anyone, but it makes me feel good.

For perfume, I choose Angel by Mugler. Bergamot whispers of fresh air, pralines evoke milk and cookies, and the patchouli and amber notes linger, a sultry reminder of feminine mystery. Edible. I slide into my 60s-inspired faux fur-lined jacket and dark brown fingerless gloves—practical for touchscreens, unlike the "tech gloves" that never work.

Before leaving, I catch my reflection in the sliding mirror doors by the kitchen. Light blush, winged eyeliner, mascara. I look good. Normal. Like someone who doesn't leave corpses cooling on stages draped with velvet curtains.

On the counter: my dinner bowl, dried streaks of olive oil cling-ing to the ceramic. The fork glints under the overhead light. I run my thumb along the prongs.

Still stained. Still sharp.

I imagine pressing it against soft flesh, dragging it up a thigh, tracing collarbone. My breath catches. I blink the image away and toss it in the sink.

People think hunger lives in the stomach. It doesn't. It lives in the brain. Behind the eyes. It's the part of you that watches blood circle the drain and wonders what it would taste like.

I rinse my hands again even though they're clean.

Then I smile at my reflection—wide, lovely, practiced—and walk out the door.

It's dead cold as I walk west. If I can get somewhere in under an hour, I prefer to walk. The subway's a filthy cesspool and taxis are just over-priced confessionals with strangers. Walking gives me exercise, solitude, and the chance to watch. Really watch. I study the couples arguing un-der their breath, the girls who pull their coats tighter as they pass men, the ones who dress like they want to be looked at and then pretend they don't. I watch their mouths when they speak. I imagine what their skin tastes like. What they'd sound like if they screamed. Central Park looms ahead. It's dark, sprawling, full of shadows to disappear into.

New Yorkers like to describe Central Park at night as if it was 1989 and "The Central Park Five" was still splashed over the headlines. The truth is most arrests in Central Park are drug related and at worse rob-bery. Still, I go around the perimeter, though straight through would be faster.

I pass by the horse-drawn carriages. The drivers are all speaking with each other, and business is slow. One waves at me, offers me a ride in his carriage. I smile, shake my head and keep walking. I imagine how romantic it must have been in 1907 with the streets lined with carriages, women in elegant dresses and parasols, and men in three-piece suits. The fantasy shatters as the stank stench of urine and body odor fills my nostrils, and I nearly trip over a homeless man curled against the wall.

The penthouse is just ahead. I give the doorman the apartment number, and he waves me in. I'll come down when Jenny's friend arrives to take him up. Men never just arrive. They come with expectations, eyes that follow you all night, invisible leashes made of politeness and fake gratitude. He's not even here yet and I already feel chained to him. Some faceless plus-one I'm meant to host like a tour guide in my own life. Tonight, I will not allow this man's presence to have power over me. It will not impact my good time. It will not detract from my enjoyment of this party. I own my power. I am responsible for my fun.

I push door 1723 open. The penthouse hums with familiar energy—chill electro music, expensive perfume, the heat of too many bodies in one gilded space. I spy the host next to the backlit built-in bar. I call him The Pug. The Pug is about 5'10", bald, with sleepy blue eyes, and his ears stick out in a cute nerdy way. He has that just-lost-about-90-pounds-by-running-marathons body. The Pug dresses nicely but understated. Tonight, he's wearing a black, well-pressed Calvin Klein dress shirt with matching slacks. He smells like ocean salt and lemongrass. He is a recent divorcé trying to live his best life and be happy. The Pug's entire penthouse is leather, chrome, crystal; very masculine and modern. It all blends handsomely. However, the vibe is broken up by these amateurish, pastel-coloured, mostly pink, floral paintings of his pugs. I'm pretty sure he commissioned them on Fiverr, maybe Etsy.

His ex-wife took his pugs in the divorce, but apparently, he still gets them every other weekend. If he catches you staring at the paintings for too long he'll walk up in an apologetic tone and say something like "Oh, those are my exes" with a chuckle. He thinks that makes it better or explains it away, but actually, it just takes a funny quirk and turns it into a heart-wrenchingly sad picture of being a single middle-aged New Yorker. He's the CEO of his brother's software company, but he'd be happier covered in rainbow glitter running naked through the woods. I walk up to him, he takes my hand, pulls me closer, and kisses each cheek. Oh so European. I've been to plenty of these parties. The faces change, but the rituals stay the same, everyone pretending they're freer than they are.

"Thank you so much for having me." I smile

"Of course, Jessie, of course, always. What can I get you?" He coos.

"Mmmm…. Coffee Patron with a splash of coke?"

He grips my waist as he hands me the drink. It's territorial, performative. I want to shove him off. Instead, I smile and let it happen. I've trained myself to tolerate it, to turn revulsion into charm, compliance into allure. I'm good at pretending it doesn't bother me. Better at pretending I don't secretly like the attention. He wanders off to entertain his other guests. I look around. The place has filled up early with the regular swinger scene. On the black leather L-shaped couch, in front of the floor to ceiling windows overlooking the city skyline, lounges Natalya. Natalya is in her late 30's, she immigrated to NYC from Russia about 10 years ago. She has 2 kids, who live in her house in Hoboken, New Jersey and are cared for almost exclusively by European au pairs that she replaces every 6 months. Her ex-husband imports gemstones and lives in China now. He's generally characterized as an inconsiderate bastard. Natalya is petite, with long, thick, dark hair and piercing grey eyes. Her personality is erratic, sadistic, self-serving and utterly addicted to drama. I would say she's a gold digger as she really seems to value people, men especially, from what she can gain; however, she is dating the DicKtator, who just slinked in next to her. The DicKtator is 6'5", lanky but well-toned, early 40s. Lives off protein shakes and supplements. He's a low-end private investigator whose greatest accomplishment is buying an asbestos-ridden apartment across from where John Lennon was shot.

He's infamous in this scene for being controlling, borderline misogynistic, and for having a cock so freakishly long it feels like a party trick. I've seen it. Everyone's seen it. He flashes it like it's a business card. Honestly, he could make a killing on the freak show circuit.

Moving on.

Standing across from them are the Fengs. They're that couple that you can't tell if they're twins or romantic partners. They got married right out of college — both virgins on their wedding night! Then, on one tropical vacation, they decide to go to a nudist beach. Their version is that this was their sexual awakening that inspired them to branch out. It's my theory, however, that she realized her husband had a micro-penis and didn't want to spend the next 60 years settling for that. They're both computer geniuses, who I believe work in IT at the same company. As I begin to approach these familiar pairings, out of the corner of my eye, I see the self-proclaimed King of Swing enter, his partner Kendra at his side. She's an absolute goddess. Five foot four, long, perfect, thin twisted dreadlocks, big dark brown eyes, long fingernails, an adorable wide-set button nose — always smells of cinnamon and five spice. He... well, in 1994, I bet he was hot. Now, he looks haggard. Dirty blonde disheveled hair, a strong square jawline with a 5:00 shadow. When he works out, he actually looks like a DILF, but lately, he's really let himself go, exemplified by the layer of fat covering a once-prominent six-pack. He has a silver ball pierced through his chin, a throwback to the early 2000s facial piercings.

He calls himself the King of Swing because he and Kendra run this swinger party in Midtown called Lick. It's open every week; most nights, it's pretty dead, but they throw about four solid, packed parties a year. Kendra took out a loan in her name to get the space—he couldn't because his credit is a disaster. She organizes the entertainment and is the main draw for the women (who make any sex party worth having or attending). But somehow, he's convinced himself, and all the men who attend, that he's the be-all-end-all of Lick and the NYC swinger scene. He never smells like anything, possibly because he's just a ghost of his former '90s self.

I run past the King and hug Kendra, running my hands over her silky silver slip dress.

"Oh my god. I haven't seen you since that whole Tinsel debacle. I am so sorry I invited her and introduced her to you. I feel terrible. She is such a fucking trollop," I say quickly, with wide eyes and a pouting mouth.

Last month, I brought Tinsel to a Lick party and introduced her to Kendra and the King of Swing. The King and Tinsel hit it off instantly, and two weeks later, I hear she's "crashing" in their spare room in Brooklyn. Which—no. That's not how this works.

Even in the wild west of ethical non-monogamy, there are rules. You don't move a girl you've known for two weeks, who you're fucking, into the home you share with your primary partner. Not without long, clear conversations and *explicit consent*. That's not polyamory. That's just asking for emotional chaos. Tinsel has a perfectly functional dorm at FIT. I'm sure she sold them some sob story about needing a place to stay, played the sad, slippery waif, and they bought it. Needless to say, the arrangement lasted all of four nights. Kendra caught the King sneaking into Tinsel's room after midnight to fuck Tinsel behind her back, and she went ballistic - started throwing kitchen chairs at him like she was auditioning for *Real Housewives: Bed-Stuy Edition.*

Of course, I feel completely and utterly humiliated. However, not surprised. I don't believe Tinsel has ever cared about how her actions impact literally anyone else, so this is pretty in line for her. I told her explicitly not to fuck around with the King, so of course, she moves in with him and makes it awkward as hell for me to go to Lick. Such a cunt. Why am I friends with her again? Kendra breaks my train of thought with a sweet laugh.

"Trollop. You are hysterical. But really, Jessie, don't even think about it. Our relationship is stable now, and you know, it wasn't your fault at all."

"Thanks." I smile shyly. "Hey, can you help me take a sexy picture to send to my girlfriend?"

Kendra smiles. "Sure thing! Of course. Okay, how about you stand in front of the window and hike up your skirt a bit to show your garter?" She directs me while snapping photos with my phone camera. We finish, and she hands me back the phone, showing me the photos.

"So sexy. I didn't know you had a girlfriend. Why didn't you bring her?" Kendra says while squeezing my hips and looking over my shoulder as I scroll through the photos, analyzing my facial expressions and body composition in each.

I look up, searching for the words to explain. "Oh yeah. I mean, it's kind of a new thing. It's not like official, I guess."

"I see." She smiles knowingly. "Well, best of luck with that." She kisses my cheek and walks over to the bar.

I sit on the sofa. Having chosen the perfect photo, I attach it to a text and send it to Tinsel with the message: *Thinking about you.*

Tinsel answers almost instantly: *Hahaha okay looking hot Raz. Where are you?*

Immediately follows that text with: *Who sends this to their friends? You crack me up.*

Honestly, I just want to go home and cry. I stare at the screen, the words blurring together in front of me:

Hahaha okay looking hot Raz. Where are you? Who sends this to their friends? You crack me up.

It feels like someone's taken my ribs in both hands and squeezed until I can't breathe. I want to scream. I want to hurl my phone across the room, watch it smash into a thousand pieces like my pride. But instead, I sit there, motionless, my thumb hovering over the keyboard, unsure if I should reply. What would I even say? Thanks? As if she doesn't know how nasty her reply was.

I remember what Mr. Wall Street told me over dinner. *Some people only know how to chase what runs from them.* That's Tinsel. She doesn't know what to do with stillness. With something real. She doesn't know how to *stay*. But I can show her. I can teach her how to feel safe in love.

I close my eyes, trying to let go of the rage pumping through my veins. We've been friends for so long. I've always been the beta to her alpha, orbiting her chaos, adjusting my gravity to suit her mood.

You crack me up. I roll it around in my mind, hearing it in a mocking tone that ricochets off my skull until my eyes sting. Our dynamic has to change. If she won't meet me halfway, I'll bring her the rest of the way myself.

Nothing worth having has ever come easily. And love is no exception.

She needs me. Her life would unravel without me. That girl can't even make a dentist appointment without moral support.

Last time her roommate ghosted her, she stopped eating for four days and tried to crash at some guy's place she met once at Barcade. I picked her up at dawn to walk with her back to her dorm because she heard 'rapists were on the rise'.

She "accidentally" overdrafted her bank account five times last year. Guess who covered her phone bill for six months of it? Who else does she even have? To everyone else, she's magic. But I'm the one who holds her hair when she's puking glitter. I just need to rewire the connection. Help her see, really see, what I am to her. It might hurt. It might hurt us both. But what is life, love without suffering?

I look back down at my phone and thumb the message: *Out with some friends. Just at this penthouse thing. You'd love it. Everyone here reminds me of you. Such a Tinsel kind of vibe. So so crazy. Let's catch up later. I seriously miss your face!! <3*

I hit send on my reply to Tinsel.

From out of the bedroom, I see Jenny moving intentionally in my direction. Sigh. He must be here. She smiles and waves while approaching.

"Hey, Hot Stuff!" She's looking cheerful, maybe even a little manic. I wonder if she's planning to have a threesome with this LA guy or what. I smile back, just enough.

Jenny continues, "He's downstairs, outside the building. Security won't let him up unless I escort him. Rules are rules." She rolls her eyes like she's been locked in battle with the doorman all night.

"Will you come with me? He's nervous, and I figured it'd be better if you two walk in together. It's more calming to show up with a badass babe." She winks.

I cringe. She's so faux feminist it's painful. Like calling me *badass* somehow cancels out the fact that she's parading me in front of her little boy toy for his evening's amusement.

"Sure," I say, though she's already halfway to the door.

13

AS THE ELEVATOR OPENS and we turn right, the hyper-polished oak concierge desk comes into view. Leaning against it is a man, about 5'8", with short, spiky black hair—*ew*—pale skin, a thin face and limbs, and a noticeable pot belly. Mid-thirties, clean-shaven. He's wearing a maroon bomber jacket, shiny nylon, not leather, over a navy shirt with a scalloped circle pattern, dark skinny jeans, and black-and-white Nike sneakers. He's leaning over the desk, schmoozing with the doorman.

An overwhelming smell of vinegar and baking soda tinged with iodine fills my nostrils. For a moment, I wonder if the cleaning crew had just been through, but no - it's him. He's a walking douchebag.

Jenny power-walks toward him. He doesn't even bother to straighten up. What the hell is he waiting for, an ass grab? Jenny links her arm in his and bumps their hips together. He turns with a feigned look of surprise, like he didn't see us stepping out of the elevator. I hate phonies. Jenny lights up beside me, eyes wide, smile syrupy. I watch the exchange, puzzled. *What does she see in him?* Then again, this is Jenny. She has a habit of collecting men like off-brand handbags, shiny, overpriced, and always a little beneath her.

Jenny's voice jumps two octaves, quick, loud, a register I've never heard from her before. They're jabbering like old friends reunited after years apart. Meanwhile, I'm swaying in my too-high heels, ruminating on the bad decisions that landed me here: saying yes to Jenny out of some outdated sense of loyalty, agreeing to escort a man I've never met, telling myself I could float above it all with grace.

Now I'm forced to witness a nauseating display of New York bull-shit colliding with LA bullshit.

The second I lay eyes on him—over-whitened teeth, gelled hair, the fake surprise like we didn't just make eye contact two seconds ago—I knew. He's the kind of man who treats parties like auditions and wom-en like props. I don't even need to hear his voice to know he'll bring up crypto before the night's over.

Jenny's already turned herself into his publicist, and I'm the bait she brought to keep him calm. This night won't end quietly. It'll unravel, loud and sloppy.

Why did I say yes? Would she have done the same for me?

Their phony eyes land on me. Jenny's cold, bony fingers lace through mine, and I'm yanked forward into the awkward theater of introduc-tions.

In this moment, I wish a massive gust of wind or a twister would scoop me up, hurling my willowy body through the towering double apartment doors, over the sprawling trees of Central Park, and toward the fantastical land of Oz. The mighty wind would drag me through the chaos of flying horse-drawn carriages, depositing me on the Yellow Brick Road in a heap of broken limbs and shattered ribs.

There, as my mangled body lay twisted and bloody, soft whimsical music would begin to play. Out of the vibrant wildflowers and tech-nicolor greenery, munchkins would emerge. Their pastel outfits and neatly curled hair framing cherubic faces would look innocent at first, but their wide, greedy eyes would betray them. Slowly, they would sur-round me, their steps tentative until the first brave one reached out, touching my splintered rib.

Then it would happen all at once. A horde of them would rush forward, their tiny hands tearing into my flesh. One would gnaw at the exposed bone of my shattered arm, while another would slurp my blood through my small intestine like a grotesque straw. They would rip and tear, their cheerful chatter drowned out by the wet, visceral sounds of their feast. The lush gardens around us would bloom crimson with the spray of my blood.

As the last scraps of me were devoured, the munchkins would recline in satisfied heaps, their distended bellies rising and falling as they sighed in contentment. Smiles of bliss would stretch across their angelic faces as they drifted into a peaceful slumber amidst the gore-soaked flowers.

And just like that, I would have provided a grotesque feast for the masses while deftly escaping this weird-as-fuck social situation.

Uh-oh. I'm supposed to say something to this guy. I straighten up, lock eyes with him, and plaster on a big, shit-eating grin. Before he can close the distance, I extend my hand and say, "Jessie. How was the flight?"

He shakes my hand with a weak grip, soft as a baby's bottom. I respond with a firm, deliberate shake and release quickly, never breaking eye contact. His perfectly manicured nails are buffed to a sheen, a stark contrast to my own: bitten, swollen, sometimes bloody. I wonder if he notices. I wonder if he likes that.

"So," he says, voice purring with self-assurance, "I'm building this thing, kind of like a wellness experience meets immersive media. Think ayahuasca meets Burning Man meets Forbes 30 Under 30. Totally disrupts the serotonin economy."

His eyes sparkle like he's handing me a diamond.

Jenny claps him on the back like he's just solved world hunger. "Isn't he a genius?"

"Sounds revolutionary," I murmur.

Jenny lights up like he just proposed.

I picture peeling off his skin like a fruit roll-up.

He keeps talking—microdosing, crypto-based art collectives, something about a silent retreat in Tulum where you scream into the ocean at sunrise to activate your throat chakra. His breath smells like pine gum and disappointment. I nod slowly, tilt my head. My silence, he decides, is intrigue. He thinks I'm captivated. Or high. Or submissive.

Perfect.

I sip my drink and drift out of my body. I watch from a distance: the ambitious man-child, the overcompensating hostess, and me—the art installation. Sharp at the corners, built for misinterpretation.

This is foreplay, in its own way. The ritual of ego, flirtation, and performance. He touches Jenny's arm. She laughs too loud. His eyes flick to me again, like he's wondering what it'd feel like to be between us. Keep wondering, buddy.

We walk back into the party. As far as I'm concerned, my obligation is fulfilled. He's through the door. Now Jenny can deal with the bullshit-spewing LAXative she invited.

I cross to the bar to top off my drink with more coffee Patrón and do a quick scan of the room. It's filling up now, littered with blonde graduate students and a few sexy Wall Street execs, plus the usual dumpy sugar daddies who always seem to be lurking. I weave through the living room, ignoring the tiresome small talk—'Oh yeah, I don't usually come to these things, but you know, I just thought, let's be wild tonight! What's the harm? You never know, it could be fun, right?!'—and head for the narrow wooden stairs tucked off to the side, leading to the rooftop deck. The Pug has lined the stairs with tea candles in silver glass holders, their soft glow casting flickers on the walls.

An arm blocks my path.

His pasty face hovers too close, leaning in like he's about to start sniffing me. His skin too tight from retinol, breath too sweet with synthetic mint.

"So what's your *real* deal?" the LAXative purrs, like he's earned access. "You've got this whole... dark, vampiric thing going on. I bet you're a freak in bed."

I look at him. Really look. He doesn't flinch. But there's a tremor behind the smile. A little boy's eagerness poorly dressed up as bravado.

"Only with people I respect," I say. Quiet. I want him to lean in to hear it.

His grin curls. "Damn. Jenny said you were intense. But I didn't realize you were *so domineering*. Let's find a room. I'll read you Anne Rice, you can show me how vampires suck."

I let a pause stretch too long. Then sip my drink, slow and bored. "You confuse disinterest for kink. Common mistake. Men like you think being ignored is foreplay."

He chuckles, smug. Like I'm negging him. Like I want to be pursued.

Dogs wag their tails right before you slam the crate door shut.

"We'll see," he mutters, already turning.

In his head, he's won something. In mine, I'm threading piano wire between his perfect front teeth, slow and gentle, just before the yank.

I duck under his arm, heels echoing softly as I climb the stairs and push open the door.

Cold air whips my face, stinging my skin and making my eyes water. I consider going back inside to grab my jacket from the coat closet, but I catch Natalya's gaze and decide to stay. Taking a deep breath, I power through the chill, goosebumps rising along my bare arms and back as I walk toward her.

Natalya is leaning against the short concrete wall separating the rooftop from a sixty-foot drop to the cement below. Her hips jut out, her right arm hanging loosely at her side while her left hand brings a Virginia Slim to her pale pink lips. She inhales deeply and tilts her head back, releasing the smoke in a slow, upward stream.

"Hey" I say not bothering to add a smile. Natalya may be completely unstable and the empress of drama, but she never makes me feel like I need to fake any type of emotion for her comfort.

I've told her things I haven't told anyone. Once, I confessed I used to fantasize about slicing open a guy I was dating, not because I hated him, but because I needed to know what lived underneath. I imagined peeling back his skin like wet fruit, slipping my fingers between muscle and bone, cupping his organs like love letters sealed in meat. I wanted to feel the heat inside him, see if his devotion pulsed in his liver, if his promises lived in his lungs. I wanted to kiss his heart mid-beat. I used to picture licking the blood off my knuckles, tasting the raw devotion he never managed to say out loud. I wanted him open—truly open—no lies, no deflection, just flesh and truth and heat.

Natalya didn't even blink. She took a drag of her cigarette, exhaled through her nose, and said, "Honestly? Same."

"Alyo" she responds in a thick Russian accent, then gets right into it. "I am so pissed off at that bastard. Did you see what he did?"

I hadn't seen what he did. I knew she was referring to the DiKtator. It must have happened when I was in the lobby picking up Jenny's ill invited LAXative.

"No, I had to go downstairs for a minute. What did he do?" I ask. Now standing next to her looking over the edge. She turned and looked at me with that steely, biting gaze of hers and replied "He fucked Erika. Fucking pathetic bastard. I told him anyone, anyone but her. And what did he fucking do?! Right in front of me on that fucking sofa."

"Oh. Wow." I calmly release a sigh and break eye contact. "What did you do?"

"I ripped her out from under him and dragged her to the hallway by her hair and kicked her out in those stupid quilt lingerie she makes. Threw the bastard's pants out the bathroom window. They both left. I don't know where. I don't care."

Damn. I definitely missed a scene. I hadn't realized Erika was even here tonight. I wasn't in the lobby for long. It must have happened fast, and everyone's already over it, no lingering tension in the party's vibe when I came back. Everyone's used to Natalya and the DicKtator's explosive relationship. Too bad Erika was collateral damage this time. She's pretty awkward but not bad.

"Well, sounds like you handled it and made your point. Why do you hate Erika again?"

"Ugh!" She groans, rolling her eyes. "She is fucking gross. So pathetic. Always lapping after us like a lost puppy without a bone. The only reason he even looks at her is because she doesn't move and whimpers when he's fucking her. He likes that. He wishes I was one of those... how do you call them? Balloon sex dolls. It's sick. Perverted. And do not even get me started on those knitted underwear she makes. Fucking peasant shit. When she pulls out her yarn and needles in the corner, I feel like I'm at a farm market or something. It's ridiculous. I do not want her peasant pussy juice on his cock, then on me. No. No. NO."

I start laughing. My laugh turns into a near-cackle as I double over, my abs straining, barely able to stand. She watches me, slightly amused. "Peasant pussy juice?! WHAT?!" I gasp out, as I continue to deteriorate into my own screaming laughter. She joins in until we're both sitting on the ground, backs against the ledge.

We calm down. She pulls out another cigarette, silently offering me one. I raise a hand and shake my head 'no' while I wipe away laughter tears. After taking another drag, she reaches back into her cigarette pack this time pulling out a little baggy with white powder and crystal rocks inside it. She takes out one of the rocks and puts it in my drink without asking. "There. Now we will both have a fun night together. MDMA, very pure, drink it."

Smiling, I say, "Thank you." And finish the rest of the drink, swallowing the little MDMA crystal. Natalya stubs out her half-finished cigarette. "It's cold. Let's go inside."

I follow her.

Inside, the room is warm and inviting, scented with vanilla and black pepper. I glance toward the bedroom at the end of the staircase. The Fengs are hurriedly getting dressed, guilt written across their faces like kids caught with their hands in the cookie jar. Jenny and the Pug are caressing each other on the armchair facing the bed. Two blonde women I don't recognize are giggling while they shut the door of the master bathroom. I think they are likely the cookies the Fengs stole from the jar. I feel Natalya's hands around my waist as she gently whispers, "I want to lay you on the bed and fuck you with a double-sided dildo. Is that okay?"

"Yes." I say a little louder than I meant to, with a slight bashful giggle in my voice.

She turns me around, sliding my dress over my head in one fluid motion. Her emerald green sequin dress shimmers in the dim light. I reach for her back, unzipping it with practiced ease. The dress falls away, pooling at her feet.

As she pushes me onto the bed, my fingers find the silk waistband of her sheer white lace briefs. Every touch feels amplified, electric, the MDMA humming through me like an extra heartbeat. My fingers slip inside, and for a moment, it's just sensation—soft skin, warmth, the steady pulse of her body against mine. I feel like Poseidon, holding the world's oceans in my hands, bending tides with my fingertips. For that brief moment, I'm not chasing anyone. I'm not running from anything. I'm in control.

Then she grabs my hair, her fingers finding the roots with a precision that sends a sharp thrill down my spine. She flips me over, her dominance igniting something feral in me as she grinds her hips toward my face. My mouth finds her thighs, the taste of her filling me with a heady mix of power and surrender. I'm aware of the room beginning to fill, shadows shifting at the edge of my vision. Eyes linger at the doorway. We both know they're watching.

Natalya and I are acutely aware of the performance. We've done this before, more than once. At parties like this, in front of people like these. We know the choreography by heart. The rhythm between us isn't improvised. It's ritual. Practiced. Honed. We move like twin flames, same height, same silhouette. If you don't look too closely, you might think we're sisters. That's the fantasy. We let them have it. Natalya knots her fingers in my hair and pulls just hard enough to blur the line between pain and permission. I arch against her, back bowed like a sacrificial lamb. Her teeth skim my collarbone. Her moan is low, almost reverent. We're not performing for the men. We're performing against them. I know this is a show. All of it. The audience, the tension, the choreography, we've built it to be consumed. But performance doesn't mean fake. That's the mistake most people make. They think masks hide you, when sometimes they reveal the truth more clearly than anything else. In the performance, I get to choose what they see. In the performance, I'm in control.

Our bodies weave a spell—soft limbs, sharp edges, the heat of skin punctuated by sudden gasps. It's not about pleasure. Not really. It's about control. We let them watch, let them hunger. But they'll never taste. Never touch. That's the violence of it. We invite them to the edge and deny them the fall.

The crowd's gaze lingers too long on her skin. So I kiss her like I want to crawl inside her, make them look away. I tilt her face to mine and kiss her like I'm devouring something rare. The air feels viscous, electric. Someone nearby exhales too loudly. Good. Let them squirm. Let them ache. This is female power—messy, holy, soaked in sex and spectacle. And it's ours.

She pulls me by my roots again, pulling me upwards. From her purse, she retrieves a pink silicone double-sided dildo, licking it slowly, theatrically. She plunges one end into me, then mounts the other, her hips grinding as her hand moves from my hair to my throat.

The MDMA intensifies every sensation—her grip, the rhythm of her body against mine. My thoughts splinter, fragments of control and chaos. I feel her power over me and relish the way I can give in without losing anything. It's all here, in this moment, balanced perfectly between us.

When we finish, we lay still for a second before slipping back into our dresses, leaving our panties on the floor. Natalya disappears into the bathroom. I head to the dressing table, smoothing my hair and applying lip balm. My reflection stares back at me, calm, collected, and untouched. The performance is over, but the mask stays on.

Stepping back into the party, I pour another drink, the warmth of the room washing over me again. Around me, the chatter and laughter continue, oblivious. For a moment, I feel the buzz of satisfaction—the kind that comes from knowing I still have control, even if it's just over this.

As I take my first sip of the cold bubbly drink, I feel an odious presence approach and lean on the wall next to me. I side eye the repugnant guest as he leans over, gently nudging my arm like we're best buddies.

"I saw you in the other room. Was that show for me?" the LAXative purrs, sidling up like he's offering me a gift. His grin is lazy, greedy, self-congratulatory, like he's just won something.

My stomach clenches. Of course this guy thinks everything revolves around him. I feel the MDMA beginning to wear off, like glitter rinsed down a drain. My skin feels too thin, my nerves too close to the surface.

I take a long, slow sip of champagne and don't answer right away. My mind floods with fantasies—none of them sexy, all of them sharp. I picture pushing his face through the mirror behind the bar. Watching the shards scatter like stardust. I imagine licking the blood from his cheek, just to watch him flinch.

Instead, I raise an eyebrow. "That's your opener? I literally don't think about you. We don't even know each other."

He chuckles, smug. The kind of laugh that begs to be bitten out of a man.

I scan the room for an exit, anyone I can cling to, distract myself with, but there's no escape hatch in sight. My hand tightens around my glass. I feel the tremor in my wrist and set it down before I shatter it. Just for a moment, I watch the condensation on the glass bleed into the marble like it's trying to vanish too.

"Well then, why don't you get to know me?" he says, like he's just offered a priceless opportunity.

"I'm good."

My eyes rake the room for an exit, a shield, a warm body to hide behind, but I'm alone. Anxiety licks at my insides, acidic and electric. I crack my knuckles, and in my mind, each pop is cartilage giving way. Tiny fingers. Tiny spines. *Snap. Snap. Snap.* I pick my glass back up. Grip tight. Too tight. The urge to squeeze until it shatters sings through my fingertips. I'd let the shards slice deep, carve rivers into my palm, watch the blood pool and bubble like champagne. Maybe then I could focus.

"Come on," he presses. "I don't know anyone here. Jenny's with her boyfriend, and I'm just… kind of floating."

His voice softens at the end, trailing off like a balloon losing air. He's not just hitting on me anymore; he's looking for an anchor. Something to tether himself to so he doesn't spiral.

It's almost touching, in a sick little way. How quickly the predators fold when they think no one's watching. All that bravado hiding a bottomless pit. I feel a flicker of something, not sympathy, not really. More like the vague thrill of knowing I could help him or wreck him. Maybe both.

"I have some coke. Do a bit with me?" he adds, eyes searching mine for permission.

The offer is tempting. The MDMA has worn off, and I wouldn't mind a little bump. I glance at him, just long enough to make him think I'm weighing something deeper.

I sigh. "Okay. Let's do some blow. Follow me."

I lead him into the powder room off the bar, and he grabs the champagne bottle on the way. On the bathroom floor, we pass the bottle and the coke, his usual bullshit flowing like a broken faucet. He tells me he's "making his mark in tech", how life-changing his Birthright trip was five years ago, and how much he loves New York's walkability. Basic bitch stuff all around.

As the champagne dwindles and the baggie empties, he turns to me. "Hey!" His tone is oddly urgent. I glance up from the compact mirror I'm about to do a line off of.

"Yeah?"

"I saw those guys out there, lots of them had boners for most of the night. How are they doing that?"

I smirk. It's actually adorable how clueless he is. His insecurity is showing. So cute.

"If you ask them, they'll say they're drug-free, drink little alcohol, and work out. That it's just their natural stamina. The truth? They're all on so much Viagra. Natalya's dude even gives himself injections, like, straight into his dick, to stay hard longer. It's freaky as fuck watching her do it for him."

A tidal wave of relief washes over his face. He definitely thought he was coming up short.

The bottle and baggie are now empty. I stand, adjusting my dress.

"Excuse me," I say, slipping out of the powder room and heading back into the kitchen, where Jenny and the Pug are posted up by the marble island, laughing over something petty and expensive.

I grab a VOSS water bottle from the counter, unscrew it, and wedge myself between them like I belong; which, here, I do.

"Your place always looks like a Dwell spread had sex with a dungeon," I tease the Pug, letting the corner of my mouth twitch up in a smirk.

He laughs, pleased. "That's the goal."

Jenny swats at him playfully, then looks at me. "She's not wrong, though. You're missing a Saint Andrew's Cross and a live-in twink."

I chuckle, take a sip, and let myself relax for a moment.

"You missed it earlier," I say to Jenny. "There was a guy in the guest bathroom yelling about how bidets are emasculating. I didn't have the heart to tell him he had a shit line smeared on the back of his boxers."

Jenny bursts out laughing, nearly spilling her champagne.

"God, I needed that," she says, wiping the corner of her eye. "You always make the down time bearable."

"Someone has to," I reply, letting just a trace of warmth peek through. This, I can manage. Polished cruelty. Dry wit. Control.

Then I feel it.

That change in air pressure. That cloying scent of ego and Axe body spray.

"I was wondering where you ran off to," the LAXative says, sliding in too close, his voice syrupy with false charm.

I turn slowly.

"There you are," he adds, grinning like we're on a second date. "Miss me?"

The smile I had been wearing shrivels at the edges. My posture shifts, just a little, shoulders straighter, chin lifted.

Jenny opens her mouth to say something, but doesn't. The Pug raises an eyebrow.

"I was just telling them about the bidet guy," I say to no one in particular, tone flat now.

"Oh man," LAX says, laughing like he's part of it. "That's hilarious."

He touches my elbow. I don't flinch. I just let my arm go limp beneath his fingers until he lets go.

There's a pause. Long enough for the energy to turn.

I lift the VOSS bottle to my lips, take a long, slow sip, then say, "Back in a sec."

No explanation. No warmth.

And then I'm gone, walking out of the kitchen, out of the penthouse, like I'm shedding a skin.

The door closes behind me, muffling the throb of music and laughter. For a moment, it's just me and the hallway—dim, still, sterile. My heels click softly against the polished floor. The sound feels too loud, like it's echoing inside my skull. I should feel powerful. I *was* powerful. The show with Natalya. The way I played LAXative like a starving dog, teasing him with the scent of meat I never planned to share. I could've taken him to the balcony, unzipped him with my mouth, and just as he closed his eyes, slit him open from navel to throat. Let his guts spill like a gift. Ride him until he stopped twitching. Moan as I gush over his dying body. I imagine peeling the skin off his face mid-orgasm, pinning his eyelids open so he could watch me smear his blood across my chest like perfume. He'd die thinking he was chosen. That's the mercy I would have gifted him. A cold breath rattles through me. I blink. The hallway returns. Stillness. Brass sconces. Beige wallpaper. But now the buzz is gone. I feel hollowed out, my skin too tight, my insides humming like a fridge about to break. The air feels cooler here. Thin. I pass a mirror above the entry console and catch my reflection—eyes smeared with shimmer, mouth flushed, hair wild from her grip. I look like I belong in that room. But I don't. I never did. I just know how to haunt a space without being caught. I press the elevator button and wrap my arms around myself, rubbing a sore spot just under my collarbone where her teeth sank too deep. The imprint still tingles.

For a second, I think about texting Tinsel.

Then I hear it. The sound of footsteps behind me. Sloppy. Hesitant. A rustle of synthetic fabric and too-loud breathing.

Turning to my right, I see the LAXative power-walking toward me. Before I can process it, he's standing next to me, word vomit spilling out of his mouth.

"Huh." My only response. I press my lips together, raise my eyebrows slightly, and nod—parrot-like. Maybe if I don't engage, he'll go away.

"So! Where to next?" His grin stretches, hopeful.

"Uh, well, it's late. I'm heading home to crash, but you could check out the Electric Room. It's fun late-night." I mutter, avoiding eye contact. Maybe if I don't look at him, he'll disappear.

"Right, yeah. I'm wiped too. Just flew in today. Totally lagged. How are you getting home?"

"Well, you know, the usual way I always get home," I say, vague. *Where the hell is this elevator?* Finally, the doors open. We step in. I hit the button for the lobby, focusing on the steel doors.

"Right on, right on." He presses on. "Well, look let me get you a cab, I want to make sure you get home safely, you know for being my date when you don't even know me."

"Um, I'm good but thank you that's thoughtful."

"Please, let me do this for you. I insist. This is New York City, I couldn't sleep knowing I sent you off to be butchered by one of those Central Park crazies."

The truth is I don't really want to walk home, and the subway is sketch this late.

I let out a nervous laugh "Okay, sure. Don't want you worrying about the butchers all night. Thanks."

Outside, he flags a cab and opens the door for me. I slide in, giving the driver my cross streets. The LAXative closes the door with a giant shit-eating grin. Relief washes over me as I sink into the worn leather seat. The backseat TV plays a broken loop of Maria Menounos waving. The driver's listening to a Quran recitation in a soothing, rhythmic chant.

Then the rear-passenger door opens. The vinegar-and-iodine stench smacks me in the face.

"Didn't realize you lived in Midtown! That's where I'm staying too. What are the odds?" He chirps as the cab pulls away.

As the taxi glides through the almost empty streets of Manhattan, the LAXative begins his usual fountain of bullshit, this time focused on the driver. I take out my phone and text Mr. Wall Street "Hey. Will you be at the apartment tonight? Miss you ;*"

He texts back immediately, "VEGAS BOYS ALL WEEKND C U WHEN I BK!" uncharacteristically bro-y and shorthanded but he seems to be having a good time. The taxi pulls up to my building. I turn to the LAXative to thank him for the taxi ride, but before I can get a word out, he casually says, "I gotta hit the head, don't mind if I come up for just a second, right?"

My pulse stutters. "Oh, um. I thought you said you were staying around here? Wouldn't it be easier to just take the same taxi there, you know, to your own bathroom?"

"Nah. I don't think I can make it. I'm about to explode. Don't worry I won't get in your hair. Quick in and out. Then I'll call an Uber. I know you said you wanted to crash." He's already stuffing cash into the taxi driver's hand and making his way towards me, basically pushing me out of the taxi.

I freeze for a breath. I could lie. I could say I have roommates. A boyfriend upstairs. That my toilet's broken. But each excuse makes me feel smaller, like I'm auditioning for the right not to be followed home. Don't let him up. But my body is already moving. I turn away, chewing my lip, leading him to the building. Maybe he really just needs to pee. The lie feels hollow. I don't even believe myself. But I can't stand the thought of a scene. Not tonight. Not when I've already given away so many pieces of myself.

The lobby is eerily empty. Where the fuck is the doorman?

I sigh and press the elevator button, feeling his presence loom behind me. His breath, too close. Too casual. Like he's earned this. The ride up is silent. But his energy is loud. When I unlock the apartment door, he's still at my heels.

And I'm already regretting everything.

"The bathroom is the only door on the left." I point in the direction as I station myself in the kitchen, my back to the knife block, listening. Piss. Flush. Water running. But then, silence. The pause stretches, setting my nerves on edge. The building feels so quiet tonight. Is it always this silent or is it that I just feel especially alone right now? The bathroom doorknob rattles. He emerges. "I have the worst cotton mouth. Mind if I grab a glass of water?" He says too comfortably, too casually.

"Yeah, no problem," I growl, sharp and forced, already regretting the words as they leave my mouth.

I grab a glass from the cabinet, my hand trembling just slightly. My whole body feels like a loaded spring—tight, coiled, ready to snap. Before I can pass it to him, he's already next to me, crowding me, plucking it from my hand like it was always his to take. The kitchen feels smaller now.

He fills it. Gulps. Refills. I watch the water slosh, wishing it were bleach.

Why did I let him in?

I try to convince myself it's easier this way - get him in, get him out. No drama. But even that sounds weak in my head. Because now he's here. In my space. Breathing my air. And I hate how practiced I am at swallowing fear and smiling through disgust. Just one drink. One minute. Then he's gone.

"So that white powder all over your bathroom counter, is that coke or what?"

I smirk "No. It's not coke. I used baking soda and vinegar to wash my hair. It's like you know, more organic than the commercial stuff. Doesn't cause as much build up."

"Ah, cool cool. Yeah." He takes another gulp of water. "Got any? Since you know, you finished all of mine."

I don't bother responding. "I need to use the bathroom," I say, locking myself in. My heart races. *How do I get him out?* I return the toilet seat to its original position, sit down and take a long overdue piss. As the urine gushes like water from a firehose out of my urethra, I have a simple solution that will probably work.

I call out "Hey, my roommate is on his way back. He doesn't really like me to invite people over. Do you want to call that Uber before he gets back and it turns awkward?"

"You mean he's coming back from Vegas? Nah, I think we have a minute." He calls back.

FUCK. That creepy motherfucker was reading my texts while pretending to bullshit with the driver. Rage and anxiety course through me, my teeth clenching so hard my jaw aches. I throw the bathroom door open, ready to scream, to threaten him with the cops, but what I see stops me cold.

He's sprawled across my bed, shoes still on, dick out, stroking himself like he's the king of the world. His head tilts back, serene, staring at the blank wall in front of him. He's confident. Too confident. He thinks he has control of this situation, of me. He's in my space, my sanctuary, treating it like his own. He came here uninvited, pushed his way in, and now he's convinced my silence means submission.

He's wrong.

I watch him, and the rage inside me doesn't just sharpen, it slithers down my spine, coils in my gut, and pulses like a second heartbeat. It's not cold. It's molten. Acidic. It wants out. I want to split him open like a rotted fruit and see what spills. He stalked me here because of my clothing, my stature. My outward femininity made him feel safe, made him believe I'd be weak, pliable. He thought if he got close enough, I'd cave. He's trying to corner me in my own fucking den.

My mind clicks into focus. Slowly, a smile creeps across my face, starting in my eyes and curling the corners of my mouth. I leave the bathroom door open, my voice calm, almost playful.

"I don't have any coke, but what about some Molly? It feels even better."

I reach under the sink where my lethal emergency pills are taped: a deadly concoction of Oxy and Prozac I prepared weeks ago. Cool, calm, and collected, I know exactly what comes next.

I don't hesitate. His position on my bed, cock out without consent, doesn't faze me. I climb onto the bed in one fluid motion, straddling him, my body pressing into his semi-hard, half-flaccid pencil dick. A playful giggle escapes me as I reach into the little baggie, pulling out two pills filled with white powder. I press them into his eager palm, watching as he greedily moves to swallow them. But then, he hesitates.

"One for me and one for you?" he asks, his smirk faltering for a moment.

I giggle again, leaning closer. "Oh I already took two when I was in the bathroom. I'm feeling so sooo good" I purr as I feel his other hand grabbing my ass. The response satisfies him and he dry swallows both pills. And why shouldn't he feel fully satisfied? This night is going *exactly* how he had planned. I reach for his phone sticking out of his pocket, grab his thumb and unlock it. "What are you doing?" He says, more defensively than he intended. "Taking a selfie of us silly. So you don't forget me!"

"Oh, heh" I lick the side of his face taking the pic. "Here, we're so cute! I'm going to text it to myself so you have my number and I'll turn on some music!" I lightheartedly exclaim as I bounce off of the bed. Walking with his phone towards my laptop behind the bed, I immediately delete the selfie and pull up his Uber app. I type in an address in Hunts Point, the Bronx. Yes! Almost immediately, it's been accepted, and a car should be here in 7 minutes. I turn on Pretty Lights and look over my shoulder at him. His dick is now completely flaccid and somewhat shriveled up looking, as he appears to be waving his fingers around in front of his face. He thinks he's seeing the visual movement trails you see when on hallucinogens. However, he's not on any hallucinogens. He's actually just a moron who swallowed pills from a woman he's known for less than 10 hours who he was intending to date rape or maybe even just straight up rape if I proved to be difficult. The Oxys I mixed in there are immediate release. He should start feeling their effects in under 30 minutes, and I'm not totally sure how long it will take for the overdose effects to start. I walk over to the bed and take a look at him. His pupils are noticeably smaller, and I can tell he's starting to melt into my bed as the euphoria of the drugs takes hold of him.

"Hey baby, how are you feeling?" I ask.

He lets out a sort of moan, "Good, good, cool. I want you to come here. Suck me off kitten. I'm so hard for you." I look at his shriveled, pale dick and just smile to myself thinking *oh buddy, you're never going to be hard again.*

"Ooooh I have such a delicious idea! I want you to fuck my ass on the rooftop, so you can cream in me while looking at the Empire State Building. It's the ultimate New York City experience."

All the muscles in his face have loosened, giving him a sagging even older appearance, but at that moment, I see his eyebrows perk up. "You know, I thought you were such a frigid bitch when we first met, but now I think I'm going to marry you. You are such a freak." He's starting to sound so slow and sleepy. He manages to make his way off the bed and slip his dick away. I grab his hand and pull him towards the door. We get in the elevator, I hit the button for the lobby. I'm not sure he can tell what's up and what's down at this point. I'm holding his hand and he's leaning quite a bit of his weight on me at this point. He can't really keep his eyes open. The elevator opens, thankfully, he's still walking forward. I nod at the doorman, who's finally slunk back to his post, eyes glassy, probably high himself.

"This guy got a little too fucked up, I guess," I say lightly.

He laughs, all sympathy and zero effort, and shuffles to open the door.

"Thank you so much!" I chirp like this is normal, like I'm not shoving a near-comatose man out of my apartment building at witching hour.

The black Camry idles out front, hazard lights blinking like a heartbeat.

I open the rear door. "Hi, Paul?"

The driver glances up from his phone. "Yes." His voice is wary. His eyes flick to LAXative—half-slumped, half-dragged.

"Come on," I whisper to LAX. "They're gonna take you home. You need sleep."

He lets out a burbling grunt, words lost somewhere behind his teeth. He smells like sweat and old pennies. I nudge him again. His feet scrape the pavement. He folds, graceless, into the seat like a dying marionette. The driver doesn't help. Just stares.

"He's fine," I smile. "Just overdid it. You know how parties are."

Paul doesn't nod. Doesn't blink.

LAXative groans, slurs something that sounds like "butter," and then, it happens.

A full-body spasm.

His knees shoot up. His head smacks the opposite door with a sickening thunk.

His mouth snaps open like a trap. Spit flecks the leather seat. Then he's convulsing, violently, his limbs flailing, body jackknifing. His skull drops, bouncing off the car frame before dangling halfway out the door.

"Jesus Christ!" the driver shouts. He lunges from the front, shoving me back as he yanks LAXative from the seat.

He lays him on the sidewalk with shaking hands, dropping to his knees to begin CPR.

"CALL 911! CALL 911!"

I don't move. Not at first.

The street is nearly empty, save for one bodega light flickering at the corner.

A woman in leggings clutches her bag tighter and crosses the street. A man walking a three-legged dog slows, rubbernecking. No one stops. It's 3 AM in Manhattan. Everyone knows what not to get involved in. I fish my phone out with fingers that don't feel like mine.

I don't dial. Not yet. I close my eyes.

Max. My first cat. Dead by the heater, stiff and still warm.

The gum they jammed into my hair in seventh grade.

Tinsel saying, "It's not that I don't love you, I just… I can't be what you need."

The tears rise. My throat tightens like it remembers how to feel. I hit the call.

"911, what's your emergency?"

"My friend—" My voice shatters on cue. "It's my friend! Something's wrong with him. He's having some kind of seizure."

"Where are you located?"

"Outside the Montrose. Thirty-eighth Street."

"We're sending an ambulance now. Is he conscious?"

"I—I don't know. He's shaking. He hit his head. He…he just collapsed." I let the sob trail off.

"Okay, ma'am, you're doing great. Stay with him. Make sure there are no sharp objects near him. If possible, turn him on his side or cushion his head. Help is on the way."

"Thank you." I hang up.

I kneel slowly, take off my coat, and fold it under his head.

He's still twitching, less now. More like a shudder. Like his body can't decide whether to keep trying. The driver's hands are still pressing his chest like he's punching the life back into him.

"He's going to be okay," I say flatly. The driver doesn't respond.

A sudden flash. Light from a phone. Someone across the street is filming.

I lock eyes with them for half a second. They turn away. And for a moment, I wonder if I should run. Just walk away. Melt into the city before it can cough me back up.

But I don't.

I stay there, coat under his head, eyes dry again.

A good friend. A girl who cares.

I stay until the ambulance comes. The driver does most of the talking. I cry. I even use my real name—I think. Or something close enough. No one asks for ID.

They say it looks like a seizure. Maybe fentanyl. The word *complications* gets tossed around. And *CPR*. I make a big show of asking if he's going to be okay. They tell me it's too soon to tell. I tell the EMTs I'll follow them to the hospital. I don't.

I go back inside. Make Sleepy Time tea. The amber bleeds like iodine through gauze. I imagine it's his blood, diluted and swirling, too thin to save. My back aches from kneeling on the pavement. My face aches from the performance.

What if he didn't die?

What if he wakes up and says I drugged him?

And that person across the street, the one who took the picture, what could they possibly do with that? No. I push those thoughts to the back of my skull. There were enough drugs in that pill to take down a horse. Between the seizure, the brutal, unnecessary CPR - he's gone. I'm sure of it.

Abandoning the tea, I head to the fridge, pulling out a package of raw ground beef and two eggs. The meat is dense and cold in my hands as I dump it into a bowl, shaping it into a pulpy, uneven lump. My fingers press into its softness, creating a crater in the center. I crack both eggs, watching the yolks spill like thick, golden, slick like liquefied fat. They slither down into the crevice like they belong there. The craving gnaws at me, primordial, putrid, throbbing like a mosquito bite. It isn't hunger. It's desecration. I need to fuck, not for pleasure, but to expel something rotting inside me.

I always keep meat on hand, even though I'm technically pescatarian. That doesn't matter. Not for this. It's the texture that matters, the raw meat, the egg yolks, the slime. Flesh-like. Organ-like. A stand-in for something more tender. More human.

Carrying the bowl to my bed, I grab my classic Rabbit vibrator and pump cool, slick lube onto the toy. My hands tremble with anticipation. I lay back, knees parted, slipping the vibrator in and out, rhythm syncing to the butcher's drumbeat in my chest.

My free hand plunges into the bowl. The cold mass squelches between my fingers, yolk oozing over my knuckles, slicking my palm. I knead it, grind it, smear it down my arm. It clings like congealed blood. My skin prickles with sensation, revulsion curdling into arousal.

I see him, the LAXative, so eager, so trusting as he dry-swallowed those pills. The way his pupils shrank, his body melting into weakness under my control. I could've saved him. The Naloxone sat untouched in the cabinet. But I didn't want to save him. I wanted him to break. His body failed quicker than expected. Oh my god, watching his body seize like that. Convulse uncontrollably, eyes rolled back, mouth open. As if he was convulsing under the weight of his own stupid assumptions.

My wrist jerks the toy faster. My hips grind. I press harder into the ground beef, my fingers sliding through egg yolk and muscle fibers. The sensation is electric, visceral. I picture Emma's eye, wide and startled, the moment the pick slid in, rupturing the membrane, splitting jelly. Oh god, how I envy that pick. Her skull crunched so delicately. I imagine kissing the hole left behind. I imagine licking the blood from the ice pick like melted popsicle.

My thighs quake. I squeeze the meat until it oozes between my fingers, yolk streaking up my forearm. I want to drown in it. Bury my face in gore. Fuck myself until the room smells like a slaughterhouse.

I cum hard, body seizing, jaw clenched like I'm birthing a demon. The smell—blood, sex, lube, meat—is all-consuming. The bowl clatters to the floor, spattering beef and yolk across the floor.

I lie there, trembling, flushed, painted in food-grade carnage. And for a moment, I feel hollowed out. Rinsed clean.

Methodically, I clean up. The bowl goes into the sink. The vibrator into its drawer. I scrub my hands raw in the shower, meat grease and cum spiraling down the drain in slow, pearled ropes.

I pull on my satin pajamas and climb into bed. Wrapped in my freshly cleaned sheets, I close my eyes. Sleep swallows me whole.

14

LAST NIGHT WAS A BLUR. I woke up with mascara crusted to my temples and a sour taste in my mouth of white powder and metal. I start the day with my usual French press marathon, the rich aroma flooding the apartment like nothing ever happened. By mid-afternoon, I'm deep cleaning, vacuuming every corner, scrubbing bathroom tiles until they shine, reorganizing my closet by color. The rhythm of order calms me. Control disguised as productivity.

I scan Google Local News. Emma's story fizzled weeks ago. No follow-up. No leads. If you scroll through the comments on the original article, you'll find a cascade of misogynistic takes that all say the same thing: if you make a living performing in underwear, you deserve to get stabbed to death.

I still search every morning. Just in case.

Nothing's been reported on LAXative. The news hasn't caught it yet. Or maybe it wasn't worth the coverage. Just another party kid overdosing on a Manhattan sidewalk.

I check his Instagram, nothing new. But the last post went out last night: a close-up of some girl's ass at the party. Not mine. I search his name on Twitter. No RIPs. No grief posts. No candle emojis. Maybe they haven't found his ID yet. Or maybe no one gives a shit.

I put my phone down and start scrubbing the stovetop. I need to relax. I need to act normal.

Between tasks, I text Tinsel. I text Wall Street.

Nothing. No buzzing reply. No read receipts. I stare at the screen longer than I mean to, willing it to light up. They're probably busy. Or asleep. Or dead. Or maybe I said too much. Maybe I'm too much. I pretend I don't care, but my chest tightens anyway. All I wanted was a reply. Something. Proof that I'm still real to someone. I put my phone down like it burned me. Then pick it up again two minutes later. Just in case.

I move on to my self-care routine. I coat my hair with coconut oil. Apparently, it's the new miracle cure—for beauty, longevity, and godlike fitness. Last year it was açaí bowls and kale. While I wait for my scalp to suck up the coconut oil super nutrients, I do two twenty-minute yoga videos - *Buns and Thighs* and *Core & Abs*. Afterward, I shower, washing out the oil, and double-shave my legs, a technique that exfoliates the dead skin away. I shave with a Venus razor with moisturizing head, then I apply shaving cream and shave a second time right after. It absolutely leaves my legs feeling unnaturally soft and supple. When I step out, I cover myself in Palmer's Cocoa Butter until my skin glows.

Wrapped in a white furry bathrobe, I open my MacBook and settle on the couch. Pochemu curls up next to me, her purr vibrating through my side like a calming hum. Halloween is a week away, and I haven't bought my costume. This, at the moment, is my highest priority.

I scroll through Yandy.com, eyeing a red tulle skirt with ruffles that screams saloon-girl-meets-stripper. Perfect. I pair it with a black and red silk corset, bunny ears, long black gloves, and a glass butt plug with a white feather rabbit tail. The absurdity makes me grin. I'll be a bunny. Since I operate solely in cash I'll have to wait for Mr. Wall Street to return before placing the purchase. I'll use his credit card and give him cash.

Still, no one has texted me back. I glance at my phone, then open OKCupid to browse potential dinner dates. Most messages are predictable drivel: "Hi." "Sup?" "You look like a friendly person!" *Do I?*

One catches my eye. His profile is Burning Man adjacent, artsy but not trying too hard. His message is long, thoughtful, referencing my profile picture: me covered in body paint, posing inside an abandoned Brighton Beach warehouse.

Whoa! Love your photos. So cool! What's that style called? Where it looks random but purposeful? It's minimal, just the right amount of color and paint. I do aesthetic design and stage builds for underground techno parties, always looking for ideas. Some live body art like this would kill it. Let's chat!

I smile. Finally, someone with potential. I type back:

I guess I'd call it minimalist urban warrior, though I doubt it's in the art history books yet, lol. You sound awesome. I've performed and helped organize similar events in Brooklyn. Surprised our paths haven't crossed. Let's chat more, shoot me a text!

I add my number, finishing with a kissing wink emoji. The ball's in his court now.

While waiting for some digital validation to remind me I exist, I scan my emails for potential income this weekend.

To my surprise, the Spaz has reached out. He's one of my regulars, a Hollywood producer who splits his time between NYC and LA. His nickname comes from his erratic spanking technique, though he's confessed he's not into kink, just a basic message and someone to talk to. Easy work.

We arrange to meet at his hotel tonight at six. He'll probably order room service for dinner. Perfect. Exactly what I'm craving.

My phone dings. Finally, it's Mr. Wall Street. He'll be back late tonight and plans to stay over. Good.

I check the time. It's almost 6:00 PM. My client will be waiting.

15

October 24, 2013

Rattling down the tracks of the Q train towards 57th Street to meet my client, The Spaz. A Hollywood legend who's been running on reruns for decades. Soft body, soft hands, a habit of spanking in light, spastic taps like he's afraid of breaking something. Mostly he likes to lie back, get a massage, and tell me about his life, his problems. I listen. He feeds me. Oysters, truffles, whatever's highest priced on the menu. Sometimes he licks food off me like it's part of the meal. Nice guy, really. Tips well. One of my favored clients.

Last night is vibrating in my head, how could it not? He must have died in the hospital. Definitely. Probably. No. Definitely. I watched the color drain from his face like cheap foundation in the rain. Watched foam bubble around his lips while I held his jaw in my lap and whispered shhh, like I was tucking him in. His eyes rolled too slow. His pulse kept fighting. When the ambulance took him, he was still alive.

Or was he?

His ribs cracked under that idiot driver's hands, pounding out amateur CPR. The EMTs were pissed. Said that might be what kills him.

The subway car smells like piss, popcorn, and perfume.

There's a man across from me eating sunflower seeds out of a sock.

A woman beside me crying without tears. Her ducts are dry, but the mascara's left rivers down her cheeks. Beautiful. I want to lick her. She reminds me of Emma. That doll-like tragic state.

But LAXative dying in front of me felt nothing like Emma. With Emma, there was music in the blood. I felt something: the cut, the warmth, the softness. It was holy. Personal. Like carving a statue from raw marble. Something sacred. I tasted her breath and it lingered. With LAX... It was trash day. A purge. A cleanup. Like cauterizing a wound. He wasn't beautiful. He didn't deserve mourning. Emma embraced me. He pushed. Pushed into the party. Pushed into my apartment. Pushed me into feeding him those deadly little pills. Called me Kitten. As if cats aren't apex predators. As if I didn't already have my claws under his skin. I toyed with that little rat of a man. Broke him, inside and out. I fed him death. Watched the drugs drown his consciousness.

Watched spasms wreck his meat-shell, push him out of the cab, crack his head on the doorframe. There was no artistry. No climax. No performance. Just silence. Like turning off a fan. Like deleting a file. With Emma, I wanted to crawl inside her. Use my teeth to gnaw her open. Slide into the blood-warm cavity and whisper secrets into her bones. With LAX, I wanted him gone. I needed to cleanse my apartment of him. A necessary nothing. And still... When he seized, his limbs jerked like puppet strings. And I felt... something. There was vomit. There was piss. Not poetic. Not pretty. But real. And that matters, too. I'm wearing the coat. The one I tucked under his head. It caught the vomit. Soaked up the blood.

It smells like him. It smells like death. I wonder if my client will notice. I wonder if he'll smell it on me. If he'll recognize it. If he knows death the way I do. I think I'm getting better at this. The mask. The rituals. Compartmentalizing.

Emma was my high.

LAX was my maintenance.

Next stop: 57th Street.

I'm in the Ritz near Central Park, sprawled across the plush king bed next to the Spaz. Empty room service trays clutter the nightstand - remnants of a champagne-soaked feast. Faroe Island salmon picked clean, martini glasses rimmed with dried cocktail sauce, the crumbs of crab cakes scattered like bones. Filet mignon sliders split and oozing Burgundy onion jam and Brie. My stomach's heavy, my skin sticky. I wipe the milk chocolate and artisanal cheese from my tits, the bits he missed with his tongue.

He's telling me about Hoffman's last set, how he's spiraling into depression, headed for a drug-induced nosedive.

"Have you ever seen someone OD? Like in front of you?" I ask, interrupting.

"Yeah. Yup. I have," he says, turning to look at me. His pale, almost translucent complexion is offset by rosy Santa Claus-red cheeks. His light brown hair, streaked with grey, is disheveled, bits sticking up like he's been electrocuted. We are both shirtless just lounging in our underwear- his loose light blue boxers dotted with navy spots and a white square tag on from that reads "Peter Miller", mine red, ruffled, cheeky. Not a notable designer but very cute.

"What did you do while it was happening?" I press, my tone innocently curious.

"I called 911, but she died anyway. Did you see someone overdose?"

"Yes." I cuddle closer, burying my face in his chest. His body is soft, cushiony, like a worn-in armchair. He hugs me with one arm, his sheer size enveloping me. He's a big guy, heavy set - think 90s era John Goodman. Maybe a touch shorter. I love this part, when people think I'm fragile and comfort me.

"And what did you do?" he asks softly, his other hand gently petting my hair.

"Not much. Not enough. I guess I called an ambulance but too late," I whisper, letting the words drop like stones in water—soft but heavy enough to ripple.

"Oh. Oh, sweetie. It's not your fault." His voice is thick with pity. His hand moves slow down my back, the well-worn stroke of a man who's learned that empathy opens legs faster than flattery.

"He was bad" I say, quieter. "I didn't want to get involved with police and paperwork, so I hesitated. But…" I trail off, letting my mouth tremble against his skin. "I don't feel very good about it."

I tilt my face up, wide-eyed, letting tears gather until they blur him. They're easy to summon when you want them—just picture Tinsel looking at me like I'm broken, like I need her. I imagine telling *her* this story instead. Imagine her pulling me close, whispering that she understands. That she loves me more for it.

He freezes for a moment, then tightens his arm around me. "Oh, you poor thing." He presses his lips into my hair. I let him hold me, let his arm lock around me like it means something. I wonder if that's how it feels to keep something, really keep it. Not just for a night. Not just until the sirens come. Next time, I think, I won't give it back.

My eyes shine wet looking up at him like a kitten left out in the rain. The tears are real this time, maybe not for him, but for the way my pulse quickens when I think of last night, of the way he went still. I'm telling it for the first time, feeling out which parts have weight, which ones draw him closer. Filing it away.

This is important. I need a story worth rehearsing—tight, repeatable, dripping with the right kind of tragedy. I was photographed beside my date as he died on the street; that image is a ticking time bomb that could explode on social media any day now. Jenny will ask. The cops might too. I have to play it small - regretful, shaken, confused.

Like I didn't go home with his last heat still clinging to my hands, slide my fingers between my legs, and rub until the phantom tremors of his seizure echoed in my own body. Like I didn't press my face into the pillow, pretending the damp fabric was his cooling skin, biting down until I tasted iron.

16

I'M ON THE ROOFTOP of the Montrose, slouched in one of the oversized designer wicker chairs. The wind bites at my cheeks, and the sun hangs high, pale but bright. It's not warm, not by a long shot, but cold enough that the chill feels cleansing, like it could scrape off the grime of the night before. I don't usually smoke, but when I do, it's Cloves.

There's something about their black paper and the way the sweet, spicy smoke lingers on my tongue. When you lick your lips afterward, it tastes like Christmas, sugar and cinnamon and something darker, like the bitterness of burnt pine needles. What kind of sick, twisted psychopath wouldn't want to taste Christmas on their lips? Obama made Cloves illegal a few years back, but you can still order them online, mostly from Thailand.

It should have been enough. I gorged myself on champagne and room service with the Spaz, let Wall Street fuck me three times. Once with my head hanging off the bed, coke spilling from the crease of my collarbone, his breath hot on my ear. He did bumps off my nipples. I let him draw lines down the slope of my back, snorted them bent over with my cunt in the air. I came until I was bruised inside.

And still, I'm starving.

If I'm honest, the way things ended with the LAXative hasn't stopped scraping at me. Sending him off in the ambulance feels wrong.

Wasteful. I should have kept him with me. Felt the exact second the life left his body, let it seep into me like heat through skin. Let his pupils go wide while I touched myself. Kept him in my bed until he went slack and cool, curled up against me like a pet gone still. I could have washed him. Brushed his hair. Made him clean for once in his miserable life.

Instead, I let strangers take him. Let them pump him full of air, drag him away while I stood on the sidewalk pretending to care. I didn't even get to feel him harden, the way muscles stiffen before they loosen into nothing. I didn't get to split him open. Didn't get to taste him.

Emma was stolen from me just as fast, her blood still warm when I had to leave her. Every body I touch gets ripped away before I'm finished. Before I can keep it, claim it, make it mine. I never get to *finish*. It's like they die twice. Once in front of me, and again when they're taken away.

Jenny texted me at 6:00 AM asking when I'd last seen him. I didn't answer. I'm not ready to put any of this into words for her.

I take the last drag of my cigarette, ember flaring like an open wound. It doesn't taste like Christmas anymore. Just char and ash. Just the aftertaste of something I didn't get to swallow.

I grind it out under my heel, eyes locked on the skyline, the city stretching on forever. The wind steals the last curl of smoke from my lips, like it's taking one more thing from me before I'm ready.

17

I TEXT TINSEL. I need to unload.

Hey Babe! Party the other night was crazy. I want to update you. Send.

I tap the top of my phone. Waiting for the *ding.* The reply. The acknowledgment.

While I wait, I pull up Instagram. Tinsel at Greenhouse last night, leaning into some guy in a Psycho Bunny T-shirt, laughing like she's in on the best joke in the world. Tinsel taking a selfie in class, pretending to be confused, eyes wide and doe-like.

I go to her profile.

Tinsel with Emma.

Tinsel between Kendra and the King of Swing (before Kendra threw chairs at her head).

Tinsel with the bass player from the night we met Emma. When did she go back to see him again?

Tinsel with everyone.

Tinsel everywhere.

But rarely me.

Why am I not the main event in her feed? I'm her best friend. We've seen each other at least once a week since high school. And yet, looking at her profile feels like scanning a stranger's yearbook. One I was never invited to sign.

Back to the Greenhouse pic. I click on the guy she's leaning against, Insta handle @Dis1tight. Standard selfies. Drunk group shots. Then, there she is again. Tinsel, wrapped in that same lazy smile, standing next to him and a crowd outside Roberta's in Bushwick. It looks like they're celebrating something.

I scan the faces. And there he is! The bass player from the loft, from the night we met Emma. How deep has she gotten into that circle? Why doesn't she tell me? Invite me? I know them. I was there. We met them together.

Is this deliberate? Is she keeping me out because she knows what happened with Emma?

I check the timestamp. Posted twenty-one hours ago, that puts it at 4:42 p.m. The Greenhouse photo went up at 1:13 a.m. - different outfit, same lipstick, same hair. So she left Bushwick, changed clothes, and still made it to the club. Who was she with in between?

I tap through pages from people in the group. Two more pics with her in the background - one outside a bodega, another in someone's apartment, laughing on a couch. I screenshot all of them, zooming in until the pixels blur. Each photo feels illicit, like catching her undressing through a keyhole, skin in dim light, her smile turning slightly toward me, even though she isn't. I can almost feel the heat of her, the weight of her thigh against mine, the faint trace of her perfume when she leans close.

My thumb hovers over the screen, but my other hand is busy tearing at my cuticles, scraping skin until I feel the sting. I file the ragged edges against my teeth, tasting the metallic burst of blood.

Maybe this is her way of telling me she disapproves. That she's choosing Emma's ghost over me. Or worse. Maybe she's just… moving on.

I blink. My phone screen is dim, warm in my hand. Three hours gone. I don't remember losing them. The photo grid is different now, open to other accounts, strangers' faces. My laptop's beside me, browser littered with tabs I don't recall opening. My camera roll is swollen with screenshots, each a blurry shard of her night. I must have been chasing her through the internet like she was leaving breadcrumbs just for me.

And maybe she was. Maybe it's her way of calling for help.

Somewhere in those missing hours, I remember her hand on my thigh, the way she leans in when she's drunk - whispers that sound like secrets but are really bait. In the haze, I see her tilting her head back, lips parted, letting me press my mouth to her pulse until the beat flutters, then falters. Her skin tastes like sweat and candy and something just past ripe, like I'm drinking from her without her ever noticing the way my teeth close in.

A loud knock rattles the apartment door. It's sharp, sudden, aimed at my skull. My heart lurches. I'm on my feet before I know it, phone clutched tight, thumb hovering over the power button like I could erase the last three hours if I pressed hard enough.

The knock comes again, harder. I shove the phone into my pocket and lick the blood from my torn cuticle. The taste steadies me.

Through the peephole: Wall Street. Mr. Wall Street.

I exhale slowly, my shoulders loosening. I don't know who I thought it would be.

I open the door and melt into his arms, giving my weight to someone just to see if they'll hold it.

"That's a more enthusiastic greeting than I expected." He pushes my bangs out of my eyes, kisses my forehead, and steps inside. "Forgot my keys in Brooklyn. Sorry if the knock surprised you."

He drops the grocery bag on the counter.

"No worries." My smile feels like it's on a delay, my brain still crawling out of the social media rabbit hole I'd been lost in for hours. But I am glad he's back. I want him to stay, for more than the night.

When he's here, the static quiets. I can almost forget Tinsel's games. Emma's last breath. The LAXative's twitching, collapsing under streetlights. With him, it all feels contained. Controlled.

I stand on tiptoe to peek into the paper bag.

On cue, he's behind me, hands at my waist, breath warm at my ear. "Stay in tonight. I want all of you to myself. I want to know you inside and out."

I turn to face him, my cheek brushing the cashmere at his chest. My eyes search his like I'm trying to decide if I believe him. "Inside and out?" I ask, smiling, soft but a little sharp. Before I can give him my answer, my gaze flicks to my phone.

Still no reply from Tinsel.

I look back at him wide-eyed, searching. He smiles, but I don't let him speak.

"There's something I should tell you."

I lead him to the bed. He sits. I fold myself into his lap like I'm meant to be there. My voice drops to the careful, broken register I've perfected.

"The night before last... I was out with someone. He overdosed. Right there on the sidewalk."

His hand stills, then cups the back of my head.

"Jesus, Jessie. Are you okay?" His tone is firm, protective, like he's already decided I'm his to protect.

"I called the ambulance, but it was too late," I whisper. "He wasn't a great guy, but still... watching him go like that..." My voice wavers, my eyes wet. "I just... I didn't want him to leave. Not yet."

His arms tighten around me, pulling me in against his chest like I'm something precious he can shelter from the world. "You don't have to talk about it if you're not ready."

"I want to. I wanted to tell you last night but…" I murmur. My fingers find the curve of his jaw, tracing it lightly. "It's strange, the things you notice. The weight of a jaw in your hand. The last flutter under your fingers, and then the stillness." My thumb brushes the pulse in his throat. "I should've kept him… just a little longer."

His eyes search mine. "You're safe now, my little dove," he says, his voice heavy with authority. "Nothing's taking you away from me tonight."

I lean closer, lips at his ear. "You'd stay, wouldn't you? You wouldn't leave me like that."

"I'm not going anywhere," he says, final, like it's a rule he's written into the universe. His hand slides down my back in a slow, grounding stroke. "You're mine tonight. All mine."

I smile against his skin. "I'll cancel my plans."

And I do, curling into him, letting the steady beat of his heart under my cheek replace the one that stopped on the pavement the other night. His words settle over me like a heavy blanket. *You're mine tonight.*

I let myself sink into it, into him. The solid warmth of his chest. The quiet authority in his voice. My fingers curl into his shirt like I'm holding on through turbulence.

He tilts my chin up with two fingers, studying me like he's checking for cracks. "Tell me what you need."

I press my lips together, pretending to think, even though I know exactly what I want. "I need you to make me forget."

His jaw tightens, and he nods once, decisive. "I can do that."

When he kisses me, it's not rushed. It's deliberate, unhurried, the way someone unwraps something fragile. His hand is firm at the back of my neck, guiding me exactly where he wants me. The control steadies me. It also makes me throb.

I let him take me apart in increments—my sweater sliding off my shoulders, the slow drag of his palm over my ribs, the press of his thigh between mine. His touch is grounding, but my mind is elsewhere. The heaviness of his body against me calls up the weight of the LAXative's head in my lap. The slack mouth. The stillness.

He feels it, and his hand comes down hard on my ass, a sharp crack that makes me gasp. "Stay with me, Jessie." His hand fists in my hair, but not to pull me away, to keep me exactly where he wants me. "That's it," he says, his other hand massaging my breast. "Stay right here with me. Don't go anywhere in that head of yours."

I bite down, just enough for him to feel it. "I'm not going anywhere" I echo. He exhales sharply when my teeth graze the skin, my mouth lingering there like I'm measuring the beat.

He groans, pulling me tighter into his chest. "Good girl."

"I've got you. I'm staying. Cum with me. Cum hard. Cum for me." he orders in a raspy growl, and there's a promise in it this time. His mouth trails down my throat, his stubble catching on my skin.

I close my eyes and picture him *really* staying—pinned in place, unbreathing, mine forever. The thought makes my hips roll against him without permission.

I moan into his mouth. I can. I will. For tonight, I'll let him anchor me. But deep down, I'm already imagining the day I won't have to settle for *pretend* stillness. The day I get to keep someone exactly as I want them.

October 29, 2013

Wall Street tucked me into bed like I was a glass doll. Kissed my forehead, rubbed my back until my breathing matched his. Whispered, "I've got you now. Don't worry." Men love to believe they're the wall between you and the world. To believe your fear belongs to them. I think he likes to imagine me as something fragile he can fix.

I let him keep me there, pressed tight against his chest, feeling his heart knock like it wanted in. I even told him about the LAXative, the polished version. He stroked my hair, said I'd done all I could. Daddy's good girl. His innocent dove.

But in my head, I was back on the sidewalk. His lips foaming. His eyes rolling. My thighs gathering up sticky warm wetness under my skirt.

I wanted to pull him inside with me. To keep him while he cooled. Lay him in the center of my bed and watch his skin go from flushed to that perfect waxy pale. Slide my fingers into the folds of his cooling flesh and see how far they could disappear.

Then there was Emma, gorgeous, perfect, phony Emma. Warm under stage lights, blood spreading beneath her cheek like a velvet curtain opening just for me. I can still smell her perfume under the iron stink, hear the soft pop of the pick leaving her skull. I wish I had been able to swing her over my shoulder and bring her home with me.

Wall Street would never understand how that kind of stillness fills a person. How keeping a body is like keeping the last note of a song, holding it so long your chest hurts, but never letting it fade.

But tonight, as he dozed off, I found myself tracing the slope of his skull with my fingertips. The smooth, solid curve beneath his cropped hair, the slight ridge at the back where my hand would fit perfectly if I ever needed to hold his head still. He didn't stir, didn't know I was mapping him.

Tinsel would understand.

I think about her hair tangled in my fists, her body slack but warm, pliant. I'd wash her in milk and honey, comb her curls until my arms ached,
dress her in silk I'd slit open just to taste her underneath. She wouldn't have
to move or speak. Just stay.

Wall Street is warm, steady, solid. I could keep him for a while. But he's
not the meal that feeds me to the bone.

She is.

And one day, I'll peel back every mask she wears, right down to the last
one. The one with her real face. The one I'll take for myself and never give
back.

18

IT'S HALLOWEEN, MY FAVORITE night of the year, and I'm
in Tinsel's dorm watching her transform. She's dressing as a sexy cave-
woman in a fur bikini that leaves nothing to the imagination. She looks
feral, edible. I can already imagine the photos she'll post later, all teeth
and skin, all hers to control. Meanwhile, I'm tightening the red tulle
skirt and black-and-red corset of my bunny look, ears waiting on the
desk like something I've hunted.

"Ack! Sorry, this room smells like bleach!" Tinsel says, wrinkling
her nose and tossing her hair like she can physically throw the smell
away. "My snot roommate keeps a bowl of bleach under her bed for her
shower shoes. So crazy!"

The air has that faint hospital tang, like the kind that clings to you
after visiting someone who's never coming home.

"She actually bleaches her shoes every day? What's she afraid of?" I
ask, fumbling with the clasps, thinking of Wall Street's fingers the other
night, how they didn't fumble at all.

"Germs, bacteria, whatever. She's totally OCD." Tinsel waves it off,
like her roommate's rituals are a personal affront. Then her gaze sharpens. "Anyway, I want the DL on your Mr. Wall Street. What's the deal?
Are you two, like, a thing now? I can't believe you just moved in with
him! Are you even dating?"

I let out a nervous laugh. "Oh, no, we're not, like, together. He's got another apartment in Brooklyn. Mostly stays there. He's really sweet, though. Genuine."

Yeah, sweet, sweet the way a palm against your throat can be sweet.

"Sweet? But are you *fucking* him?" Her eyes bug slightly, hungry for details but not the right ones.

"Yeah, of course," I giggle, half because it feels like she's interrogating me, half because I keep picturing Wall Street's mouth between my legs, whispering how good I taste. The way his voice dipped low when I told him about the overdose. My rehearsed lines sliding off my tongue like silk, like sin. How it was supposed to be her I told, if she only bothered to text me back.

She grins, leaning closer, close enough I could bite the slope of her shoulder. "How's the sex? Do you think it'll turn into something serious?"

"The sex is good. He's super gentle, very caring. But…" I let my voice drop, like I'm confiding a secret, "…he's got this emotional love triangle thing. Still hung up on his ex, the one he cheated on, and now he lives in the same building as the mistress. She's apparently batshit crazy, threatens to slit her wrists or jump off the Brooklyn Bridge, so he feels… responsible for her."

Tinsel smirks, fastening my garters to my stockings. Her fingers brush my thigh, and the touch sends a jolt through me. "He's sweet, but it's messy," I add. "Also, he definitely sees himself marrying an Asian girl. He's got a thing."

Tinsel stands, arching an eyebrow. "Wow. That's… a lot. But cool he lets you live there, though."

"Yeah. Totally." I watch her fluff her hair in the mirror, the light catching on her lip gloss. She's beautiful in the way that makes you feel like she's holding out on you. I mentally begin to file through all the social media pictures, all the strangers she tags, all the places she goes and tells me nothing about. "So," I say, forcing brightness into my voice, "what about you? How's Connecticut guy?"

"Wildthing?" She rolls her eyes. "Over it. He's been clingy and dull. But I did hit him up yesterday, and he came down from Connecticut. Left us some treats for tonight."

"What treats?"

She grins. "Ecstasy and acid."

"Oh my god! Candy flipping on Halloween?"

"YES."

We squeal in unison, but my brain is already skipping ahead to Tinsel in someone else's arms on another dance floor, laughing like she does when she's drunk, lips wet, hips loose.

"This is going to be amazing!" I say. "So, what's the plan? Parade first?"

"Yes, and then the girls down the hall are going to Benny Benassi at Pacha. PhD's having a thing, too."

"Or we could do Bang On! in Brooklyn, maybe hit a loft after-party." I smile, pretending my mind isn't categorizing every stranger she's smiled at in the last month.

"We could," she says, "but I'm thinking we ride with the girl crew. Bottle-service guys, free drinks, maybe get them to cover cab fare later."

"Strategic."

She grins. "The girls down the hall? Total FIT bobbleheads. Probably listening to Gaga and taking tequila shots. But they're nice enough."

"Bobbleheads?" I laugh.

"You know like wiggly heads. No real use except to be looked at."

I slide on my gloves. "Got it."

Yeah, bobbleheads hollow, nodding at whatever's in front of them. Maybe that's how she sees me now. A prop in her personal set. She's still talking, but I'm somewhere else, imagining her Instagram feed as a map, a code I could crack if I stared long enough. Imagining her pulling me into a bathroom stall, whispering my name like she did that one time in high school, before she left me for her boy toy flavor of the week. My phone in my bag is heavy. I want to check it. I want to see if she's posted anything without me in it.

Instead, I follow her into the hall.

Tinsel knocks on the big metal door. It swings open instantly, and the scent of every Victoria's Secret perfume ever made hits me like a sugary slap, stinging my eyes. Standing there is a six-foot ethereal blonde with pale gray eyes and a smile so perfect it's offensive. Suede shorts, barely four inches of fabric, hug her hips, and a hot-pink bra peeks out from under a fringe vest. Pink and yellow flowers are braided into her near-white hair. Hippie costume, I assume. The kind of hippie who would monetize peace and love to pay for her Botox.

Behind her, the room glitters with girls who look like they've been bred for beauty. They're all impossibly tall, skin like Photoshop. If this were Lord of the Rings, Tinsel and I would be hobbits stumbling into Rivendell. Except these elves aren't immortal. They're temporary, their glow dimming with every camera flash and drink poured down their throats.

"Hi, Melinda! This is my ride-or-die BFF, Razor! We are totally psyched for Pacha!" Tinsel says, her voice bubbling over in a tone I haven't heard in weeks.

Melinda beams at her like they're sisters. "Ah! I can't believe you're coming! Razor, was it? Oh my god, Tinsel is a riot. We love her!" She takes my hand like we have a history and pulls me inside, her perfume heavy enough to taste.

The others lounge around a desk with a Costco-sized Grey Goose, their laughter bright and sharp.

Briar: tight leather jumpsuit, cat ears, braids that end at an ass sculpted like it has its own insurance policy.

Ragan: ginger with a bleach-tipped faux-hawk, Leeloo bandage bodysuit, a smirk like she knows the punchline before you do.

Lani: curvy, pink wig, candy bra, skirt made of candy bars. Her clear purse stuffed with Ring Pops that she'll probably hand-feed to strangers.

I smile, hug, play the game. But my eyes keep darting back to Tinsel—how easily she slots herself into their circle, the way they touch her shoulder or lean into her laugh. How she acted like she barely knew these girls, but watching her now, she's glowing for them. She tilts her head just so, exposing the soft stretch of her neck like an offering, and they drink it in. How is it that I can be so tuned into every twitch of her body, every flicker of her eyes, and yet she seems more connected to everyone else?

Someone hands me a shot. I blink, and the glass is empty, my throat burning, music louder. Laughter crashes against my ears. I don't remember lifting it. The Grey Goose bottle is lower now. The candy girl is talking, but I can't catch the words. Tinsel's face swims in the corner of my vision, haloed in light from the desk lamp, like she's already far away.

We duck into the bathroom. The light overhead buzzes like an insect. Tinsel hands me half an ecstasy pill and slips the other half into her own mouth, acid blotter tucked under her tongue. We look in the mirror at the same time. Her reflection is flushed, alive. Mine looks like it's watching her through glass.

She grins at me, *ride or die*, her mouth seems to say, and I can't stop the thought: *She doesn't know how true that is.*

I imagine her body pliant under my hands, warm like Emma's was before the light left her. If Tinsel were mine, I'd keep her past the moment she stopped moving. I'd make her mine in every way.

We step out, grinning, following the perfume-cloud of Melinda's crew. And I promise myself she'll leave with me tonight.

We decide to walk the twenty minutes to Greenwich Village for the parade. Halloween in New York is the only time the city really feels like it's on my wavelength. Every shadow is alive, every face a mask, and the air thick with the sweet rot of anticipation. The streets are clogged with pirates, demons, glittering angels; weed smoke and cold air curl together in my lungs like lovers.

We're a spectacle ourselves, the kind that turns heads without trying. Melinda's crew moves like they own the sidewalk, all height and hair and limbs that don't have to ask for space. Tinsel's in the middle of them, glowing like they've been waiting for her all along. I catch myself counting how many times they touch her shoulder, lean in for a joke, pull her into the center of their orbit. It's been hours, and she still hasn't pulled me into it.

By the time we reach the parade route, it's chaos, sweaty chaos. A guy in a Nixon mask and toilet seat necklace leans against a barricade, waving like we're old friends. A bumblebee girl stumbles past, sloshing a neon-blue drink that splashes down the front of Lani's candy skirt. The smell of sugar and vodka mixes with the bleach still clinging to my nostrils from Tinsel's dorm.

The group freezes. For a moment it feels like the crowd thins, the noise dampens.

Then Lani turns on her heel. Without a word, she kicks the bumblebee square in the ass. The girl goes down hard, face kissing the pavement. Before anyone can react, Lani's heel comes down on the back of her head—one, two, three times. A wet crack. Blood blooms across the asphalt like it's been waiting for her.

The bumblebee screams, choking on it. Her teeth are wrong now. One is hanging by a string of gum. No one moves to help her. People glance, then glance away, like it's just another performance piece in the Village.

But my mind locks onto the image, the gush of crimson spilling over her lips, her scream sharp enough to slice the cold air in two. Who knew there was that much blood in a face? And Lani, calm, deliberate, like she'd been rehearsing for this. Her boot came down without hesitation, precise and merciless, the crunch of bone reverberating in my skull. Her head buckled like a cheap Halloween mask.

It's almost… inspiring.

I imagine sliding my fingertips along those jagged gashes, feeling the heat pulse against my skin, the stickiness clinging like a second layer. She didn't just hurt her. She finished her. And in that moment, I knew Lani wasn't like the others.

Tinsel tugs my arm, voice low. "We should go."

The others hesitate, glancing over their shoulders like prey animals waiting to see if the predator will follow.

"Run!" Ragan finally yells, and we're off! Six-inch heels slapping the pavement, skirts flying, the parade dissolving behind us in a blur of masks and lights. A block and a half later, we stop. Panting. Staring at Lani.

"I can't believe you did that," I say first, laughter spilling out before I can stop it. It's high-pitched, involuntary, almost giddy.

Tinsel's looking at me now, not like she's in on the joke but like she's just noticed I'm not laughing for the same reasons as everyone else. Her hand hovers like she might touch my arm, then she doesn't.

Lani glances at me, searching for a read. I wink. She exhales. Relief? Excitement? She laughs too, quiet at first, then harder, and it's just us in it for a second, like we're the only ones who understand what it feels like to *do* something irreversible and walk away intact.

Melinda finally snaps out of it and flags a cab. We pile in, limbs folding over each other in a tangle of tulle and leather and glitter. I'm wedged on Briar's lap; Tinsel's perched on Ragan's. The driver doesn't blink, just tilts the rearview to get a better look.

I lean back into Briar's vanilla-scented warmth, my fingers gliding absently along Tinsel's thigh. Her skin is impossibly soft. The ecstasy deepens, the acid edges in, and peacock feathers bloom in the corners of my vision.

God, I love how soft women are.

We pull up to Pacha, the red cherry sign throbbing like a pulse, throwing wet light over the crowd outside. The line coils around the block, hundreds of costumes shifting and twitching, cheap fabric brushing against cheap fabric. The smell is wet polyester and human heat. I can't go in like this. Not through that line. Not while I look this good. Not while I'm coming up.

Ragan's hand finds mine. "We don't wait in that line," she says, her voice curling in my ear like smoke.

Relief floods me too quickly, it feels suspicious. The bass from inside is already in my chest, like the building's heart is trying to sync with mine.

Melinda drifts toward the doorman like she's on a moving walkway I can't see. She hugs him, her perfume cloud swallowing him whole. Briar's nails rest on his shoulder—long, sharp, a little too close to the vein in his neck.

That's when I see it: movement two blocks down. A thin figure steps from an alley, legs telescoping with every step until it's eight feet tall, dressed in black-and-white stripes, face painted like a mime. My pulse quickens. The air between us warps like heat off asphalt. Its legs keep stretching. I can't look away.

I grab Tinsel's arm. "How is he so long?" My voice sounds like it's coming from inside a fish tank.

She giggles, pulling me in, her breath warm on my ear. "I think he's on stilts, sweetbum."

"Oh… yeah…" I say, though I'm still watching him glide past. I want to touch his knees just to see if he'd fall.

Briar calls out, "We're in!" A Skeleton-faced person waves us toward a side door. The stairwell is tight, each step too small, the rail sticky under my hand. The bass seeps through the walls, sliding into my bones. One step, ball of foot, push, lean forward. I keep forgetting and remembering I'm walking.

The red leather door swings open into a balcony dripping with velvet and glass. Below us, the dance floor is a writhing ocean of masks and limbs, every beat sending ripples through it. In our little VIP alcove, the vodka glows under the table light like molten silver. I feel absurdly grateful for this tiny, controlled island in the chaos. Plush seats, a perfect view of the dance floor. It's one enormous, breathing animal, pulsing to Benny Benassi's beat. Lights slice across the room, white petals blooming and closing, blooming and closing. I can't tell if the petals are made of light or knives.

The table to the right of us is men in suits with farm animal masks on and women in leather BDSM wear. To the left is a smaller table of guys dressed as classic horror monsters - Dracula, Dr. Frankenstein, Dorian Grey, Werewolf of Paris and Mr. Hyde. Dracula's cape looks expensive, real satin, not from Party City. I pour pineapple juice, just to have something in my hand. Below us, the crowd moves like one body. Circus creatures in black-and-white swirls blow whistles from perches, their movements jerky and too slow at the same time. I wonder if they're human or just costumes filled with light. Tinsel sits beside me. Her thighs are warm against mine. I keep catching the way people lean into her, laugh a little harder for her, watch her mouth when she speaks. I want to wrap my hand around her throat just to make her hold still, make her look only at me.

I nudge her arm. "Want to talk to those guys?"

She smirks and nods toward the monsters. We cross the VIP like we own it. My fingers trail over the couch backs, leaving invisible marks. Tinsel's smile widens as she slides into Dracula's lap without hesitation. My pulse skips. By the time I'm in front of Dr. Frankenstein, I'm already touching him, brushing the lightning bolt stitching on his jacket like I'm claiming it.

"I love that you're the doctor instead of the monster," I say.

He grins. "Well, he was the real monster. Wasn't he?"

"So true," I murmur, stepping closer.

He offers me a seat. I straddle his lap instead. His stubble scrapes my skin, and my hand slides under his shirt, tracing the lines of his ribs. They flex under my palm, fragile in a way that makes me want to press harder. I think about splitting him open, peeling him back, seeing if he's as hollow as he looks.

I lean in, my lips grazing his ear. "You'd let me do anything to you, wouldn't you?"

He nods before I've even pulled back. My clit throbs.

His hands grip my hips, testing my weight. The bass below us swells until I'm sure the floor is breathing. Every face on the dance floor tilts upward for a second. Do they see me? Or is it just the acid folding the night in on itself?

I kiss him, deep and deliberate, syncing my tongue to the beat. My thoughts keep breaking apart and reforming: Tinsel in Dracula's lap → my hand on Frankenstein's ribs → Tinsel's throat in my palm → the mime's endless legs stepping over me like I'm nothing. When we finally break apart, my head's buzzing, my skin electric. He pours me juice with a splash of vodka, and I let our fingers brush just a little too long.

Below, the dance floor heaves and shifts. I swear I see the bumblebee girl's bloody mouth in the crowd, grinning up at me.

The night blurs into a kaleidoscope of flashing lights, demented clowns blowing whistles, and sweaty bodies colliding on the dance floor. Sloppy costumed yuppies spill their drinks down my corset while electronic beats pulse through my neurons, colors and serotonin splashing over me like waves. By 4:45 AM, our two groups finally stumble out of Pacha and onto the dimly lit streets of the Meatpacking District.

Plans have shifted; now we're heading to Dracula's penthouse, just a few blocks away. The guys summon a fleet of black cars waiting outside. Technology really can feel like magic sometimes. We pile in, and eight minutes later, we're climbing out again.

Dracula unlocks a massive black steel door, leading us up a newly shellacked pine staircase to yet another heavy steel barrier. Three bolted locks later, the door swings open, releasing a fake warmth scent of pumpkin spice and apple crisp from Air Wick fresheners.

The open kitchen gleams with a marble island and sleek black cabinetry. Dracula invites us to kick off our shoes and make ourselves comfortable. Plush white herringbone carpet that swallows my stockinged feet, grey sofa like an altar, massive driftwood table in the center.

We spill in, shoes off, bodies slouching into the U-shape. I let Dr. Frankenstein guide me to one side, my legs draped over his lap, my shoulder brushing Tinsel's. She smells like cheap vodka and men's cologne and the acid still blossoming in my bloodstream.

Melinda, Briar, Lani, and Ragan sprawl across the sofa and floor, tangling with Mr. Hyde, Dorian Gray, and the Werewolf of Paris. Dracula reappears with a tray: chamomile tea steaming in glass cups, a blunt, an ashtray, a lighter that snaps like a gun. We pass the blunt clockwise, lips slick from gloss and smoke. I inhale deep. The grape wrap clings to my tongue, and my heart does this strange accordion thing — expanding too far, contracting too tight. The room starts bending at the edges. The carpet moves like fur under my hands. Every color has a pulse. Every pulse has a face.

I rise from the sofa and lean into Dracula, my lips grazing the shell of his ear. "Where's your restroom?"

"Second door on the right," he murmurs, low, like he already knows I'll snoop.

The hallway feels longer than it should be, like I'm walking down the inside of a throat, the carpet soft and wet as tongue. The bass from the club is still pulsing in my head but it isn't music anymore; it's a heartbeat, steady and slow, vibrating through the walls. My heartbeat? Tinsel's?

The bathroom is *too white*. The marble walls ripple faintly, like they're underwater. Navy cabinets inhale, exhale. The gold fixtures wink at me in unison, conspiratorial. I go straight to the medicine cabinet, my reflection flickering, wide pupils, too-big grin, every time the light above me hums.

Inside: Adderall prescription. Predictable. A box of Her Pleasure condoms, their foil catching the light like they're laughing. Rows of hair products lined up like soldiers. And then… the straight razor.

It hums before I touch it. Heavier than I expected when I lift it, as if it's full of something alive. The blade catches the light in a slow, liquid shimmer. I run my fingertip along the edge, not pressing, just feeling that whisper-thin promise.

Through the walls, I hear it: Tinsel's laugh. Muffled but close, too close. It slides into my ears like silk, then turns sharp, not laughter, but the quick, shallow pant of someone gasping for air. It's rhythmic, synced with the bass in my brain, synced with the pulse in my throat.

Her face blooms in my mind. Warm skin under my palm. I imagine parting her with this. The first slice so clean she wouldn't even know she'd been opened. Her gasp would be confusion before it was pain. The warmth would spill over my hands, dripping into my mouth until I could taste her — salt, sugar, and the copper that makes her impossible to let go of.

The thought loops. I see her laughing, gasping, still. Then not still at all. Each version sharper, bloodier. I can't tell if it's fantasy or memory, if I've already done it or if I'm rehearsing for when I finally do.

The bass slows until each beat feels like a footstep coming down the hallway. My breath is shallow now, the marble under my palm cold enough to sting. I force the razor back into its spot, aligning it perfectly like nothing happened. Not tonight. This dress leaves no room for souvenirs.

When I catch my reflection again, my pupils look even bigger. Like they're swallowing the rest of me whole.

I wash my hands, let the cool water ground me, and step back into the living room, and stop.

When I come back, the scene has shifted. It's like I blinked, and everyone rearranged themselves into a living sex mural: Briar and Lani tangled together, tongues glittering wet; Dorian Gray groping Lani's breast while undressing Melinda; Ragan licking the Werewolf's bald head like it's the last lollipop on earth.

And there's Tinsel. Always Tinsel.

She's wedged between Dracula and Dr. Frankenstein. *My* Dr. Frankenstein. Their hands roam over her like they're memorizing every inch for themselves. Frankenstein's mouth is on her neck, the same spot his lips were on mine an hour ago. She's laughing, tossing her hair, turning her head to kiss one, then the other. Their hands moving over her like she's the only warm thing left in the world. She's laughing, leaning into each man in turn. Her laughter is so bright it stings my teeth. My skin starts to hum.

It's so different from Wall Street's touch.

His hands hold me like I'm a fragile, expensive thing. Tinsel's game is the opposite — she gives herself away like candy on Halloween, daring you to grab as much as you can before someone else does. Wall Street makes me feel contained. Tinsel makes me feel like I could dissolve.

A sharp, stupid ache festers in my chest. I want to unzip her from her sternum and see if her insides twitch in my hands.

But then I see Lani, flushed, pupils blown wide, candy bra slightly askew. She's looking at me like I'm the one worth devouring.

Fine. If Tinsel wants to play with my toys, I'll make her watch me play with hers.

I slide onto the carpet beside Lani. My fingers find her thigh, then slip beneath the candy skirt. She gasps, a sharp inhale that makes my own pulse skip. I work her slow, then faster, every sound she makes syncing perfectly with the bass still vibrating through my bones.

Across the room, Tinsel's head turns. Our eyes meet.

I don't look away.

Lani moans louder now, hips tilting into my hand. I keep going until she shudders apart, sugary sweat dampening my wrist. Only then do I pull back, licking my fingers while holding Tinsel's gaze.

And just like that, she's crossing the room. Dropping to her knees in front of me.

Her mouth crashes against mine. Not gentle. Not playful. Posses-sive. Her hands undo my corset, sliding down to graze the curve of my ass. It's always like this: she drags me to the edge, lets me hang there, then yanks me back with a single touch.

We sink to the carpet. My mouth traces her collarbone, her stom-ach, until I'm between her legs. She tastes like sweat, ecstasy, and pain. The world narrows to nothing but her breathing and the heat in my mouth.

She's laughing again, but softer now, like it's only for me.

And I know, no matter how many other people are in this room, no matter how far I have to go to get her attention, she's mine.

For now.

We slip out of Dracula's penthouse just before sunrise, leaving the smell of weed and sex clinging to our hair and clothes. The others peel off into cabs, their voices fading into the city's early-morning hum, but Tinsel decides we should walk. She says it's "good for the high" and "refreshes the soul," like she's some barefoot shaman in a fur bikini.

The streets are quieter now, just a few stragglers wobbling home in costumes missing crucial pieces. The acid's still breathing in the edges of things—streetlamps pulse, puddles glitter like oil slick gal-axies. My legs feel too long and too short at the same time, but I match her pace. We walk side by side, her arm brushing mine, and every time it happens, I want to hook my fingers through hers just to keep her tethered.

We're cutting across Ninth when she says, almost lazily, "You were… kinda weird about that girl at the parade."

My stomach shifts. "What girl?"

"The bumblebee. The one Lani kicked." She glances at me, quick and assessing. "You laughed like... I don't know. Like it turned you on."

The air between us feels thinner. I manage a half-smile. "Maybe it did. You didn't like it?"

She laughs, but it's short, clipped. "I mean, she got *wrecked*. I think everyone else was a little freaked out."

I nod like I'm agreeing, but inside it's a blur - her body between Dracula and Frankenstein, their hands on her hips like they owned her; her laughing with them instead of me. Every touch they took from her felt like something stolen. And now she's looking at me like I'm the stranger in the room.

"I just... didn't think it was that deep," I say, soft enough to make her lean closer to hear me. "You know me."

Her eyes linger a second too long. "Yeah. I do."

But the way she says it makes my chest go cold, like she's filing me away. Like she's already moving toward someone else.

"I mean—" My voice comes out smaller than I expect it to. "I didn't think it was a big deal. No one got arrested. We were fine."

But she's not looking at me anymore. She's scanning the street, watching her reflection in shop windows, like she's already walking somewhere else in her mind. And suddenly I'm back in that Instagram rabbit hole—hours of scrolling, chasing her through photos of other people's nights, her leaning into strangers, smiling at jokes I wasn't there to hear. The same low, acid hum of dread unfurls in my stomach: *She's pulling away.*

The sky's bruising into morning, she tosses her hair and laughs at something I don't hear, and it hits me, hard and hot, that I have to do something before she's gone completely. Something to remind her where she belongs. Something to make her stay.

I match her pace, close enough that our shoulders brush, close enough to smell her skin under the stale perfume and club smoke. She doesn't push me away. That's good. That means there's still time. But not much.

By the time we reach her block, I've already started imagining it - how her face will look when she realizes no one else can love her the way I do.

She hugs me goodnight, warm and casual, like nothing's wrong. I hold her tighter, inhaling the scent of sweat, perfume, and smoke like I'm trying to keep it inside me forever.

I don't let go first.

November 1, 2013

Tinsel thinks I was "weird" last night. She said it like a joke, but her eyes were measuring me. We both know what that means: she's deciding where I fit, how much I'm allowed in her world. I can feel the line tightening, pulling me back, like she's testing how far she can let me drift before I disappear.

She doesn't understand. It's not about Lani, or the bumblebee girl, or anything that happened last night. It's about her choosing who gets her attention, who gets her heat, who she lets lean in close enough to smell her hair and touch her wrist.

I can't watch her drift into other people's nights anymore. I was here first. I am here first. She's mine.

I'll be careful. Patient. Sweet. I'll keep her close without her feeling the rope. Then I'll pull it, slow, slower, slowest, until she's not sure when she moved. She'll think it was her idea even. And once she's here, fully here, she'll never want to leave. Never ever. Ever. Ever.

19

IT'S 4:00 PM ON a cold November day, and I'm barefoot on a lavender mat at Yoga to the People on St. Mark's Place.

Mr. Wall Street came by this morning, all crisp wool coat and cashmere scarf, and insisted we go furniture shopping. "It's depressing to think of you sleeping on an air mattress," he'd said, picking out a queen-sized bed, a hammock chair, a kitchen table set. He even chose the sheets, blue, 1500 thread count, and the kind of pillows that stay cool all night. The same kind he has. He swears by them.

Then, like static, Halloween cuts through: Lani's boot coming down, the crack of bone, the bumblebee girl's mouth opening in that high, wet scream.

And my laughter.

The laughter Tinsel judged, sharp enough to cut me, even through the ecstasy haze.

It's all so loud in my head, I can almost hear it echo in this quiet room. I shut it out, or try to, breathing deeper.

Mr. Wall Street's steadiness is quieter, cleaner. He's been texting more since that night, since the night he said he'd stay, and did. The night he didn't vanish into someone else's plans, or slip away before sunrise to someone else's bed. Tinsel always leaves. Always finds a new sun to orbit.

The instructor's voice is warm and steady, guiding us into child's pose.

"Let your hips sink back. Begin connecting with your breath. Deep ujjayi breaths, in through the nose, out through the nose. Like Darth Vader," she says with a soft laugh.

I press my forehead into the mat. In. Out. In. Out. I try to stay in the here and now, but my mind drifts—his hand on my back in the store aisle, the slow weight of his palm, his voice dropping into those deep, reassuring growls, like he already knows what I need before I do.

For a split second, I see it—him cooking breakfast in the kitchen, my head still on the pillow, the sheets he picked wrapped around me. The air smells like coffee, instead of bleach or sweat or someone else's perfume. It's so simple, it's almost absurd.

I exhale, slowly, and push the image away before it can make itself at home.

"Lately," the instructor says, "I've been reflecting on a Yogi Sutra: 'To one established in non-stealing, all wealth comes.'"

Her voice glides over the room. "In this city, it's easy to be greedy. For more time, more money, more… everything. But the more we take, the emptier we feel. True wealth is freedom from desire."

Freedom from desire.

Her words settle in the air, heavy and impossible to ignore.

I move into downward-facing dog, arms shaking just slightly. Freedom from desire. Desire for what? Desire for whom?

The thought pushes its way in, uninvited but familiar, like a stray cat at the door. Could I release Tinsel? Could I be released from her?

I try to picture it - a life without her. It's blurry at first, then sharpens into something hollow: me waking up alone in an apartment too quiet, the air heavy with silence. Nights spent scrolling through meaningless messages. Holidays passing without her chaos to light them up. The stillness I'm supposed to crave feels suffocating.

When I look back at my mat, I see him instead. Mr. Wall Street. The easy grin. The slow touch. The way he said he'd stay, and did. I wonder if I could want less. If I could be the kind of woman who only needs one person, one safe, steady person. Could I be enough for him?

We rise into tree pose, one foot pressed into the other leg, arms reaching overhead. My balance wavers immediately. My gaze shifts from the instructor's hands to the girl next to me, then to my own reflection. Every flicker of attention makes my body sway. Steady your gaze, I remind myself. Pick one point. Hold it.

I think of Wall Street's grin, the way his voice softened when he said, "I'm staying." How my body relaxed just hearing it. Maybe I could learn to stay there.

But the thought unravels almost as soon as it forms. I picture Tinsel—her hair in my fingers, her laugh cutting through a crowded room, the heat of her eyes on mine. Even here, in this quiet, she rushes in, flooding every empty space until I'm tilting toward her again.

My foot slips. I catch myself before I fall, laughing under my breath. Maybe that's all it is, a matter of where I let my eyes land. Maybe the difference between falling and holding steady is just… picking the right point to fix on.

"Smile," the instructor says as we move into warrior pose. "Plague this city with happiness. Should we die in a minute, let us die laughing, drowning in joy."

The image makes me smirk. Drowning in joy. If only it were that simple.

I stretch deeper into the pose, my breath pulling me back into my body. Maybe there's something here—this slow, steady care that doesn't vanish when the night's over. Maybe the constant wanting, the hunger, doesn't have to be the whole story. Maybe.

20

I DIDN'T SLEEP WELL last night. My dreams were fever-bright and sticky. Tinsel and I sitting at a long Thanksgiving table, the china pristine, the silver polished to a mirror's gleam. But instead of turkey and mashed potatoes, we were carving Emma and the LAXative. Their bodies lay splayed across the linen tablecloth, steam rising from split-open torsos.

I took my time, slicing thin ribbons of LAXative's flank, dipping them in cranberry sauce before pressing them to my tongue. The meat collapsed in my mouth, tender, blood-warm, fat melting like butter against the roof of my mouth. Every chew sent hot juice dribbling down my chin.

Tinsel was beautiful in the candlelight, her fingers buried wrist-deep in Emma's ribcage, fishing out a lung slick with blood. She bit into it like a ripe peach, juice spilling over her lips. I laughed. Until her face twisted.

She started to gag, then vomit, not bile, but hair and bloody fingernails, long and curling, knotted with saliva. They spilled from her mouth in thick ropes, pattering wetly onto the china. She stared at me the whole time, eyes glinting with accusation.

Before I could speak, she lunged across the table, her nails hooking into my cheek, trying to rip the smile from my face. I reached for Emma's tongue, still slick and pink on the platter, but Tinsel's weight crashed into me and the whole table went over—cutlery, candles, bodies hitting the floor.

And then I saw it—no chair for him. No plate. No Mr. Wall Street at our table. He wouldn't be here, wouldn't lean in for the heart or lick the juices from his fingers. He'd stand in the doorway, watching, not understanding. Maybe afraid. Maybe disgusted.

I woke gasping, my mouth wet, the taste of iron clinging to the back of my throat.

I tell myself the dream means she's jealous, jealous that I'm devouring Emma instead of her. That's easier than considering the alternative.

By morning, I'm wrapped in a blanket with coffee, letting YouTube autoplay whatever comes next. Hunting videos. Skinning tutorials. "How to quarter a deer in the field." It's easy to tell myself this is harmless. Like chewing nicotine gum to keep from smoking. I can watch other people make the cuts. Feel the shape of the act without doing it.

Here's what I've learned:

After making the kill, you must immediately field dress or quarter your prey to cool it down, especially if the temperature is above 40°F. Bacteria grows fast—doubling every 20 minutes—threatening to spoil the meat. Efficiency is critical.

Slitting the throat? Overrated. Removing the heart and lungs is faster and cleaner.

Seven tools are essential for decapitation and preparation:

A high-quality hunting or butcher-grade boning knife, at least 3.5 inches long.

A whetstone or diamond stone for sharpening as you work.

A compact saw with bone-cutting blades.

Quarter-inch cotton rope to hold the prey in place—nylon slips won't hold tight knots.

A tarp to keep everything off the ground.

Five Alaskan cloth game bags for transferring meat.

An external frame backpack for easy carry-out.

Optional but recommended: a hoist and gambrel system. Paper towels help with the blood, but that's more for neat freaks than necessity.

What strikes me most is how accessible this all is. Walmart, outdoor stores, even Salvation Army, they all carry these tools. It's almost too easy, like the world is practically inviting you to try it. The thought lingers as I scroll to the next video, a big woodsy guy standing over a skinned bear carcass, its blood drained, muscles laid bare like an anatomical diagram.

How does this disconnect happen? How do people see this bear as any different from their neighbor or their brother? If this were a video of a guy methodically dismembering a Starbucks barista, the world would implode. Outrage would flood every corner of the internet. But here? The murder and dismemberment of this bear is calmly narrated and enthusiastically explained, as if it's a craft project.

I tilt my head, studying the glint of the hunter's knife as it slides through sinew. The smooth efficiency. The reverence in his tone. It's accepted. It's normal. I simply do not understand.

But maybe—if I watch enough of these videos—I won't have so many cravings. Maybe I'll stop imagining slicing and devouring everyone I love. This could be the path to normalcy. I could be... good. A good housewife. *His good girl.*

Tinsel might never look at me again the way she did the morning after Halloween—*I know you*—those words dripping with judgment, oozing from between her teeth like something rotten. Perhaps she'd choose to stay on her own if I just... relaxed. I can live vicariously. I can make it work. For a while.

The yoga teacher's voice from yesterday drifts in: *True wealth isn't money; it's freedom from desire.*

I laugh under my breath. Freedom from desire would mean never replaying that night on stage with Emma—the wet pop as the pick pierced her eyeball. Never touching myself to the sound of her last gasp, closer to a moan of pleasure. Of acceptance. Of thanks.

It would mean not imagining Tinsel lying still beneath me, her warmth fading, my hands working to keep her preserved and perfect forever.

That would be freedom from desire. Aspirational. Impossible.

21

I OPEN MY EYES the next morning, the quiet stillness of the room wrapping around me like a cocoon. My fully furnished apartment feels surreal, a stark contrast to the empty shell it had been. Rolling over, I lay my head on Wall Street's chest, his thick, dark curls brushing my cheek. His body is lean but softened, the hair on his chest thicker than the layer of fat beneath it.

Pochemu is curled in the hammock chair, snoring and purring, a sound so soft it almost blends with the hum of the heater. Outside, fat snowflakes drift down, blanketing the city in white. Everything feels untouched, hushed, like the world has paused for just this moment. I allow myself to think: maybe this is it. Maybe this could be my every morning. I breathe in. Own this calm. You deserve this.

I slide out of bed, brush my fingers across the mahogany stand of the hammock chair on my way to the kitchenette. As the kettle starts to boil, Wall Street's phone rings, its sharp tone cutting the stillness in half.

"Hello?" His voice is low, rough from sleep. A pause. "Do you know what this is in regards to?... mhm... I see. Well, tell him we're on our way and send him up in twenty minutes. Thank you. Bye."

I glance over, curiosity prickling with something darker. He meets my eyes, reading the question on my face.

"That was the doorman," he says evenly. "A cop is here. Wants to speak to you about something. Do you know what this is about?"

The question lands like a pebble in still water, ripples spreading fast: Ubers, LAXative's seizure, prescription cocktails. And then Emma. Emma like a photograph developing in black room fluid. Blood. The ice pick. Her body folding. My stomach tightens. Those keys jingling right before I made my exit.

"I have no idea," I lie, smooth as silk.

He studies me for a beat, then nods. "Alright. He'll be up in twenty. Get dressed."

I pull the baby blue Ralph Lauren sweater from the closet—my perfect yuppie armor. In the bathroom mirror, I gather my hair into a ballerina bun, enough makeup to look fresh but not hiding. My chest feels hot and tight. What if this *is* about her? What if they know? I grip the counter until my knuckles blanch. Breathe. It's nothing. It has to be nothing.

Twenty-six minutes later, Wall Street answers the door. He's wearing a loose-fitting black and brown Prada wool and cashmere crew-neck sweater with a mouliné knit. His hair is slicked back with pomade, giving him the effortless polish of someone who's used to being in control. He fills the doorway like it's his by right, shoulder against the frame, hand resting just high enough to block entry. His tone is calm but edged.

"Hello. How may I help you?"

"Good morning. I'm Officer Pickens, and this is Officer Perot. Is this where Jessie Anne Getty lives?"

"Yes. What's this regarding?" His voice doesn't waver.

"We have a few routine questions regarding a young lady she may know."

Wall Street doesn't flinch. His hand remains steady on the doorframe, forming a physical barrier between the officers and the apartment. "Sure. Jessie?" he says evenly, turning his head just enough to call me over without breaking eye contact with them.

I step forward, my breath caught somewhere between my chest and throat. Wall Street lowers his arm from the doorframe, letting me pass but still maintaining his presence near the door.

"Hi," I say with what I hope looks like a nervous but cooperative smile.

"Hello. Are you Jessie Anne Getty?"

His voice is casual, but my stomach drops anyway.

"That's me," I say, curling my fingers around the doorframe so I don't fidget.

He offers a polite smile. "Detective Pickens. Just following up on a tip about an investigation we're working on, Emma Heard. Can I ask you a few questions?"

Emma. Her name feels loud in the hallway. I hear it in Tinsel's voice, like she's just said it behind his shoulder, whispering it into his ear with my name attached. I hear those keys again - *jingle, jangle, jingle, jangle.*

"Sure," I say, keeping my smile steady.

"Did you know Emma Heard?"

"Knew of her," I say. My words float out while the inside of my head tightens, coils. *Don't flinch. Don't blink. If you blink it looks like you're remembering something. If you remember something they'll see it on your face.*

"When did you meet her?"

I check my phone for the date. "October 8th, at a Brooklyn loft party."

Not too exact, not too vague. Casual, like I'm talking about the weather or groceries. Not like I'm thinking about the warmth leaving her body. Not like I'm thinking about the way her last breath caught in her throat, how soft the skin under her eye was right before the pop.

"Did you see her again after that night?"

"No." The word is too short. I pad it out. "We weren't really friends, I guess. I just remember her from that one night." Don't picture the stage. Don't picture the ice pick. Don't picture the way her knees buckled. Don't think about how Tinsel was right there in the room, sitting in the audience, watching it all. Maybe she saw more than she lets on. *I know you, Raz. I know you.* Tinsel's voice bounces off the inside of my skull, drilling behind my eyes.

"At the party, did she seem upset? Worried?"

"She seemed fine. Having fun."

Fun. Yes. That's the right word. Not desperate. Not doomed. Fun.

They keep going—who she was with, who else saw her, if she left alone. Every question is a fishing line, the hook just grazing my skin. I keep my voice even, but inside it's looping: *Did Tinsel send them? Was my name the only one she gave? If they knew anything real, they wouldn't be here asking. They'd already have me in a holding cell.*

Finally: "If you think of anything else, will you reach us at this number?"

I nod, take the card, and shut the door.

Wall Street is in front of me immediately, hand cupping the back of my neck, thumb brushing my jaw. "You okay?" His voice is low, grounding.

"Yeah." I set the card on the counter. "They just wanted to talk about Emma."

"Who is Emma, baby?"

"Some burlesque dancer who got murdered. We were at the same party, but that's it. More Tinsel's friend than mine."

His eyes stay on mine for a long moment. Then his palm slides to my lower back. "You have nothing to worry about, my dove. Let's grab breakfast at Sarabeth's. I want you to tell me all about Tinsel, these parties—everything."

I spill everything across from him in the corner table, tucked into the back. The clients, how Tinsel makes me feel, how she stole Emma that night we first met her, how LAXative forced his way into my apartment. I talk until my throat feels raw.

He doesn't interrupt. Not once. Just sits back with his coffee, fingers loose around the cup, eyes steady on me like I'm the only thing in the room worth watching.

When I finally run out of steam, the silence between us is thick enough to feel. My mind races. Was that too much? Did I just make myself sound pathetic?

He breaks the silence by reaching into his jacket, pulling out a black Amex, and sliding it across the table. "No more hotel rooms with strangers," he says evenly. "You don't need to do that. Not for money, not for anything. I'm not asking you to be monogamous. I don't care about that. But you need to take better care of yourself. Make safe decisions. Your mental health will thank you for it."

I stare at the card, half-expecting it to vanish before I touch it. "But... how would I pay you the five hundred a month we agreed on for rent?"

He laughs, low and amused. "Jessie, we both know that's symbolic. It barely covers the coke we do together."

The weight in my chest loosens, replaced by something warmer. Not the wild, burning high of Tinsel, but a steadier heat. The kind that might last if I let it.

The laugh sticks to me, warm and easy. Something unravels in me. I can't remember anyone ever wanting me safe without an ulterior motive. Not my parents. Not my clients. Not even Tinsel. Maybe this is what the yoga teacher meant, freedom from desire, not wanting the wrong people to want you. Or maybe that's just another thing I'll never get right.

And then, uninvited, Tinsel flickers across my mind—laughing in some stranger's lap, eyes darting past me toward someone else. I blink, push it down. Not now. Not here.

I nod, eyes dropping to the card again. "Okay," I say quietly, meaning it in a way I don't usually mean things.

Mr. Wall Street left about an hour ago. My brain's buzzing, chewing itself into knots. Breakfast wasn't supposed to go like that. I thought—no, I *knew*—there was at least a fifty percent chance he'd ask me to leave, that he'd never want to see me again. Cops show up at the door, I spill the almost-truth about my life... and instead of cutting me loose, he tightens his grip. Doubles down. Holds on harder.

But the cops.

How did they get my name?

It keeps circling. Not in a straight line, more like a spiral—tightening, squeezing, over and over. Who told them? Who would tell them? I see Tinsel's face in my mind, lit up in that Halloween dorm bathroom light, lipstick smudged, pupils wide. She'd say it was a joke, a throwaway, that she just "mentioned" me. She'd shrug and make it sound harmless.

But I can *hear* her voice saying my name to them, in that slow, deliberate way she uses when she wants something to stick.

And then… maybe I didn't just *hear* it in my head. Maybe I *heard* it.

Her voice, that easy high-sugar tone she uses when she wants to charm someone.

"Oh yeah, Jessie? She was at that party. Knows a little bit about Emma. Let me text you her address."

A low male voice responding.

"Thanks for your help, miss."

And then the click of a pen.

She was giggling, flirting. They couldn't resist her.

I wasn't there. I couldn't have been there. But the sound of it feels *real*, lodged somewhere between memory and dream, like I only have to close my eyes and it'll sharpen into a full scene.

And here's the part that won't let me go: what did she get in return?

A drink? A free ride home? His phone number? His eyes dipping down her chest as he scribbled my name into his little notebook. Did she tilt her head that way she does, like she's letting him in on a secret, only this time, the secret was me?

I Google Emma Heard again. Nothing new. No follow-up article. Just the same grainy photo, the same vague write-up. Her social media's rotting in real time, half grieving fans and flirty "you were an angel" types, half basement-dwelling, woman-hating creeps. Do the cops knock on *their* doors?

I open Facebook. Jenny's friends list. There. Him. Smug-ass LAX-ative. His profile is public, of course. A guy like him wouldn't deny the world his thoughts, his status updates, his artfully filtered beach photos. The top post from October 20th is some plastic blonde named Ashley Goldberg—perfect teeth, nose job, new tits, maybe a little baby Botox—writing about how her "soul is heavy" because one of "our tribe" has passed. She lists the time of death down to the minute, like she was in the room holding his hand. St. Barnabas Hospital. October 18th, 7:09 a.m.

The comments section is a wake without a casket, all God and Hos and Bros and platitudes:

"I am so sorry. May he Rest In Peace."

"Too Young, Too Soon."

"I had a dream about him last night. I woke up crying."

"Weren't we just having margaritas? Miss you, Sonic my hedgehog." (I actually laugh out loud at this one.)

"Such a good boy lost to addiction. Please, Just Say NO. The high is not worth the loss of such precious life."

Nothing like a death to turn people into moral preachers. Why not just post, *I told you so, junkie*' and be done with it?

More comments:

"Pouring one out for all the hos we fux, all the bucks we made, and all the pus you gonna miss."

"The most painful goodbyes are the ones that are never said."

"LEGENDS NEVER DIE!"

Over 120 variations on the same thing. I click the funeral fundraiser link—$425.73 of a $5,000 goal. Who donates seventy-three cents?

Karlita Lopez gave $5 and linked a non-profit rehab in Oakland. Her *own* non-profit. A hustle's a hustle, I guess.

I copy-paste his full name into Google. A vague obituary. No news coverage. No deep dive. Just another dead party boy in the big city.

And still, underneath it all, that phantom memory—Tinsel, smiling at some cop, my name leaving her lips. Maybe it never happened. But maybe it did. And now my name's in a cop's notebook. Inked. Permanent.

As I peel at the dry, cracking skin around my thumbnail, a flap tears loose, and a hot ribbon of blood streams. I press my tongue to it out of habit, metallic and faintly sweet.

My phone dings. Her name. Tinsel.

It glows on the screen like it's burning through the glass.

I almost scream. The phone slips from my hand, clattering across the floor, still lit, her name watching me like an unblinking eye.

The ding keeps echoing. Once. Twice. Again. But the phone is silent now. No new message, just the ghost of the sound reverberating inside my skull. My ears feel full, stuffed with cotton and static, as if the air pressure in the room has shifted.

How did she know? Did she send the cops? Did she smell it on me, on my coat—Emma's blood, the iron tang I swore I'd scrubbed from my hands? The heat of it, the way it steamed in the cold air, the way my pulse synced with hers until it stopped? She was sitting in the audience, of course she saw it. And she's jealous. Jealous she's not my first. No. *The theater was empty; stop saying Tinsel was there.* I dig my teeth deeper into my cuticle bed.

I picture her somewhere else now—phone in hand, smiling as she presses send. Smiling because she knows exactly what this will do to me.

It's not just a message. It's a hook. And she's tugging. I feel it snag behind my ribs, sharp and cold, threading straight through my spine. The pull makes my shoulders jerk, my breath catch. My vision tightens at the edges, tunneling toward that one word—her name—burning on the screen. It's as if she's reeling me in, slow and steady, and I don't even want to fight it.

The static sharpens into a high, wet ringing. And then, her hands. Warm, sure, sliding over my shoulders from behind. Not comfort.

Claim. Her fingers curl over my collarbones, her hooks, tugging me toward her.

I can feel her lips graze my ear.

"I know you," she whispers.

The room tilts. My stomach lurches. I whip around.

No one's there.

Just the phone, still glowing on the floor. Her name.

Still watching.

November 5, 2013

There was a knock at the door and I flinched so hard I dropped my tea.

Jasmine with honey. The mug shattered across the hardwood and it looked like a crime scene. Perfect. I thought they were coming back. I thought they forgot something. Or maybe they lied when they said it was routine, when they smiled like fucking flight attendants and asked if I knew a girl named Emma.

Like they hadn't already decided I did it.

Like Tinsel hadn't already told them.

I could see it in her eyes—the slight drag in her breath when she said my name like it tasted like rot.

She gave them my fucking name.

An hour later, Mr. Wall Street buzzed in.

Said he wanted to take my mind off things.

Said he missed my energy.

Said he bought new powder.

I cut a fourth line with the corner of my library card.

The powder burns going in, then chills my spine like someone dragging a razorblade down it.

I moan. Out loud.

Like a slut in heat.

He laughs.

"God, I love watching you do that."

I don't laugh back.

My jaw's locked, but my thighs are shaking.

That's the problem. The drugs are just a prelude.

What I really crave is skin splitting.

The little sounds they make when they realize I'm not kidding.

The heat of a fresh wound pressed against my clit.

I'm trying so hard to be normal.

But baby, it's so hard not to cum when they scream.

I can hear Tinsel screaming.

Again and again in my head.

I have her gagged with her own hair.

Nails gone.

Knees trembling.

When I tell her I know.

I know everything.

And I forgive her.

Right before I take my ice pick and jam it into her cunt,

over and over again.

When she's done cuming all over my pick—

screaming my name, screaming like I always wanted her to, choked and melodic, like worship on fire.

Her insides begin to slough out in ribbons.

Her cunt spasms like it wants more.

But I decide it's enough.

She doesn't deserve more.

I may forgive her, but she'll have to earn back my generosity.

So I pull the ice pick out slowly, dragging tissue behind it like pink taffy.

And then I shove it in her mouth.

All the way down.

So she never speaks my name again.

Never.

The club he took me to was on the Lower East Side.

It looked like a cave inside and they served tropical cocktails.

He held my hand at the club.

Let me lean on him like I was something soft.

He doesn't ask questions.

He doesn't look too close.

He just lets me be.

Gives me his peace.

I could die for him.

Or die beside him.

And I was good.

I didn't drag a broken wine glass across anyone's neck.

Didn't follow the bitch in the red latex to the bathroom just to hear her beg with her face in the toilet.

I was normal.

I was fine.

I was someone else's dream girl.

That's why he'll stay.

Even after Tinsel rots.

He'll stay with me.

I know it.

I came home and filled the tub.

I didn't get in.
Just stared at the water.

Imagined slicing my thigh open and painting the surface with it.
Imagined floating in it like soup, marrow leaking out, ribs stewing soft.
The water stays clear.
Tomorrow I'll drink green juice.
Tomorrow I'll smile like a woman who's never tasted blood.
Tomorrow I'll go to yoga and hum through the exhale.
But tonight...
Tonight, I press a steak knife between my thighs
and whisper,
"I miss you, baby."
"I miss you, Tinsel."
I miss the version of you I can cut open and keep.

22

NOW THAT I STOPPED seeing clients, I have more time on my
hands. No emails to answer. No Craigslist ads to refresh. No panic
texts from married men who can't find parking and want to know if I'll
still "count the hour." I sleep in more. Eat slower. My ass doesn't ache
from hours over the laps of middle-aged men playing out a schoolgirl
fantasy. It should feel like freedom. And in some ways, it does. But part
of me worries I've made a mistake. This arrangement with Mr. Wall
Street is comfortable, easy. He likes having me around. He likes feeding
me. He likes fucking me when the markets close green. But what if that
changes? What if he gets sick of my moods, my mess, my mania? What
happens when the Amex stops working? What happens when I've giv-
en up my clientele, my income, my fallback plan and all I have left is
a closet full of designer clothes and no one to undress me? There's a
version of me—older, smarter, with better boundaries—who wouldn't
have let herself get soft.

But she doesn't live here anymore.

I replied to Tinsel about an hour ago. She wants to see me tonight. I
haven't seen her since Halloween, which was less than a week ago, but
between the cops, the coke, and Mr. Wall Street's Amex card, it feels

like a lifetime. I'm nervous. Not the kind that makes your hands shake, the kind that simmers just under the skin, like a rash. The kind that makes your own reflection hard to look at.

So I dress. Not for her. Not for him. Just to feel like there's at least one thing in my control.

I start with the lingerie—black mesh thong, no lining. Matching bra, the one with the underwire that leaves a faint red groove if I wear it long enough.

Then a silk slip. Then tights. Black, sheer.

Over that, a dress: charcoal satin, slashed neckline, cut for a body that makes no apologies.

I add the belt with the knife clip. Just for fun.

Jewelry next. Gold hoops. A chain around my neck with a charm that doesn't mean anything.

Makeup is meditation.

Foundation. Blush to resurrect the cheekbones.

Winged liner so sharp I could dissect someone with a blink.

Lipstick: red, blue-toned, cruel.

I line the bottom lashes last.

Always last. It's the part that makes me feel finished. I stare at myself in the mirror. Hold the gaze. Smile without showing teeth.

"I'm okay," I whisper.

Just once. Just to see if the glass believes me.

I wait outside the restaurant on Orchard, hands stuffed in the pockets of my coat like they might behave in the dark. It's colder than I expected. Or maybe I'm just thinner now. I keep shifting my weight, heel to heel, pretending I'm not nervous. I check my phone even though I know what time it is. Tinsel's late. Of course she is.

She texts: Be there in 5 bringing friends 😋

Friends. I stare at the emoji like it's mocking me.

She arrives laughing, in a vintage leather jacket that isn't hers. Her lips are stained wine-dark and smudged at the corners like she's already had a drink. Behind her trail two men: tall, cologne-heavy, and so clearly Turkish it feels like a punchline.

"Razor!" she sings, like she didn't just blindside me with a double date.

"These are the Turks I told you about from my textiles class. Aren't they cute?"

I smile like a corpse. Shake hands. She never told me about anyone from class. I let one of them kiss my cheek and pretend I don't flinch.

Inside, the restaurant is warm, buzzing, candlelit. Everything is amber and shadow, intimate in a way that feels designed to hide things. Tinsel slides into the booth beside me. Her thigh brushes mine. One of the guys sits across from us. The other pulls up a chair.

I order something with gin in it. Something that won't taste like anything. Tinsel's telling a story. She's animated, glowing, backlit by candlelight like some drunk little goddess. I can't bring up the cops now. Not in front of these random guys. It's like she planned this double date to avoid the pink elephant in the room.

And then I see him.

Mr. Wall Street.

Across the room. Corner booth. Leaning in. Laughing.

With her.

The girl from Brooklyn.

Tall. Long neck. Black velvet blouse. Her hand is curled around a wine glass like she was born to be adored. She looks like a Korean supermodel.

She laughs at something he says. Her teeth are perfect. She doesn't look insane. She doesn't look like someone who paints the walls with blood and destroys record collections.

He's smiling like I've never seen him smile. Like he's *relaxed*. Like he's *real*. He touches her hand. And I feel mine curl into a fist around the stem of my glass. My drink goes down too fast. So does the next.

Tinsel notices. "Hey," she whispers. "You good?"

I nod, too hard. She doesn't believe me. She scoots closer. Her hand finds my knee under the table. I want to snap her wrist. I want to sob into her shoulder. I want to peel her open and sleep inside her like a second skin.

"I'm fine," I say.

Tinsel tilts her head. Frowns.

Reaches under the table and touches my hand. Hers is warm, soft, coated in lotion that smells like lavender and sugar.

"Let's go to the bathroom," she says.

Not a question.

She's already pulling me off the seat before I can protest.

The Turkish guys barely register. One of them makes a joke I don't hear. The other raises his glass like this is charming. Tinsel loops her arm through mine and leads me past the bar, down the narrow hallway with the flickering exit sign.

Inside the bathroom, she locks the door behind us and turns to face me.

"You're shaking," she says. "What happened?"

I stare at my reflection over her shoulder. My lipstick is perfect. My eyes are too wide. I look like someone wearing a human suit. I look like a bad imitation of a girl who belongs here.

She takes my face in both hands. Thumbs grazing my cheekbones. Her fingers smell like mint and mezze.

"I'm fine," I say again. Quieter this time. More childlike.

"No, you're not." She hugs me. That's all it takes.

She just wraps her arms around me like I'm real. Like I'm fragile. Like I'm hers.

And something inside me gives.

Not loudly. Not violently. Just a soft snap, like wet cartilage pulled loose. I don't cry. I just stand there, letting her hold me. Breathing in her perfume—something vanilla, something spoiled.

She says, "I missed you."

And I say, "I know."

But what I mean is: *You didn't forget me. You didn't abandon me. You still love me enough to drag me to a bathroom and press your body against mine and pretend I'm worth saving.* Tinsel pulls back, but not far. Her hands stay on my arms. She looks at me the way she used to back in high school, when I got nosebleeds in the middle of class and tried to pretend it was nothing. Like she knows I'm not fine. Like I'm a project she's not ready to give up on.

"What happened?" she asks again. Quieter now.

I glance at the sink, the warped mirror, the hand soap shaped like a seashell.

I shouldn't say it.

But she's here.

She's *here.*

So I do.

"I saw Mr. Wall Street."

I swallow hard.

"With another girl. In the booth. Right now. Back corner."

She blinks. Waits.

"They're laughing. Touching. She looked like someone. Polished. Put together. Not crazy. Not me." I don't cry. I won't. But I feel my throat catch anyway, a flicker of nausea curling around my ribs.

Tinsel lets out a small breath. Not a gasp. Not surprised. Just a sigh.

"Oh, babe." She shakes her head. "Men are always gonna do that shit. That doesn't mean you're not special. You know that, right?"

I stare at her.

"He likes you. You've said that, and I've seen it."

She leans back against the wall like she's about to give a TED Talk on Emotional Stability.

"But if he's not being straight with you, you gotta protect your peace. You've done so much work to get stable again. You seem so much calmer lately."

Calmer.

Right.

"I just—" My voice cracks. I recover. "I gave up everything to be with him. I stopped seeing clients. I made room in my life."

I look down at my hands.

"I don't want to go back to that. To being touched by strangers for cash just to afford rent. I like being taken care of." Now I look up at her, my eyes wide.

Tinsel nods like she understands. Like she knows what it means to have men take slices of you one hour at a time. Maybe she does. In her own way.

"So don't," she says. "Don't go back to that." She tucks a strand of hair behind my ear.

"You've got options. You've got me."

That's all I need.

The sentence slides out before I can stop it. Soft. Casual. I rehearse it like a joke so she won't know it's a proposal.

"You should move in." I smile, small. Playful. "Seriously. We basically lived together back in the day. So, like, why not?"

Tinsel tilts her head.

"Move in?"

"Just think about it," I say quickly. "I've been lonely. It'd be fun. Like a sleepover every night. We'd cook. We're always together, right?"

She chews her bottom lip.

Considers.

I see it happening behind her eyes. The mental math. The weight of her current roommate. Her laundry pile. Her need to always be running somewhere.

Then she smiles. "Maybe. That'd be cute."

And just like that, she says the word I needed.

Cute.

She thinks it's cute.

She's *not* running. Not tonight.

Tinsel kisses my cheek before she unlocks the door.

"You'll feel better after we eat," she says.

Like food fixes everything. Like I didn't just offer her my life and ask her to move in as if it was no big deal. She disappears back into the warm blur of the restaurant.

And I stay. Just for a second. Just to breathe.

The light in here is too blue. Too harsh.

I walk to the sink, press my hands against the counter.

My palms are sweating. I close my eyes. And then my forehead meets the mirror. A soft thud. Glass against skin.

"Please," I whisper. "Please don't fuck this up."

The mirror doesn't answer.

I pull my lipstick from my bag and reapply without blinking. Blot once on a square of toilet paper. Toss it in the trash like a body. Then I straighten my dress. Lift my chin. And go back out. The music's louder now. The table's louder too.

Tinsel's laughing at something someone said. Her eyes are shiny. Her hand is resting casually on my thigh like she owns me and forgot to mention it.

I sit. Smile. Nod. Swallow water. Breathe.

But my eyes go back, again and again, to the booth across the room.

He's still there. They're still there. Mr. Wall Street and his *other* life. She doesn't look crazy.

He said she was. He made it sound like she was unstable, dramatic, *a problem.*

What does he say about me? Does he even say anything? Or am I just the dirty little secret he fucks between deals?

This is what we agreed to, I remind myself. *No rules. No labels.*

But I didn't think he'd love her *like that.* I didn't think it would feel like this.

How can he not see me? Does she fill his eyes so completely that the rest of the room just disappears?

She laughs at something he says and he looks proud of himself. Like he earned that laugh. Like he's being rewarded for doing the bare minimum with someone who's *not me.*

I grip my thigh under the table, fingers digging through the mesh of my tights.

Tinsel turns to me, her mouth brushing my ear.

"You okay?"

"I'm good," I lie. Again.

Inside, I am *not good*. Inside, I'm thinking about her.

About *him*. About how I gave up everything. About how I'm replaceable. Disposable. About how she said maybe. About how *maybe*, *cute* just isn't enough.

The dinner moves along in a blur of laughter, flirtation and clinking silverware. Tinsel keeps her hand on my thigh. She talks too loud. Laughs too hard. Orders dessert for the table. I nod when I'm supposed to. Smile on cue. Across the restaurant, he's still there. Still smiling. Still completely enveloped by her presence.

Eventually, it ends.

The Turkish guys want to keep the night going—karaoke or someone's rooftop.

Tinsel giggles, makes promises, then turns to me.

"You coming?"

I shake my head. Feigned sweetness. "I'm wiped. But you go. I'm glad we got to talk tonight."

Her smile softens. She leans in and hugs me. Tight. Familiar. Warm. Like she still has *no idea* what kind of monster I am.

"Text me when you get home," she says.

"I will."

I wait until she's down the block. Then I turn and head the other direction.

Mr. Wall Street and the mistress are leaving the restaurant.

He's hailing a cab. She's fixing her scarf. I follow them half a block behind.

Close enough to watch his hand on her lower back as he opens the door for her. Of course he opens the door. Always the gentleman.

I slip into another cab. Give the driver an intersection in Brooklyn I remember him casually mentioning when I asked what part of Brooklyn he was in. We follow at a distance.

Their cab weaves through downtown. Over the bridge. Past memories I don't want. The streets get quieter. Residential. When their cab stops, I do too. I watch from the corner. She kisses him before going inside. Long. Familiar. Like they've done it a hundred times.

Like he belongs to *her*. He turns and walks back toward the street, pulling out his phone.

I duck.

Hold my breath.

Watch him disappear into a building right next door like nothing happened. I thought he would go inside with her. Why didn't he? It's a small consolation but doesn't distinguish the rage I feel building up deep in my stomach waiting to boil over.

I walk.

I don't remember deciding to, but my feet take over. Out of the neighborhood. Past bodegas and shuttered wine bars. Toward the edge of the city where the sky opens and Manhattan glows like a wound. I take the train. Stand the whole time. Stare at the black window, reflection flickering, eyes hollow. I get off at 72nd. Keep walking. No aim. No direction. Just the cold wind peeling at my skin. When I finally look up, I'm in Central Park.

The trees loom over me, skeletal branches curling like claws against the sky.

The path ahead is dimly lit, winding deeper into the park.

I don't think. I just move.

My boots crunch against the icy gravel like teeth grinding in a locked jaw.

Then I see it.

A yellow tent, blazing against the muted grays and blacks of the park. It glows like a beacon. Like it was placed there just for me. I freeze, staring at it, my breath visible in the cold night air. The weight of my

purse tugs at my shoulder. My fingers brush the zipper and I feel it—
the ice pick. I'd left it there simply because I didn't know where else to
put it. Now it feels like fate. I approach the tent and unzip it slowly.

The smell hits me first—piss, sweat, and decay. Inside, a man stirs.
Bundled in a navy blazer. Face in shadow. He's alive. But barely.

A living thing. A target. Something to *focus the storm* raging inside
me. Before I can stop myself, I'm straddling him. The ice pick flashes
in the faint light. He blinks. Mouth opens. Then he lunges. A syringe
comes out of nowhere. Cracked plastic, brown fluid, maybe blood, maybe dope. I grab his wrist before the needle hits my neck. He screams.
High, wheezing, feral. I twist. His arm snaps with a sick pop. He swings
with the other hand, clawing at my face. His fingernails rake down my
cheek. I feel skin split. Then I bring the pick down.

Once.

Twice.

Again.

Into his shoulder. His stomach. His throat. He shrieks, gurgling
through a throat full of blood and regret. His hands flail, punching at
my sides. I dodge. Slam his head down. I stab his eye.

It punctures like a blister under pressure. Oozing from the hole.
Blood sprays—hot, sticky, *delicious*—drenching my coat, slicking my
hands. I lose count. I stop trying. Every stroke is broad, manic, deeper.
Each one cracks something open inside me. He tries to crawl out from
under me, but I drag him back by the collar of his blazer.

This isn't over. Not until I say it is.

The air in the tent thickens with the reek of copper and death. My
breath comes in sharp gasps, shallow and uneven, until it suddenly
steadies. The storm inside me is gone. Everything feels... quiet. The silence is so strange it feels funny. It loops, ludicrous and relentless, until I
can't hold it back. I say it out loud, rolling the words off my tongue like

some kind of mantra, a chant from my childhood: "Merry Christmas, you filthy animal."

I laugh.

The sound bursts out of me, uncontrollable and wild, filling the tiny, blood-soaked tent.

The absurdity of it all—this moment, this line, this *release*, makes the laughter sharper, louder, until it echoes off the flimsy fabric walls. I laugh and laugh, until I don't know if I'll ever stop. I slip the ice pick back into my purse, my fingers trembling.

My coat is soaked through with blood. I peel it off and toss it onto the man's lifeless body. The yellow tent sways gently in the wind as I step out into the cold night, leaving the chaos behind. The streets are quiet as I hail a cab. The driver doesn't look twice at me.

This city never does. I sink into the back seat, staring out the window as the lights blur past. By the time I reach my building, I feel nothing at all.

23

I **UNDRESS THE SECOND** I step through the door. Dress. Tights. Bra. All of it peels off like skin I don't need anymore. I leave it in a trail across the floor. Let it rot there. Let it tell the story.

The shower is scalding. I don't ease into it. I just step in and start scrubbing. Hard. Deep. Desperate. There's blood under my nails. Grime in my scalp. A smudge of something dark and elastic stuck in the bend of my elbow. Tissue? Hair? I don't know. I don't want to know. I wash it all. Scrub until my skin is raw, pink and trembling. The thing in the tent, it barely feels real. Like a movie I half-watched on Ambien. Like something that happened to someone else. But the ache in my wrist is real. The bruises erupting on my thighs are real.

The scratch across my cheek burns when the water hits it. I stay under until the water runs cold. Until my fingers wrinkle. Until I feel clean enough to pretend I don't remember what I did. When I step out, I'm calmer. Not better. Not whole. Just... quieter. I towel dry my hair, slow and mechanical, staring at nothing. Then I hear it.

Ding.

The familiar chime from my phone, somewhere tangled in the sheets. I walk naked through the apartment, dripping. Pick it up. A single text.

Mr. Wall Street: *Awake?*

I stare at the screen. Glowing. Buzzing. His name lighting up like a command. Reaching out. The hurt creeps back in—soft, slithering, romantic. I want to ignore him. But this?

This is my fix. Just one word from him and suddenly I exist again. Visible. Touchable. Real.

I want to drown him in the bathtub. Hold him under until the thrashing stops. Then let him up, gasping, grateful, only to take it away again. I want to hear the wet panic in his throat. I want his mouth open under mine, pleading through bubbles. I want to curl into his chest right after. Inhale his cologne. Bury myself in the soft cotton of his expensive shirts. Feel his pulse against mine and believe, just for a second, that I'm loved. Owned. Understood.

That's the problem. I want to kill him and kiss him in the same breath. The text pulses. Waiting. Blinking like a heartbeat. Like a dare. I type.

Jessie: *Not really. What's up?*

Mr. Wall Street: *Can't sleep. I miss your voice. I'm thinking about your curves.*

Jessie: *Oh.*

Jessie: *Maybe tomorrow or something. It's late.*

(Pause. He types. Deletes. Types again.)

Mr. Wall Street: *Everything okay?*

No. Nothing's okay. I bite my lips, staring at the screen. He starts typing again.

Mr. Wall Street: *I saw you tonight.*

He saw me. Does he mean at the restaurant? Or….Brooklyn?

Mr. Wall Street: *I saw you Jessie. Let me come over.*

Mr. Wall Street: *Please.*

I want to cry but my body feels dry. Drained.

I want to scream, but there's nothing left inside me. My power is low. I'm almost dead.

I reply.

Jessie: *Tomorrow?*

Mr. Wall Street: *Tomorrow. Goodnight Beautiful.*

I plug in my phone. Pull on black cotton boy shorts and a threadbare CBGB T-shirt. Crawl into bed. The last thing I feel before drifting off into a restless, gore-drenched dream world is Pochemu's soft fur on top of my left hand like a prayer.

I dream.

A man, faceless, no, not faceless. Just forgettable. Shirtless and tied to my kitchen chair with duct tape and dental floss. He's crying. Or maybe laughing.

Doesn't matter.

I'm kneeling in front of him with my box cutter, the one with the grip worn smooth from use. I drag it across his sternum, slow and careful, like opening a Christmas present. He twitches. I giggle. Blood arcs up and paints my chest, my lips, my neck. It smells like pennies and power.

I wake up sweating. Panting. My boy shorts are soaked. Not with blood. I peel them off and throw them on the floor. Then curl back under the blanket, still shaking, and let sleep take me again.

24

MY BODY HURTS. Everything aches like I've been dragged across asphalt. My muscles are pulled tight like piano wires. My cheek is swollen, hot, tender, like it remembers something my brain won't admit. Yesterday is fog. A film of static across my mind. I remember the bathroom. Tinsel's hands. The word *"cute."* She said it'd be *cute* to live together. Not *no.* Not *stop.* Not a laugh. Not a shove. Just... maybe. I could've lived inside that maybe forever. But something leaked through. Rage. Disbelief. It slipped out of the corners of my eyes like tears made of gasoline. Mr. Wall Street. His not-so-crazy supermodel. The One. The One he moved to Brooklyn for. He told me about her. Day one. No promises. No rules. No betrayals. And still. I hate it. Hate *her.* I frown and feel it pull the sore spot on my face. Pochemu meows from the foot of the bed like she's asking what I did. I pour her dry food, scratch the base of her tail. She purrs. Always supportive. Always on my side.

I catch my reflection in the closet mirror. What the fuck. I look... wrong. Bruised. Pale. Like I went out and got jumped by my own reflection. What am I supposed to tell people? Wall Street? Tinsel? I dig through my purse. The ice pick's still there. Clean. Too clean. A flash in my mind. Yellow tent. Glowing like a lantern in the dark. Rot. Piss. A needle rising toward me. No. That's not real. Is it? Maybe I was mugged. My coat is gone. But my wallet's here.

My phone is charging. Nothing makes sense. But the smell lingers in my nose— metal, mildew, a whisper of something dying.

My phone rings. I jump like it bit me.

I stare at the screen like it's something unfamiliar, writhing. **Mr. Wall Street.**

His name soft and venomous in the glow. I yank the charger out. Knock my water bottle to the floor with a plastic clunk.

I answer. Voice small. Raspy. "Hi."

"Good morning, Gorgeous."

His voice—low, warm, smooth. "I'm at Swallow Café. Everything bagel with tofu veggie cream cheese, right?"

"...Yeah," I say.

Smile cracking through like light under a door.

"That's my favorite."

"Alright, baby. I'll see you soon."

The line goes dead. But his voice stays in the room like a fog. Warm. Heavy. Seductive.

He's coming.

I drag myself to the closet. My hip catches the edge of the kitchen table and I gasp—sharp pain radiating across my side. There'll be bruises. There *are* bruises. I pull up my shirt and see them: purple bursts along my ribs, a smear of red down my thigh like a handprint from a ghost I don't remember touching me. It looks like I've been in a fight. Or fucked by someone mean. Or both. He can't see this. I pick my softest black high-rise Jeggings, modest and clean—a ribbed tank top under a slightly oversized gray sweater, made of cashmere blend.

One of the ones he complimented before. Soft against my skin. Covers everything. Still, I feel raw underneath. Unstitched. I move to the mirror.

My face looks worse under the light. Cheek flushed. A scrape near my temple. Something pale and broken in my eyes. I start with concealer. Layered thick. Then foundation.

Blush only on the good side. Highlighter, but subtle, just enough to distract.

Eyes next. Winged liner. Thick mascara. I blink. Still look haunted. So, I add more. Smoke out the corners. Make my eyes look deliberate instead of damaged. A light pink gloss over my lips to balance it out. Perfume: behind the ears, wrists, cleavage. The scent is vanilla, leather, something spiced. It smells like me, but better.

I grab my purse. Check for the ice pick. It's still there. At the bottom. Unmoving. I tuck my purse away at the bottom of the closet. Just knowing it's there makes my spine settle.

I stare in the mirror, telling myself *Be soft and sane and glowing.* I take my curling iron and create loose waves around my face. Smooth in the de-frizz cream. The more polished and together the makeup, the clothes, and the hair appear, the harder it'll be for him to pick up on the bruises, the pain and the confusion. Spray one more veil of perfume, just in case I start to rot underneath.

My hand trembles as I pick up my coffee mug. It's empty. I just need something to hold. I pace. One circle around the apartment. Make the bed. Fluff the pillow. Light a candle.

My pulse quickens. I dab at my lip with my fingertip and taste foundation, powder, rose. Then a knock. Three polite taps. The keys unlocking the door.

Then he's standing there holding a brown paper bag, two coffees and a bouquet of lilacs.

Smiling. That Wall Street smile. Devastating. Unbothered. His hair still damp from the shower, his gray coat is open, trusting.

"Morning," he says.

I blink.

Smile.

Tilt my head.

"Hi," I say, like I don't fantasize about choking him out while I cum.

He sets down the bag and coffee, then walks over and wraps his arms around me. Hard. Long. I let go first. Pull back. Search his eyes for... something. I don't know what.

I look at the bouquet.

"Lilacs."

"They remind you of spring," he says. "And your mom, right?"

"You remembered." Almost smiling. Almost crying.

"Of course I did." He pauses, glancing at me. "You look..."

Broken? Ravaged? Deranged?

"...Good."

He hands me a coffee and sits down like we're about to review quarterly losses. "Look," he says, "I saw you at the restaurant last night. I could tell you were hurt. Let's talk about it."

I look at him.

Sigh.

I'm not sure where to start. I'm not really even sure how I'm feeling. He's not breaking eye contact.

"You said she was crazy. You made it seem like she was a burden, like some responsibility you couldn't shake. But she was gorgeous. Flawless. Graceful. You were laughing. You looked happy."

"Yeah, Jessie, she is gorgeous. But she's also crazy, needy, and borderline." His voice is slow. Calm. "She's layered. Just like you. And yes, I care about her. I never said I didn't. But my relationship with her doesn't diminish what I have with you."

I look down.

"I'm scared", I whisper.

"What scares you, dove?" His voice goes low. Warm.

"That I'll become dependent on you... and then you'll get bored. You'll throw me out. I'll be alone. Abandoned."

He inhales sharply. Stares at me for what feels like an eternity.

I look up but can't hold his gaze. His eyes are steady, warm, strong.

"You're my peace, Jessie. I'm not turning my back on you. I want you in my life. I want you in every part of my life."

He holds my hands and kisses me. Long and deep.

"Tell me you understand that. Tell me you believe it."

"Yes. I do." I say, voice cracking, eyes wide. And I do want to believe him. I want to believe him with my whole being.

I sip my coffee. Trying to take it down a notch. Not let him see how deeply his words hit me.

He breathes. I breathe.

Then he leans back in "I've been thinking." His tone is casual, but there's weight under it.

"I want to take you to something next weekend. A party on the Upper West Side. Industry people, hedge fund types. Black tie. A real scene."

He leans back, opens his chest, like he's showing me he has nothing to hide.

"I want to show you off," he adds. "Get you something to wear. A dress. We'll go shopping this week."

My heart flutters like a spooked bird. He wants to introduce me to his friends. His co-workers. That should mean something, right? But what comes out is, "You want to take me shopping?"

He grins. "I want you looking expensive."

Then softer: "Because you are."

The words sink under my skin like warm water.

He stands. Walks toward me, angles his body over mine, and whis-

pers into my ear: "You have nothing to be jealous of. I know how blessed I am to have you. And if that means sharing you with Tinsel, or
anyone else, I'll cherish the moments you give me."

My breath catches. I didn't realize he knew how deeply I felt about
Tinsel.

And he accepts it.

My body leans toward him before I can stop it. I want to crawl into
his lap. I want to unzip his fly and forgive everything.

He tucks a piece of hair behind my ear.

"I miss touching you," he says, and it's almost a whisper. "Miss that
filthy little mouth."

My pulse goes wild. I shift toward him, slow, teasing. He pushes
my sweater up over my head, breathing in the scent of my neck before
biting down. His eyes drop.

Then— He freezes.

"Wait." His brows draw. "What's that?"

I blink. "What?"

He reaches forward and gently touches the bruise on my rib, just
above my waistband. The one I missed.

"What the fuck is this?"

I freeze.

"Did someone hurt you?"

His voice sharpens. "Jessie. Did you see a client?"

"No," I say too fast.

He pulls back. Face darkening.

"Don't lie to me."

"I'm not," I breathe. "I swear. I haven't seen anyone. I haven't—"

My throat closes. Panic swells in my chest.

"Then who did this? Those guys you were at dinner with?" His eyes
are fired. No seduction, no smirk. Just heat and fear and fury.

"I—"

My voice breaks. I don't mean to cry, but something in me cracks wide open.

"I walked through Central Park last night," I say. "Late. After dinner. I wasn't thinking. I didn't want to go home."

He's still staring.

"I got jumped. Some bum. He took my jacket. I think—I think he hit me. I don't know. It's fuzzy."

I press a hand to my temple, to sell it. Maybe to believe it.

Wall Street blinks, processing.

He softens just a little. But not much.

"You should've called me," he says. "You don't walk through the fucking park alone at night."

"I know."

He sighs. "Jesus, Jessie." He stands. Runs both hands through his hair.

He touches the bruise again, more gently this time. "Why didn't you tell me last night?"

His voice is low now. Hoarse.

"I didn't want to ruin anything. Like I figured you were with her." My voice breaks just a little. Just enough.

He closes his eyes like that hurts worse. "You could've been—" He doesn't finish the sentence. Just pulls me into his chest.

"Don't ever do that again," he says into my hair. "I swear to god, Jess. Next time, call me. I'll come. I don't care what time it is. I don't care who I have to bail on."

He kisses the back of my neck. Just once. Then again, slower. Warmer. His hand slides under my tank top, palm splaying flat across my stomach. My skin flinches under his touch. Not from fear. From feeling. He shifts behind me, breathing deeper now.

"You still want this?" His voice is soft. Careful.

I nod. "Yes." My voice is steadier than I thought it would be.

He moves slowly. Lifts the shirt inch by inch, revealing more bruises. He doesn't say anything at first, just traces them with his fingers. Each touch lingers. Gentle. Healing.

Like he's trying to memorize where I was hurt so he won't add to it. I roll onto my back, arms open. He leans over me, eyes dark and searching.

"Tell me what you need," he whispers.

"Just you. Only you."

He kisses me long and deep. No rush. His mouth is warm and forgiving, and I arch into him, thirsty for more. Clothes come off slowly. He undresses me like I'm made of glass, pausing at every mark. A bruise above my hip makes him stop.

"Does this hurt?" he asks.

"No," I lie.

His hands are so careful, it makes me ache. Like he thinks if he touches me right, he can fix whatever broke. When he finally pushes inside, it's slow. Deep. He moves like he's trying to be gentle with a storm. I wrap my arms around him. My fingers dig into his back.

I let him think I'm healed. His eyes never leave mine.

"I've got you," he says again.

His thrusts stay steady. Measured. Every time he pushes in, I feel myself stretch to hold him.

To keep him. The room smells like sweat and lilacs. Like ruin and rebirth. I moan into his mouth. Let him love me.

After, he stays inside me a little too long. Breathing heavy against my shoulder.

"I'm here," he says.

I nod against his cheek. I want to believe it.

But all I can feel is the ice pick, still zipped in my purse.

I can feel it going into a man's neck.

Chest.

Stomach.

Stabbing over and over and over.

The weight of a blood-soaked coat thrown away.

The yellow tent.

The blood splattered yellow tent.

November 8, 2013

I've been losing more time. The sun sets faster now. Conversations smear. Tinsel texts me to confirm plans I don't remember making.

Something happened in Central Park. I don't know. I'm not sure. There was a tent. Yellow. Glowing from the inside like it had a soul. I keep picturing his face. Or not a face. Just a blur. A man-shape. Filthy. Hollow-eyed. Arms flailing. A mouth foaming. Like he was screaming. Or laughing. Or praying to me.

And the sound. Like meat slapping concrete. Like something bursting open.

Like I wasn't just cutting.

Like I was scooping.

I was carving a cradle inside him.

Digging through his belly like wet clay. A second mouth opening in his stomach. Begging. Gurgling. I wanted to crawl in, make it my home. Live there, so I wouldn't have to rot alone.

But the bruises. The split near my eyebrow, already scabbing. Those are real. Those are proof. That maybe I was in a yellow tent. That maybe I was born. Or fed. Or worshipped.

I think Mr. Wall Street is real too. As real as he can be. As real as his mask allows. He came over yesterday to talk about the Brooklyn girl. To reassure me. He held me like I was real.

Like I was made of plush and porcelain, not razor blades.

Like he could fix it.

Like he wanted to.

He kissed the bruises. Fucked me slow.

He wants to buy me a dress. Introduce me to his people. Show me off. Keep me.

And I want that. God, I want that.

I want to be kept. Pinned. Framed. Pressed in glass like a butterfly someone loved too hard.

But I feel it creeping again. That itch. That hunger. That need to ruin what touches me. To worship it by carving it open. I wanted to keep Tinsel. Now I want to keep him too. Not just have him. Keep him. It's not obsession. It's not wanting. It's deeper. Worse. It's inside-out wanting.

I imagine opening his chest with a Jousaku knife. I'm just so curious. What color is his heart? Does it beat faster when he thinks of me? I want to hold his face underwater. Gently. Just until he starts to thrash. Then kiss him while he gasps. Let him surface. Then take it away again. What will his eyes look like when he thinks I'd let him go? What kind of relief will he feel when I lift him up again to receive a deep hard kiss?

I want to keep his eyes. Just the eyes. To watch me forever. To remember me. I'd slip them inside me, like Kegel weights. So he can see my insides. Just like I worshipped his. So he can really see me. All of me. I could carry him with me. Always.

Isn't that what love is?

25

I'M IN A USED bookstore on St. Mark's Place, pretending to read *The Stranger*. My fingers stick to the pages. I can't focus. I keep seeing the cops. Their cheap shoes. That airline smile. The word "Emma" in their mouths like gum they've been chewing too long. They came to my door on a hunch. A *tip*. From who? Only one person knows where I live. Only one person could've said my name. My address. And it wasn't a fucking coincidence. There's no lease. No paper trail. My name's not tied to anything. She gave me up. I *know* she did. I can hear her voice in my head, laughing. Pretending it's a joke. Giving me away like a secret she couldn't wait to tell. They haven't been back. Thank God. But they will be. The night we went to dinner with those guys from her textiles class, before I realized it was a setup, before I knew it was a double date, I was going to confront her. Rip the smile off her fucking face. But then I saw him. Wall Street. With her. The Brooklyn girl. Shiny and beautiful. And I crumbled. Tinsel took me to the bathroom. Held me like she could put me back together. Listened when I said she should move in. She didn't say yes. But she didn't laugh. That was enough to shut me up. For now.

Still… I hear her voice sometimes. Like a radio in the walls. Telling them everything. Feeding me to them.

I'm supposed to meet her in 40 minutes. Bryant Park. Ice skating. We do it every year, first week it opens. Tradition. Girlfriends. I'll be shocked if she mentions the cops. She'll probably skate backwards and tell me about some dream she had. Some guy she kissed. Some vintage dress she found. If the subject comes up, it'll be me who brings it there.

Me, again, cleaning up the mess.

The copy of *The Stranger* is still in my hands when I leave the bookstore. I don't buy it. I just slip it in my purse and walk out like I'm not spiraling. No one notices. I'm invisible to almost everyone. It never matters what I do.

Outside, the wind is sharp. Knifing. It makes my eyes tear up instantly, which feels cathartic, like my body is crying for me. I head toward Bryant Park. The closer I get, the more crowded the sidewalks become, the holiday lights strung across the awnings, tourists clutching paper cups, school kids in unzipped coats chasing pigeons.

Everything smells like hot dogs and baking chocolate.

Bryant Park is already glowing. Skaters spiral across the ice like wind-up dolls, all flushed cheeks and cheap scarves. Children wobble and shriek. Everything glitters. It's nauseating. I spot Tinsel before she sees me. She's standing near the rental booth, holding two hot chocolates, her cheeks pink from the wind. Her hair's up in a stupid, messy bun, and she's wearing that old aviator coat she found at a flea market last year; the one I told her made her look like a sexy pilot.

She laughed for ten minutes.

I meant it.

My stomach twists. She's smiling at a kid who just fell on the ice. She's always smiling at strangers. Like they deserve it. I walk up slowly.

"Hey," I say, trying not to sound like I've been narrating her betrayal in my head for the last three hours.

"Raz!" She beams. Hands me a hot chocolate. "Extra cinnamon, like you like it." Of course she remembered. She's always extra sweet when she thinks I'm teetering on the edge.

I take it. Sip. It burns my tongue.

"Cute crowd this year," she says, eyeing the rink. Her voice is syrupy, excited, completely unbothered. Not a word about the cops. We sit on a bench near the rink and start lacing up our skates. My hands tremble as I thread mine. I blame the cold. She chatters on about her fashion history class, her weird TA, some girl who tried to copy her midterm concept. I nod along like I'm here. Like I'm present. But all I'm thinking about is how easy it would be to crack her head against the ice.

Just once.

A clean, cinematic sound.

A spray of blood against snow.

"Hey," she says, nudging me with her knee. "Where'd you go just now?"

"What?" I clench my fists inside my gloves.

"You zoned out." She squints at me. "You okay?"

I blink. Smile. "Yeah. Just tired."

She eyes me for a second longer, then lets it go.

We skate. Circles. Spirals. Laughter. I trail behind her like a ghost. We fall once and laugh like idiots. She helps me up. For a second, her hand stays in mine. Warm.

Soft. Strong. I wonder if she can feel the pulse in my palm. After a while, we sit on the bench again, breathless. She pulls off one glove and brushes snow from my shoulder.

"I'm really glad we're doing this," she says.

"Me too." I want this to be a lie. But I am glad.

Even if she betrayed me.

Even if she gave my name to the police.

Even if she twists her treacherous knife into my soul just to pull it out and tongue fuck the gaping hole she left behind.

I'm glad.

Because she's here.

Because this is ours.

Because maybe, if I play it right, she'll still say yes.

To moving in.

To choosing me.

To loving me like I love her.

She walks me to the M train. We pass a group of cops laughing in front of the entrance. I look at her too long. Daring her to say something. She pulls me into a hug.

"Have fun, sweetbum! Let me know what that sugar daddy of yours dresses you up in."

She winks, skips off.

I descend into the cesspool of the NYC subway system. My brain tears itself in half—love and rage, disgust and admiration. What glue does she use to keep that mask of denial in place? It's flawless. Unmoving. Like she was *born* with it.

The train screeches out of the dark. Wind slaps my face. What if I just throw myself into the speeding side? Just for a second. Just to see how it feels.

I get on. It's crowded. I hold onto a greasy pole as the doors close behind me. We lurch forward. Up the tracks toward Madison Avenue. Mr. Wall Street is waiting at Dolce & Gabbana.

The boutique is hushed. Lit like a chapel. All glass, mirrors and the scent of rose water with a hint of citrus. The air feels expensive. I step inside and immediately feel a sense of unease.

He's already here.

Standing near a chaise lounge, flipping through his phone like he owns the building.

Maybe he does.

When he looks up, his whole face softens.

"There she is," he says.

He walks over and kisses me on the cheek, then slides his palm down my arm like he's checking for cracks.

"Ready to be spoiled?"

"Always," I say, pretending like my back hasn't started sweating.

A sales associate appears out of nowhere. Perfect blowout, red lips, heels like needles.

"We're looking for something black tie," he says. "Classic. Sensual."

"Of course," she purrs. "Right this way."

She brings dresses like offerings to a god. Silk, velvet, organza. Blood red. Oil slick black.

I disappear into the dressing room. The curtains close behind me.

Under the boutique lighting, my skin looks unreal. My bruises are easy to miss if you don't know where to look.

I try on the red first.

It hugs like hands. Makes my waist look obscene. My tits like an invitation.

"Let me see," he calls.

I pull the curtain back.

He exhales like I kicked him in the chest.

"Jesus, Jess. You're going to kill them."

He steps forward. Fingers trail my hip.

"You look like sin."

I smile. I tilt. I pose.

I wonder what he's seeing. What he's clocking as his eyes wander up and down my body. Would I see myself differently if I wore his skull as a mask?

We try six more. Each one tighter. Lower. Meaner.

I slip into a sheer lace midi dress, with a sweetheart neckline. It looks like it was tailored for me. I pull my hair up tight enough to tug the corners of my eyes. I pout my lips. This could be my life. If he falls for me completely, he'll keep me. Rich people are all mental cases anyway. Maybe this is where I belong. In his world. Maybe that's why I'm his peace, because I'm his missing puzzle piece he needs to navigate his own sick twisted existence of privilege, excess and depravity.

He slips inside the dressing room. "This one," he says, eyes on the neckline. "This is the one."

His hand drags slowly down my spine. I feel like silk could melt. Like if he pressed any harder, I'd bleed right through the fabric.

I nod.

I want him to choose me. I want to be the most desirable thing in the room. Seen. Seen by him. His people. Accepted.

He kisses my shoulder. "Let's get you heels to match."

At the counter, he slides his Amex card across the glass like he was tipping for good service. He buys the dress. The heels. The lipstick the salesgirl picked out. The perfume I pretended not to want. And lastly, a black wool single-breasted trench coat to replace the one I lost.

The associate hands me the bag like it contains a new identity.

Outside, the city glares. He hails a car, kisses my temple.

"You're going to own that party," he says.

"Thank you" I whisper. "I really appreciate you. And you know… everything."

He squeezes my hand before disappearing into the yellow cab.

I imagine dancing under chandeliers. Imagine smiling with blood on my teeth.

Back home, I drape the dress over my bed. It gleams under the overhead light, sleek and black and already humming, ready to be worn, ready to be torn off. I curl into the hammock chair, knees to chest, fingers laced tight. The Dolce and Gabbana bag rests on the floor beside me like a totem. Like proof I've been chosen.

I stare at the dress. This is how Wall Street owns me. Possesses me. Loves me. Through creature comforts. Care-taking. He ensures my body is safe, fed and very well clothed. If the outside is perfected, he assumes the inside is satisfied.

He said he didn't mind sharing me with Tinsel. Said it without flinching. But does he know how *I* desire to own, to love, to possess? Would he still be so generous if he knew I wanted to keep Tinsel in a freezer? Would he still say I was his peace if he knew I fantasized about slicing her open and preserving the best parts? Could he love a girl who keeps people like perfume bottles?

What if he's like me? What if he doesn't flinch at the sight of blood? What if he gets hard when he smells it? I imagine him in that dressing room again. Palming the small of my back like he owns me. What if I turned to face him and opened my chest with a blade? Showed him my real shape? Would he reach in and hold my heart in his hand, or would he fuck the cavity until we both went blind? I want to unzip myself for him. Let him see the rot. The maggots, the hunger, the split parts of me I keep packed in ice. If I built us a home out of ribs and skulls, burnt my secrets into the bone, painted the walls dark red and moist - would he crawl inside. Hold me while I slept?

He sees me. I know he sees me. But does he see *all* of me? Because I want to be worshipped and I want to be ruined. I want to be kept like a secret and gutted like a sin. Maybe love, our love won't be Valentine's cards and kiss emojis. Maybe it will be matching bruises. Bloodstains that no one bothers to clean.

Maybe I'm finally ready to be the one kept. Pinned. Preserved. Still breathing in the jar.

26

THE PITCHER OF MIMOSAS is half full. Fluffy pancakes and berries litter the serving tray like offerings no one touched.

I made Mr. Wall Street brunch. Sunday morning style.

His hand is on my thigh as he scrolls through graphs and lists of numbers on his laptop.

I'm staring into space, champagne glass in one hand, the other working over Pochemu's ears, chin, and shoulders. She purrs. Kneads her claws into my thigh like she's testing my pain tolerance.

He looks up from his laptop. "Maybe you should bring Tinsel tonight."

I thought I misheard. "Why would we do that?" I ask.

He reached into his pocket. Pulls out his keys and a small bag of white powder. Takes a bump Passes it to me. I do the same. It burns in the best way.

"Everyone there's connected. Thought you might want a familiar face. Someone who gets you."

What? Doesn't he get me? My heart starts racing. Maybe from the coke. Maybe from the swelling panic attack pulsing between my ribs like a second heartbeat. I stare at him like he's glitching.

"Don't...don't *you* get me? Aren't *you* my familiar face?"

He closes the laptop, finally. Looks at me full on.

"Of course I get you, Jessie. I've memorized every inch of you. I see you."

He reaches for my hand. Warm. Steady. Like he believes what he's saying. "But I thought maybe you'd want her there too. She matters to you. That matters to me."

I stare at him. Something sharp curls inside me. He means it. I think. And still— Still, I can't stop the thought: If I matter to him, why does he want her in the room with us?

"You don't really know her." I say "She can be a bit of a wild card." I look past him. Over his shoulder. Not quite sure what the right answer is. Would it be more fun if Tinsel were there? Or would she destroy everything?

"It's a party Jess. This could be a great time to get to know her better. But it's up to you. I want you to have fun tonight. Whatever that looks like."

My fingers twitch under his. I force a smile.

"Okay," I say.

Just one word. Just enough.

But I'm already wondering how the light will hit her face at that party. What will pour out of her mouth. And how much of it I'll have to clean up.

I step into the bathroom and shut the door. The light is soft, flattering. Yet I still manage to look haunted in it. Disturbed.

I pull out my phone.

Jessie: *Want to come to a party tonight? Upper West Side. Wall Street crowd. Fancy.*

Jessie: *Should be fun.*

I stare at the messages. My reflection in the mirror tilts its head like it's not sure who sent them.

She replies almost immediately:

Tinsel: *omg yes. I have a dress that's DYING to be seen.*

Of course she does.

I sit on the edge of the tub, phone still glowing in my hand. My stomach turns — not with dread exactly, but with something stickier. Like glue. Like bile.

She's going to say something.

She's going to laugh too loud or call Mr. Wall Street my *sugar daddy.*

Flirt with the wrong man.

Strike that.

Every man.

She's going to shine.

And I'll have to smile like it's fine. Like I'm not dying. Like she's not grabbing my breasts, one in each hand, and pulling until my skin rips, reaching past my ribs to devour my heart. Twist my lungs into balloon animals. Turn my spleen into a clip hat for her Fashion History final.

I think about giving her rules.

Don't drink too much.

Don't tell anyone where I live.

Don't mention Emma. Or Halloween. Or the dreams I told you about.

But that would make me look crazy. And worse, it might make her start to *wonder.*

No.

I'll manage her the way I always do. With compliments. With drugs. With the promise of a good time.

I close my eyes and see myself in the dress, in the heels, holding Wall Street's hand. Smiling. Graceful. Demure.

Tonight is mine.

I'll make sure of it.

I'm standing in front of the mirror, half-dressed and barely breathing. The dress clings like morning mist. The lighting makes my skin look airbrushed.

Almost holy.

Almost unreal.

Behind me, I feel him.

Mr. Wall Street's hands slide around my waist—warm, sure, like they've always belonged there.

He pulls the zipper up my spine, slow and reverent, like sealing me into something sacred. His mouth follows the line, kisses brushed between vertebrae, slow and spaced like prayer beads.

"Stunning," he murmurs at the nape of my neck.

"Just missing one thing."

He reaches into his pocket and pulls out a thin gold choker, delicate, antique-looking, with a single oval ruby at the center. It swings slightly between his fingers like a pendulum.

The air stills. My throat closes.

I gasp.

I can't help it.

"Tonight," he says, fastening it around my neck, "I want you to feel, without a doubt, that you are mine."

The ruby settles just below my throat, catching the light like it was always meant to live there.

It's perfect. Too perfect.

It makes me dizzy.

I turn. Look up at him. Kiss him deep, like I'm trying to say a hundred things I don't know how to confess.

When I finally pull back, I whisper, "You're perfect. It's perfect. It's too much."

He cups my face, his thumb brushing the corner of my mouth.

"No. It's not enough," he says. His voice is low. Certain. Almost terrifying in its calm.

"You deserve more. I'll never stop until you have the moon."

He pulls me in again.

I breathe him in. Cartier oud, champagne, skin.

That oaky, clean heat that always makes me feel like a person worth keeping.

For a moment, the world shrinks to this: his arms, his scent, his certainty.

But then, like a flicker behind my eyelids, I wonder:

If he knew the version of me that wants to cut out his heart and wear it in a locket,

Would he still want to give me the moon?

Or would he hang me from it?

Mr. Wall Street pulls around the corner in his silver Jaguar XF, the car gleaming under the streetlights like a predator in heat. Quiet, powerful, waiting to pounce. "What do you think?" he asks, gesturing to the polished dashboard. "Bought it last year on a whim," he says, brushing the wheel like it's a woman he tames for fun. "Thought I'd drive out of the city more often, but somehow never managed. Maybe this spring, we could take it through New England. See the coast."`

"It's beautiful," I say, running my hand over the smooth leather seat. "And that sounds lovely." It's not the car that gets me. It's the effort. The wanting-to-impress. That's what hooks me every time.

"Are we picking Tinsel up?" he asks, glancing at me with just a hint of curiosity.

"No, I told her to meet us at the address."

"Cool." His tone is relaxed, his focus back on the road as he smoothly maneuvers through the city. One hand on the steering wheel, the other slides up my skirt, his touch sending a jolt through me. I bite my lip, stifling a gasp as my body responds.

As my hips shift slightly, betraying my pleasure, he reaches to turn up the music with a casual confidence that makes me melt. His eyes never leave the road, but his smirk tells me he knows exactly what he's doing.

When we pull up to the brownstone, he finally removes his hand, and without hesitation, slips his fingers into my mouth. I clean them with deliberate slowness, my tongue curling around them, never breaking eye contact. His smile widens, full of satisfaction, a winner's smile.

I glance up at the brownstone. There's Tinsel, leaning casually against the stone railing, a cigarette balanced in one hand as she animates her words with the other. She's deep in conversation with a slick-looking blond in a designer pinstriped suit, his expression completely captivated, hanging on her every syllable.

Mr. Wall Street follows my gaze. "That's her?"

"Yeah," I sigh.

"She's not as pretty as I thought she'd be."

I can't help the smirk tugging at my lips. "You lie. But I'll take it."

He chuckles and steps out of the car first, circling around to open my door and offer his hand. Ever the gentleman. I take it, stepping into the cold night air as Tinsel spots me. Her face lights up, and before I can say anything, she's rushing toward me, arms wide.

"Raz!" she squeals, barreling into me, lips smashing mine in a kiss too eager to be platonic. My pulse hiccups. Just like that, she's in my bloodstream again. "Oh my god, I've missed you!"

I can barely get a word in before she's spinning me around, her voice tumbling over itself. "Is this Wall Street? Is this the guy you've been blowing me off for?" She winks, sticking her tongue out playfully. "You look amazing!"

"No, stop. You do," I counter, running my hand down the front of her gold strapless dress. She's shimmering from head to toe, her high ponytail braided with crystals that catch the streetlights. She looks like a walking firework, and all the negative thoughts I've been harboring about her evaporate in an instant.

Mr. Wall Street steps forward, his gaze warm but amused by her whirlwind energy. "Hi there. You must be Tinsel," he says, extending a hand.

"It's a pleasure," she replies, flashing him a bright smile that could disarm anyone. She's charming. Too charming. Effortless. I feel suddenly overdressed and underloved.

His smile lingers just a second too long. Did it? Is that even a thing? I know what she does to people. I've seen it too many times. That brightness. That helium voice. The way men orbit her like moths too stupid to register the burn.

"All right, ladies," he says, glancing between us, his grin widening. "It's freezing out here. Let's head in." His hand brushes the small of my back, possessive, grounding, but I still feel untethered. Like I've just introduced my favorite blade to my softest wound. And now I'm supposed to walk into a room with them both.

As we move toward the door, the blond in the pinstripe suit pipes up. "Hey, man. Long time no see," he says, patting Mr. Wall Street on the back.

Mr. Wall Street nods and claps him lightly on the shoulder. "Good to see you," he says, his tone friendly but brief.

And just like that, we're swallowed whole by the glittering mouth of the party — heat, light, champagne fizzing like acid.

The house is thumping with low bass, emitting a pulse I haven't quite put my finger on yet. Everywhere I look: tailored suits, watches that cost more than a year's rent, and girls who don't look old enough to drink, their bodies lacquered in platinum lamé and highlighter. Their giggles float above the murmur of mergers and IPOs like bait on a hook. Their dresses sparkle like fishing lures—flashy, sharp, meant to be swallowed.

I grip Mr. Wall Street's arm tighter. He's solid. Steady. But my skin prickles anyway. Something in the air feels wrong. Like the party has teeth. My dress feels suddenly obscene, like I showed up wrapped in raw meat.

We slip into a side room, a darker chamber off the main hall. A leather-accented bar. A mahogany billiards table glinting under low light like a sacrificial altar. Tinsel is just behind us, already armed with a champagne flute, her eyes darting around the room like a cat who just spotted a dozen red laser dots. She doesn't look fazed. She never does. I wonder what she's registering. I wonder if she feels the static in the air, too. Or if this kind of environment tastes like home to her.

Wall Street pulls me closer as we approach the bar. "Come on," he says, voice low, buttery, like we're slipping into a performance. "I'll introduce you to a few people."

But something's changed. His tone is too smooth. His smile, too wide. Not the one from the car. This one is for them. For here. It's sharper. Glossier. A new mask sliding into place. He's playing a role. We all are.

And I'm the only one who didn't read the script.

I feel eyes on me assessing, cataloging, appraising. I wonder what they see. My stomach curls. This isn't a party. It's a showroom.

He penetrates the group of men around the bar, their sharp jaw-lines, executive haircuts, laughter too loud, their words laced with insider jargon and soft misogyny.

Mr. Wall Street slides into their rhythm like he was born there. Handshakes. Back slaps. His voice lifts to meet theirs. He looks taller somehow. Broader. His movements exaggerated, theatrical. His laugh, deep and booming, startles me. I've never heard it like that.

It's like watching someone else wearing his skin.

I hover nearby, smiling when I'm supposed to, nodding at jokes I don't hear. But my chest tightens. The air turns wet. The room smaller. I scan the men—one continuous face with a thousand teeth. Power and privilege melting into one other. They're laughing too loud. Watching the girls too hard.

I don't belong here. Not really. Not in this world of shiny shoes and shark grins.

I'm the trick mirror in a room full of polished chrome.

"Jessie, you good?" Wall Street glances over his shoulder as he hands me an Aviation cocktail, his hand resting on my arm for a moment. It should feel grounding, but his touch feels foreign, like it belongs to someone else.

"Yeah", I manage to croak out. But when I look back at him, his face shifts. For a split second, I swear his features distort, his jaw elongates, his eyes darken, his smile twists into something too wide. I blink hard. He's back to normal, but the image lingers, clawing at my mind.

Tinsel appears at my side like she's been summoned. "Dividends, like who even cares?" she giggles in my ear. "These are all finance guys, right? So where's the coke, Raz?"

The knot in my chest loosens, but not completely. Yeah, who the fuck cares about dividends? I laugh, but it comes out strange, high-pitched. Like I'm trying it on. I take her hand. It's warm, soft, familiar.

I squeeze it a little too hard.

Then I lean in and whisper to Wall Street, "Where can we do coke here?"

He turns to me, and for a moment, he's back. The warmth in his eyes, the boyish tilt of his grin, it's all there again.

"At this party, sweetheart," he murmurs, reaching over the bar, "just pick a spot and get comfortable."

He pulls out a white-and-blue porcelain plate, then reaches into his blazer, producing a fat bag of coke, a gold straw, and his platinum card in one smooth motion.

"And hey," he adds with a wink, "don't be afraid to share. There's plenty more where that came from."

Then he's gone again. Reabsorbed into the sea of chuckling sharks.

Tinsel and I kick off our shoes and climb on top of the billiards table like it's our stage. I chop up the coke fast. Mechanical. Like muscle memory, learned from the Bowling Green Bull himself.

She leans close, her breath hot in my ear. "You first."

I stare at her. She glows like a hallucination. Her skin, her eyes, her teeth. If I die tonight, I want her to be the last thing I see.

"No," I say, voice low. "You."

She doesn't argue. Just lowers herself gracefully, one hand pressed to the table for balance, and snorts a clean, vicious line. The sound it makes is delicate, almost ladylike, like a straw sucking marrow through fine china. When she lifts her head, her eyes are wild. Her grin is wider than ever.

"Oh yeah," she whispers, voice sticky with satisfaction. "That's the good shit."

I follow. The burn rockets up my nose like firecrackers shoved into my skull. It hits my brain like glass shattering. For one sharp second, the world crystallizes: light, sound, heat. Then it all smears at the edges again, soft and bright and *wrong*.

We're laughing now. Hysterical. Our feet dangle off the edge of the table like we're kids on a swing set. The suits have stopped pretending not to watch. Their stares crawl over us—slimy, possessive.

"What do you think of this scene?" I ask, words spilling out loose and sideways. "Like… these girls look pretty young. Younger than us, even."

Tinsel glances around, then back to me. "Um, yeah," she says, nonchalantly. "They do look a bit young. But, babe, you look pretty young too and you're legal." Her tongue darts across her lips. "I'm having fun though. And Wall Street seems really nice."

I want to tear her away. Away from the gaze of those men, away from the mirrors and smoke and flashing teeth. I want to fold her up like a paper doll and tuck her into my chest. Keep her.

Her eyes lock onto mine. And for a moment, it's just us. The music fades. The bodies blur. The party drops away like a rotten fruit peel. And I feel it again.

That ache.

That *tether*.

The one that ties me to her, no matter how hard I try to chew through it.

Before I can respond, one of the suits slinks closer—tall, tailored, the kind of man who wears generational wealth like aftershave. His hair's too perfect. His teeth too white. His eyes scan Tinsel like she's a car he's thinking about leasing.

"Ladies," he says, voice low and wet. "Mind if I join?"

Tinsel laughs, throws her head back, all teeth and sparkle. "Sure," she purrs. "But you better keep up."

He grins like he's already won, plucks the straw from the plate with too much confidence, and bends down for a line. I glance toward the bar.

Mr. Wall Street is watching.

He's still smiling, barely, but the warmth is gone. He doesn't look jealous. He looks... calculating. Recalibrating. His fingers drum once against his glass, then go still. He turns back toward the men he was with, but I feel the shift. A drop in barometric pressure.

"Is that your boyfriend?" the suit asks, jerking his chin toward him.

I open my mouth, but Tinsel beats me to it.

"Nope," she says. Sugar over cyanide. "She doesn't really do boy-friends."

My blood rushes upward, hot and spiked. I feel my whole body heat. "Tinsel..."

She cuts me off with a shrug, coy and dismissive. "I'm just saying, babe. You're...free-range. That's your thing."

Then the suit moves. Puts a hand on Tinsel's thigh, his fingers spidering upward, automatic, entitled. Like a man who can't hear when a woman says no.

She catches his wrist mid-creep. Nails digging deep into his skin.

"Excuse me?" Her voice is still honey, but it's been left out too long. Spoiling.

Her eyes sharpen. Surgical. Locking on his like they're lining up an incision.

He blinks. Laughs. Tries to play it off.

But she's not laughing anymore. And I'm frozen, watching behind glass.

She doesn't let go. Her grip tightens. He winces. Confused. Embarrassed.

"I said," she repeats, "excuse me?"

He gathers himself. Tries to reframe.

"Come on, baby. If you like it rough, we can go downstairs. Let me show you rough."

She drops his wrist with a sound of pure disgust.

"I'm not interested."

He moves in closer.

My pulse spikes. My body goes hot, then cold. The itch behind my teeth begins to burn.

I want to brake the coke plate against his skull.

Use the shards to carve the edges of his grin so he never stops smiling. Then pack his filthy mouth with the sharp, jagged pieces until it's nothing but pulp and broken teeth.

My hand wraps around the 8 ball next to my knee. Cool. Solid. Heavy. My smile spreads, too wide. Too calm. One crack to the temple. I'd be on him like a rabid baboon tearing open an intruder.

I shift forward.

"Everything all right over here?" The voice cuts through like a hot wire.

Mr. Wall Street.

He's calm. Pleasant. Almost amused. But there's warning in his eyes.

The suit pauses. Recalculates.

"We're just chatting. Trying to help these ladies loosen up. They look like they could use it."

Wall Street claps him lightly on the back. "Appreciate that," voice like smoke curling off a loaded gun. Lazy, but lethal. "Why don't you grab yourself a drink?"

The suit sizes him up. Looks from him to me to Tinsel. Decides against it. Slithers off into the gold-dusted depravity of the party.

Wall Street turns to us, his hand grazing the small of my back, grounding, but barely. "Ladies," he says. Smooth as scotch. "You're drawing quite the crowd."

Tinsel exhales sharply, flipping her ponytail. "What a fucking creep. I'm going to grab a shot at the bar. You want?"

"I'm okay." My voice is flat. My grip still tight around the 8 ball. My pulse won't slow down. My smile doesn't fade. Not yet.

Wall Street looks at me. Really looks.

"Let's find a quieter corner," he says.

Then, lower, just for me, "Come back to me, Jess."

We slip into a darker corner, away from the clink of ice and sharp wolf laughter. A hallway lined with books no one's read, the carpet plush and sound-swallowing. Mr. Wall Street leans close, his breath warm against my temple.

"You okay?" he murmurs, pulling a little glass vial from his pocket like he's offering a cure. "Want another bump?"

I shake my head. My heart's already rattling the cage. I'm grinning, but it's made of glass.

"I'm better now that he's gone," I say, leaning into him. "I was about to make a scene."

He smiles, slow and crooked. "Would've paid to see that."

I study his face. That beautiful, confident face. Would he really like it? Would he still touch me after seeing my lips dripping with blood? Would he still kiss me if I cracked that man's skull open like a crème brûlée?

His hand is warm on my lower back. I shiver.

"Jessie," he says. "You're glowing."

I don't know what to do with that, so I nod.

Then a voice, light and high and suddenly very close.

"There you are," Tinsel says, sliding up behind me. Her hand brushes my arm. "I was starting to think you two eloped."

Mr. Wall Street chuckles and lets me go, his touch replaced by her perfume and static. She slips an arm around my waist. I stiffen.

"You good?" she asks. "You looked like you were about to take that guy's eyes out."

"I was," I say.

Tinsel laughs, tossing her braid over one shoulder. "Thanks for being ready to throw down for me."

She presses a quick kiss to my cheek. Too quick. Too soft. I want to grab her face. Make her mean it. My whole body flares. Possessiveness, arousal, something hungrier. So I do. I grab her waist, pull her in, and kiss her deeply, sliding my tongue between her teeth. Playful. Friendly. I taste champagne and lip gloss. But underneath, it's metallic. Sharp. Like biting a battery. I imagine tugging her lower lip until it snaps. I want to know if there's glitter in her blood.

Tinsel grins. "Careful," she teases. "We'll make everyone jealous."

"You two are absolutely trouble." Wall Street grabs two flutes of something sparkling, something amber from a passing tray. Handing them to us, "Come on," he says. "We're dancing."

He takes Tinsel's hand, then mine. Pulls us toward the heartbeat of the party—pulsing bass, sweating chandeliers. The crowd parts like we've been expected.

I let him lead. One hand on my hip. One on hers. Tinsel spins, laughing. I sway between them. Caught. Buzzing. Electric.

They don't notice I'm not really dancing. Not here. Not with them.

I'm already gone, evaporating into perfumed air, melting into smoke and pulse.

In my mind, I'm back at the billiards table, hand curling around the 8-ball, swinging it into that smug fuck's temple.

Crack.

His skull splits open like overripe fruit, brain leaking out in warm ropes. I drop to all fours, lapping it up like a dog. Then Wall Street's behind me, cock hard, thrusting into me while Tinsel grabs my hair and licks the brain-matter off my face like frosting. A threesome soaked in blood and revenge. A 21st-century trinity.

The music is molten. A low-slung bassline crawling up my spine.

I move because I'm supposed to. Because bodies are supposed to sway when music like this throbs through your ribs. But I feel like a mannequin in someone else's hallucination.

Mr. Wall Street is behind me, hands firm on my hips, steady, claiming.

Tinsel's in front, hips circling, hair wild, her gold dress catching the strobes like a living flame.

She laughs at something he says, leans in too close, and her hand brushes his chest like she's done it before.

I feel it then.

The tilt.

The slant.

Like the floor's not flat anymore.

The music pulses, but it sounds underwater. My jaw tightens.

I picture it again: Tinsel's lip splitting under my teeth. A flower of blood blooming where her gloss once was. I could make it beautiful. I could make her still.

Wall Street leans down to say something in my ear. His lips graze my skin. I nod, not hearing a word. I'm watching the room twist. Watching his hand slide from my hip to her waist. Friendly. Familiar.

My vision halos red.

It's not that they're touching. It's that they could leave me.

Together.

I squeeze my eyes shut. Breathe.

Tinsel spins again, catching my hands in hers, pulling me between them. We're dancing, the three of us, like some dark little trio. But I'm the one in the middle. The glue. The grenade.

I laugh, too loud. I can't tell if it's real.

"I love you guys," I say, the words come out easy, and dripping with gruesome longing.

Tinsel beams. Wall Street kisses my neck.

Leaning into Wall Street, not letting go of Tinsel's fingers, I announce,

"I think I could use a drink and some air."

He nods. "Let's go up. The roof's quieter."

We make our way deeper into the party. The hall narrows, the music softens, and the crowd thins into whispers and shadows. A cracked door reveals too much: an older man kneels beside a bed, guiding a syringe into the soft inner elbow of a blonde girl drooping against him, her limbs boneless, her eyes rolling back.

Tinsel gasps. I stop breathing.

Mr. Wall Street doesn't flinch. He just reaches back, calmly shuts the door. "Come on," he murmurs. "Let's not get pulled into someone else's mess."

I follow, but something itches beneath my skin. I glance at Tinsel. Her mouth is tight, eyes wide. She doesn't say a word.

We don't make it to the stairs. Two men step out from the shadows, predators in suits. Calculated, hungry. Their smiles too precise. They zero in on Mr. Wall Street like he owes them blood.

He straightens, pulling me close. "Gentlemen," he says smoothly, "been a while."

The taller one is carved out of marble and cruelty. Silver suit, silver tie, eyes like frostbite. The other's shorter, red shirt, black jacket, gold wolf brooch gleaming on his collar. If this is who he used to run with, no wonder he's so good at pretending.

"Hard to get a hold of lately," Frost Bite says. "Thought you were ducking us."

Mr. Wall Street smirks, casual. "Just been busy. You know how it is. Deals. Travel."

Red Shirt coughs, dry and deliberate. "Yeah? SEC's been busy too. Your name keeps showing up. It's starting to look...interesting."

For a split second, he stills. Just long enough for me to feel it in his fingers, tightening slightly on my waist. Then the smile returns, just a touch too late.

"They always sniff. Never bite," he says. "Besides, they've got nothing."

The beasts stare. Frost Bite tilts his head, studying him. "Hope so. Would hate to see you lose all this." His eyes flick toward me. Then Tinsel. "You've got a lot riding on this. And so do we."

I can't tell if it's a threat or a promise.

They shake hands. Wall Street's grip is firm. Performed. The men melt back into the party.

We're left in the hallway. My ears are ringing. The air is too still.

"Who were they?" I ask.

"Old friends," he says, brushing it off. "Just business. Don't worry about it."

But I *do* worry. Because I felt it.

That hitch in his breath. That half-second where the mask slipped.

I don't ask again. I could. I should. But I don't.

I let him lead us up the stairs toward the roof, because if I look too closely, I might not like what I see.

And right now, I want to be the girl in the necklace. The one worth spoiling. The one who gets to play dumb.

I've done this before — been paid to kneel, trained to obey. I know the script, the cues, the right sounds to make.

But this isn't that.

With him, there's no safe word. Just the hush of silk and the weight of the choker. I imagine myself on a velvet leash. His show pony, his freak.

And the sick part is: I like it better this way. Not for money. Not for safety. Just to be chosen. I've learned not to ask questions that turn gods into men.

We climb the final staircase in this labyrinth of a townhouse. The rooftop door creaks open into a burst of cold that slices straight through my tights. Goosebumps rise on my arms and legs.

Without missing a beat, Mr. Wall Street slips off his suit jacket and drapes it over my shoulders. Like I'm something to protect. Something delicate.

We make our way toward the seating area. It's a cluster of modern loungers arranged around a sleek electric fireplace. The flames flicker behind glass, all glow, no heat. Dead potted plants line the perimeter like little graves.

"Oh, baby," he says, kissing the top of my head, "let me grab us a bottle and some glasses." Then he disappears back through the door.

Tinsel nestles beside me, close enough that our hips touch. I slip my hand into the inside pocket of Wall Street's jacket and fish out my cloves. Offer her one without looking.

"What are these, Sweetbum?" she giggles, inspecting the black paper.

"My cigs." I shrug, lighting mine. The smoke curls between us like a signal.

She squints. "Babe, I didn't even know you smoked. What are these? Witch cigarettes?"

I laugh, exhale. "Guess you don't know everything."

She sighs, smiling. "You and your secrets, Raz."

I turn. Meet her eyes.

"My secrets?"

She freezes. Just a beat. Like a deer catching scent. Her smile falters.

She looks small now. Fragile. Like a doe, lost in the woods, left behind by her herd. A few steps from the hunter's cabin.

I take a drag. Let the moment hang in the cold. Then:

"How about those cops."

Flat. Precise. A knife slid under the skin.

I don't blink. I just watch her. Watch her choose her next move.

Tinsel blinks. Tilts her head. "The cops?" she echoes, like I've just mentioned a movie we saw last year.

She waves a hand through the smoke. "Oh right! That little thing. I totally forgot."

A laugh. Dismissive. Paper-thin. "I mean, they didn't even ask real questions. Just, like, weird vibe stuff, you know? It was nothing."

She takes a drag, blows the smoke towards my face. Grins.

"Why? Did they talk to you too?" she asks, feigning wide-eyed innocence like it's a game. Like she didn't just tip over my entire life with a flick of her tongue.

I stare at her.

She's too calm.

Too floaty.

Like she believes if she keeps the tone light enough, the truth won't stick.

She bumps my shoulder.

"Don't look at me like that. I didn't say anything. They probably just... found your name somewhere, I don't know. People talk. I mean, we've been seen together, right? You were with Emma. At Glasslands, weren't you?"

That name.

Like she's putting her cigarette out between my ribs.

She keeps talking. Too fast now, laughing too much.

"God, remember those double stacks? You were such a mess. I told you not to mix it with vodka. You probably don't even remember half of it."

She giggles again. Leans her head on my shoulder like this is just girl talk.

"I mean... what even happened to Emma?" she says, syrupy-sweet. "It's not like she was anyone's best friend."

My jaw tightens. My cigarette's burned down to the filter. I don't speak. I just smile.

Let her hear the ice cracking under us.

Her words smear into static, buzzing in my skull.

I sip the clove-flavored smoke like it's champagne.

And in my mind, I'm grabbing her hair.

Stuffing her face into the fire pit. Holding it down as her skin peels, blackens, screams.

But she can't scream. Not really.

The smoke's choking her. The shock's too strong.

I could slice her open right here. On this rooftop. Lay her guts across the dead plants like a garland. Make her into something beautiful. Finally.

Maybe I'd keep her lips. Just the lips. Sew them shut so she can't tell another story.

Or keep her throat. Press it to my ear like a conch shell.

Let it whisper: "*I didn't mean it.*"

She laughs again. A cat in heat. Whining. Howling. Too loud. Too desperate.

I smile at her. I think I'm smiling.

Then the rooftop door swings open.

Mr. Wall Street steps through, bottle in one hand, crystal glasses clinking in the other.

His smile is wide, bright. Too bright for this hour.

"God, it's cold," he says, setting the glasses down. "But you two—"

His gaze lands on me. Pauses.

"—look like you've warmed up fine."

I blink.

Tinsel's jawless face is still flickering behind my eyes like a film reel catching fire.

"Perfect timing," I purr, mask sliding back into place. "We were just catching up."

Tinsel giggles, reaching for the bottle like nothing happened.

And I let her.

Wall Street pours. I raise my glass.

"To the twisted little stories we tell ourselves just to make the world feel softer. Just to make people stay a little longer."

He smirks, that polished Wall Street smirk, and downs his glass.

Tinsel giggles, clueless, and follows suit.

I watch her mouth curl around the rim, those pretty lying lips swallowing bubbles like secrets.

I turn to him. "It's freezing. Let's go back inside."

What I mean is: *Just fucking save me already.*

What I mean is: *Save me from myself. Save me from her.*

The music is softer now. The crowd has thinned. Heels echo louder on the hardwood. Laughter has dulled into murmurs.

"I think I'm gonna head out," Tinsel announces, adjusting her glittering gold dress. Her cheeks are flushed. Her pupils still huge from the coke, but her voice is steady.

I blink. "You sure?"

She shrugs, nonchalant. "Yeah. Early class tomorrow. And—" she leans in, conspiratorial, "you two look like you could use some alone time."

I force a smile. She doesn't need to make pretend excuses to leave, but whatever.

"Let me walk you out."

Outside, the air slices clean through my skin. We linger at the curb, steam rising from our breath.

Tinsel rubs my arms like we're still friends. "Tonight was fun."

I nod. "Totally."

A beat of silence. Her eyes flicker. I wonder if she's remembering the rooftop. The cops. Emma's name falling from her mouth like it didn't cost anything.

"Text me tomorrow," she says, already stepping back. "Love you, sweetbum."

I watch her disappear into the dark, her gold dress catching the last flickers of streetlight. I can't believe she didn't bother to wear a jacket. What's that about?

The cold creeps in slower now. Like it's coming from inside.

I should feel better. She's gone. The threat has left the building. But I don't feel better.

I feel like she took something with her.

Bringing her tonight was a mistake. Not because she embarrassed me. Not because she laughed too loud or sparkled too hard. But because I saw it. Him looking at her. The way his eyes lingered, even if just for a second. The way her fingers brushed his chest. Like I'd invited the demise of my own relationship and served it up on a gold sequin platter.

I hate that they were in the same room. Breathing the same air. Drinking from the same glass. I hate that she knew it would fuck with me and did it anyway, grinning the whole time.

She calls me secretive, but she's the one who dropped my name to the cops and acted like it was nothing. Like it was a misplaced coffee order.

Emma's name didn't belong in her mouth. Not with that tone. Not with that lie. She pretends she forgot. I don't believe her.

I never did.

And yet...some twisted, raw part of me is glad she came. Because for one tiny moment, we were close again. For one moment, I felt her choose me. But Tinsel always leaves.

And she always leaves me with the mess. I wrap Wall Street's blazer tighter around myself.

The hem still smells like his cologne—oud and something darker.

I'm not ready to go back inside, but I do. I step back over the threshold. And I start looking for him.

The hallway off the kitchen is half-lit and lined with empty wine crates and framed bullshit—artsy prints of horses and women's backs.

I should turn around. But something draws me forward. A sound. A breath. A door cracked open. The glow of a red bulb leaking through.

I push it.

It creaks.

Music pulses faintly through the floor.

I walk into the basement.

At the bottom there's a black metal bed with a cage underneath. Two of the girls I saw earlier are inside, one gagged, the other biting and pulling on her own nipples.

On the mattress, men surround it pissing, jacking off onto a brunette with a pixie cut. She's on all fours, mouth open, lapping up the fluids. Bruises flourish along her arms. Her legs and ass look cut up. Scarred. Her eyes are glassy. Her expression, vacant.

My breath catches. "Fuck."

I stumble backward, the door swinging shut with a sickening thud. I'm halfway up the stairs before I even hear my feet.

The music upstairs has thinned to Crystalize by The XX. Low. Slippery.

The crowd is lighter now. Quieter. Hungover in advance.

I spot Wall Street across the room, just past the bar, half-silhouetted in gold light, deep in conversation. The two men from earlier flank him. Sharp suits. Sharp smiles. They're close, shoulders tucked in, voices low.

I can't hear what they're saying, but their faces are wrong.

Too still. Too serious. Wall Street runs a hand down his face. Not like he's tired. Like he's cornered. I freeze in the hallway's shadow, heart rattling. He's not performing anymore. Not for me. Not for them.

He looks like a man calculating risk. One of them nods toward the door. Wall Street glances around. His eyes brush over mine. He sees me. His face flickers. Guilt? Concern? Something else? He breaks away from them. Crosses the room. Not hurried. Not casual. Controlled.

"Hey," he says gently, palm brushing my back. "Did Tinsel head out?"

"Yeah. But there's these girls," I whisper. "In the basement. I think they're—its like pretty scary, even by my standards."

He cuts me off, firm but soft. "I know. You shouldn't' have gone down there."

He looks past me towards the stairs. "I think it's time to leave."

He *Knows*.

It coils in my gut like a wire tightening.

I nod. But my mind is turning over the implications.

He knows.

And he didn't stop it. Didn't even flinch.

He brought me here. *These* are his people.

This isn't just a crack in his mask.

This is a whole second face.

And I want it ripped off. And eat it like thinly cut prosciutto on rosemary focaccia slices.

I give him his blazer back. He helps me onto my black wool coat, buttoning the front and kissing my forehead. "You were amazing tonight, dove." I allow myself to melt just a little. Somewhere in the depth of my intestines I know our days are numbered.

The car glides through Manhattan like it's skating over glass. Mr. Wall Street's hand rests on my thigh, gentle, familiar, but my skin crawls beneath it. He's humming. Some low R&B song from the late 90s. The kind of song men like to fuck to because they think it's romantic.

Like nothing happened.

Like he didn't look me dead in the eye and say: *I know.*

I stare out the window. The buildings warp. Streetlights stretch into halos, and the shadows between them are bloated with the stench of skank and regret. I imagine the girl in the basement is still there. On her knees. The cage clanking shut again.

"You were perfect tonight," he says, squeezing my leg. "Every guy in that room wanted to fuck you. But you were mine."

Mine.

Mine.

Mine.

His praise slides over me like oil over raw meat.

Back at the apartment, he unbuttons my coat with deliberate slowness. His lips graze my collarbone. Gently. So, so gently.

"You have no idea what you do to me."

He pushes the coat from my shoulders, lets it puddle to the floor. His hands roam like he's checking for damage—thumbs pressing gently into my hips, the bruises beneath my ribs.

He's reclaiming me.

And I let him.

Because if he's touching me, maybe he's not thinking about the girl on her knees.

Because if he's inside me, maybe he won't notice the rot curling behind my eyes.

This is how he reclaims his peace. This is how he compartmentalizes.

The bedroom is dim. Soft amber light. The R&B rhythm still twisting its way through my neurons into my brain stem. His mouth finds mine, greedy, worshipping, like he's trying to exorcise something through my tongue.

I taste power.

And rot.

He strips slowly, savoring it. Then slides my dress over my head fluid, like spilled milk drenching to floor. I'm naked before I realize it.

"You're so fucking beautiful," he whispers. "So fucking good."

When he pushes inside me, something fractures.

His face changes.

Not once. Over and over.

Wall Street.

The man from the basement.

The suit who touched Tinsel.

Tinsel herself—mouth open, pupils blown, laughing as her skin melts.

I blink, but the images keep sliding. Like someone's shuffled a deck of faces and is slapping them down, one after the other.

He fucks me like he's trying to prove something.

I let him.

My nails drag down his back. I picture them carving through skin, hitting vertebrae. I wonder how deep I'd have to go to get to his real face.

Show me who you are.

"You like that?" he pants.

I nod, but I'm somewhere else. Somewhere lower. Beneath the mattress. Beneath the floorboards. My mind peels open.

I'm slicing his stomach. Scooping out the guts. Bathing in them.

I'm pushing my hand into his mouth, past the tongue, until I feel the scream rattle in his throat.

And still—he thrusts.

And still—I moan.

Because this is what love is, isn't it? Mouths full of blood and pleasure.

Fucking the thing you want to destroy, just to keep it closer.

After, we lie in silence.

His breath slows.

He's asleep.

His arm drapes across my waist like he owns me. Like I'm safe. Like he didn't bring me to a house where girls were used up like party favors and left in basements to rot.

I stare at the ceiling fan as it spins and spins—blades, ribs, knives. A carousel of masks and meat.

He let them have her.

And maybe I wasn't brave enough to speak up. Not then.

But I felt it. That need. Not to save her. Not really.

To *keep* her. Those eyes of glass. That vacant empty expression. Maybe it could be brought back to life if it was only cared for properly.

Carve a bit of her into my soul. Like I did with Emma. In someway, like I did with LAXative. Make her matter.

That's the difference. He looks at suffering and looks away. I want to crawl inside it and never leave. He'll never understand that. He'll never understand *me*. And I can't let someone hold me who doesn't know what's behind my eyes. That's the real problem with masks. Eventually, someone has to take them off.

And I want to be the one to do it.

Slowly.

Lovingly.

So I can keep his face forever.

November 11, 2013

It's 3:46 a.m. My throat still tastes like his spit and champagne. I can feel the coke dissolving down the back of my nasal cavity. I'll have a sore throat in the morning.

He's snoring beside me, soft and dumb, face slack with dreams, the mask half-fallen. I wonder what he's dreaming of. Stocks. Blood. My mouth.

I want to unzip him. I want to split the seam of his chest like a Brooks Brothers jacket and crawl inside. See if the pieces match the pitch.

Because something in him isn't right.

The face he wore tonight wasn't the one he used with me.

It wasn't the one that kissed my bruises.

It wasn't the one that said, I see you.

So where is that face?

Where does it go when the cold, hard, boys-club mask comes on?

He saw those girls.

236

Saw what those men were doing.

And all he said was, "I know."

Like he wasn't made of the same meat. Like one of those girls couldn't have been me.

Like he was the hunter, cheerfully dismembering the bear on YouTube.

I'd start with his face.

Not to destroy it. To find it.

Scrape off each layer, one by one.

Eyebrows. Eyelids. Cheek.

The lips peeled back like citrus rind.

I'll keep what's honest. Feed the rest to the drain.

I want to slit his stomach and pull out his intestines like a magician's ribbon trick.

Kiss each coil. Wrap them around my neck like pearls.

Chew the knots of bile and memory.

He told me I was his peace.

But peace doesn't wear masks.

Peace doesn't ignore rape dungeons in the basement while pouring you Veuve and brushing your spine like you're his fucking Persian cat.

I want to pry his ribs open to see if anything inside hasn't lied to me.

Shove my fingers into his pancreas.

Crack his sternum and suck out the marrow like soup.

I want to vomit into his mouth and kiss him so hard we fuse at the uvula.

Would he still call me beautiful with his tongue nailed to the ceiling?

Would he still reach for me if his arms were roasting in my oven?

I want to peel the skin off his face and wear it to bed.

Not out of hate, but out of need.

To be closer.

To understand.

To make him mine in a way no one else ever could.

I'll sew his eyelids open. Force him to watch me.

The real me.

The one who dreams of cracking heads like eggshells.

The one who cums hardest at the edge of a scream.

I'll fuck him while he bleeds.

I'll keep him on ice.

I'll whisper Tinsel's name into the wound.

I'll call it closure.

He let those girls rot.

But I'm not rotting. I'm flowering into something holy. And holy things demand sacrifice.

I know what I have to do now.

I'll turn him into a bouquet. Organs arranged like roses and foliage. And I'll bury my face in it and breathe.

27

THE SUN'S ALREADY SINKING. My blackout curtains turn it to twilight, but I can feel the heat pressing against the windows, a reminder that I slept through an entire day.

The bed's empty. Sheets cold.

He's gone.

Not just gone. Erased.

His jacket is folded on the chair. There's a neat roll of hundreds on the kitchen counter, tucked inside a paper bag of leftover macarons. Next to it, a fresh gram. No note. Not even a text.

My phone's in my hand like an extra appendage. I check Instagram. Tinsel posted a blurry picture from the party. Us on the billiards table, her laughing, me blurred in the background. Her caption: "gold & glitter & the girls that bite #UptownFeral"

She hasn't responded to my last three texts.

Jessie: *awake?*

Jessie: *luv catching up with you last night <3*

Jessie: *are you mad at me or something lol*

I stare at the screen like it might twitch. Nothing.

I scroll through her Instagram.

She's out again. Somewhere downtown. Laughter, cocktails, velvet booths, too many men in one frame. One of them has his arm slung around her shoulder. My vision blurs. I close the app.

I pace.

Circle the kitchen. Light a clove. Don't inhale. Put it out.

Wall Street doesn't do socials. Annoying. I check his texts.

Nothing since: "Sleep well, dove. You were fucking radiant tonight."

4:47 a.m.

I stare at the money again. The coke. The curated silence.

What is this?

A thank you?

A goodbye?

A payout?

I text him.

Jessie: *Everything ok?*

Jessie: *Miss You* 🥺

Jessie: *?*

I sit on the floor and claw through last night:

- Tinsel's face glowing in the streetlight.
- Wall Street's hand on her hip.
- The thing in the basement.
- His voice: "I know."
- The way he ran his hand down his face, talking to those men.

What am I supposed to believe?

I rub the sore spot behind my eyes. My nose still aches from the coke. My body's a split screen — tight and electric, numb and heavy.

The quiet scratches at me.

Pochemu stares from the windowsill, unblinking.

"I'm fine," I say out loud, just to hear it.

Then I'm crying.

Then I'm laughing.

Then I'm standing in front of the mirror, leftover mascara smeared, eyes wide, looking for the crack in my face. Trying to find which version of me survived the night.

Was it the one they smiled at?

The one they ignored?

The one still waiting to be chosen?

I don't know where I'm going. I just get dressed.

Short skirt. No bra. Smokey eyes. The girl in the mirror: wide-eyed, waxy, already dissociating. I take a bump off the corner of the bathroom sink. No dinner. My stomach's a garbage disposal. I leave the apartment like it's a murder scene. The street is too loud. Cabs scream by like dying animals. I don't check my phone. If I see Tinsel's Insta one more time, I'll throw myself under a Citi Bike.

First bar is dark, red-lit, half-full. I slide into a booth. A man buys me a drink without asking what I want. It's gin. I drink it. He talks too close. His voice buzzes like a mosquito in my ear.

He's not *him*. Not even close.

I laugh at something he says. It wasn't funny. I touch his thigh under the table. His pulse jumps. I ask if he wants to come outside with me. He follows like a puppy. Around the corner, I push him against the brick wall. Our mouths crash together. I picture his lips peeling off like wet scabs. He tastes like mouthwash and desperation.

"You're intense," he says, breathless.

"You're basic," I say back. Then I walk away.

Next bar. Next drink. Next mistake.

I'm slipping sideways through the night, untethered, unowned. Nobody knows me. Nobody can see me. I bump into a girl with black glitter lipstick who tells me I smell amazing. I almost kiss her.

At some point I end up in a bathroom stall, knees spread, panties pulled to the side, getting eaten out by a stranger. I get my period in his mouth. He tries to pull away at first, I push his head back down. He doesn't fight it. By the end his face is covered in blood. I tell him to clean up and walk away.

I stop in front of a glass storefront at 3:02 a.m., stare at my reflection. My pupils are blown. My lipstick is gone. I look like someone trying to crawl out of her own body.

He let them touch her.

He let them keep touching her.

And now he's gone. Silent.

What was I expecting?

I check my phone again. Still nothing. From either of them.

I start walking home barefoot, heels dangling from my fingers. I pass a closed deli. In the reflection of the window, I see something behind me. A flicker. A shadow. A version of me smiling too wide. Holding a knife behind her back.

I don't stop walking. I don't go home. I get on the train heading to Brooklyn. I get off at his stop. I walk to the cross streets. I sit in the shadows between two buildings across from his.

I wait.

I watch.

I don't remember closing my eyes.

I just remember the cold. The sharp, stomach-sickening kind that creeps under your coat and into your bones. When I open them again, it's still dark. Early. Or late. The kind of hour that doesn't belong to anyone sane.

There's a woman standing over me.

She's old.

Wool hat. Long coat. Face like a crumpled paper bag, softened with too much kindness or not enough sleep.

In her hand: a plastic bodega bag with two small bottles of water and a banana. The kind they give out at marathon finish lines.

"You okay, sweetheart?"

Her voice is soft. It has the wet warmth of oatmeal. Not prying. Not afraid. Just... there.

I blink up at her, dizzy. My legs are numb. There's a crust of vomit near my knee.

"I'm fine," I say, but my voice cracks on the F.

She kneels beside me anyway. Presses a water bottle into my hand.

"You looked cold," she says. "Didn't want to leave you like this. Lot of bad people out here."

She glances across the street.

"You've got blood on your thighs."

She dabs my face with a tissue, like she's done this before.

"They always do when they wake up in front of his house."

My stomach turns. "Who?"

The woman smiles. No teeth.

"You know who."

I follow her gaze to his apartment.

Dark windows. No light. No movement.

Just the long silence of a place that no longer wants you.

When I look back, she's already gone.

The tissue is clean.

My phone says 4:44 a.m.

But when I look back down, the banana and water have been placed gently beside me. No bag.

I sit there for another ten minutes. Maybe twenty. I sip the water. I don't touch the banana.

Then I flag a taxi home. My thighs ache. My shoes are gone. I don't remember taking them off.

In my pocket, my phone buzzes.

But when I check it —

Still nothing.

From either of them.

The apartment smells like Lysol and wine.

I don't remember cleaning.

I don't remember drinking.

But the sink is full of broken glass, and my toothbrush is floating in a mug of red.

I drop my keys too loudly. The sound ricochets off the walls like a gunshot.

I stand there in the dark, coat still on, purse still slung over one shoulder, like I'm waiting for someone to greet me.

No one does.

I turn on the light.

My reflection in the mirror startles me. Mascara crusted into spider legs. A faint trickle of blood down one shin. Lips bitten raw.

My phone buzzes in my coat pocket. For a second, my stomach lurches—Wall Street?

No.

Tinsel.

Tinsel: *Hey babe. Wanna come to this wild-ass performance thing to-night? Some art chick at Grace. She's supposed to strip and transform or whatever. Come be weird with me.*

I stare at it.

My fingers hover. I don't type anything.

Not right away.

I sit on the edge of the bathtub, lights off. I can still smell the cheap booze from last night. Still hear the old ladies voice replaying in my head, like a warning or a spell.

Jessie : *What time?*

Tinsel : *Show starts at 8. I'll save you a seat, sweetbum*

The air inside Grace Exhibition Space is hot, metallic, and filled with something that smells like incense and melted microphones. The space buzzes like a hive. Everyone looks like they've smoked something or swallowed something. Eyes too wide. Skin too open.

Tinsel's next to me, her fingers trailing my wrist like she's not sure if I'm real.

"You'll love this one," she whispers, her breath sticky with boxed wine.

I don't respond. I'm still trying to blink the morning fog out of my eyes. Still wondering if that old woman was ever really there.

The lights dim. Chatter dies. The room inhales.

Then—

Birdsong.

Branches creaking.

A growl so low and primal it feels like it crawled up from my womb.

A spotlight snaps on.

She's there.

Perched on a stool.

Long blonde hair glowing. Blue eyes like knives.

She's wrapped in a sheer red robe, and for a second, I wonder if it's wet. If it dripped its way in from some scene of carnage. Bloodwater. Wine. Amniotic fluid. Whatever.

Her voice is velvet and iron.

"There is a beast whose appearance resembles a fox…"

The story spills from her lips like prophecy.

Nine tails. Seduction.

Shapeshifting. A woman who isn't one.

A mask that wears masks.

I watch as she peels the blonde wig away, her face calm. Divine.

Then her skin shifts. Again.

Again.

Until the face staring back at us is a new woman entirely.

A Black woman with a perfect halo of hair. No pretense. No costume. Just her.

But even that—how do I know it's the final face?

I swallow hard. The air feels thick.

Tinsel squeezes my hand. "Isn't she fucking incredible?"

My skin itches. I can't answer. I can't breathe.

"In one hand, I hold a basket of gold coins…" the woman says.

"My other hand is empty. I will close my eyes. You may take a coin… or kiss my lips."

The lights flicker.

My brain does too.

We're outside, sitting on the curb. Tinsel lights a cigarette, legs crossed like a ballerina. Around us, the crowd trickles out—leather-clad hipsters and prairie girls with bird-skull earrings that swing like pendulums. Waves of mismatched boots and bad dye jobs blur past.

I stare into the night, still half-possessed by that performance. The woman peeling off her face. The voice. The mask beneath the mask.

"I think Wall Street's collecting girls," I say flatly.

Tinsel coughs on her first drag. "What?"

"I'm serious." I turn to her. "The party. That basement. Those girls. He saw it. He knew. And he just said we should leave. Like it was no big deal. Like it was part of the fucking aesthetic."

Tinsel shifts uncomfortably. "Okay, but maybe he was freaked out too? Maybe he didn't know what to do."

"No." I shake my head. "He brought me there. He knew the men. He knew the faces. He knew the rules. What if that's his role? What if that's his role? Not just a guest. A supplier."

She stares at me. "You think Mr. Wall Street is some kind of... what? Trafficker?"

"I think he wears a different face for every room he walks into."

She goes quiet.

"And where is he now?" I snap. "Why hasn't he called? Why ghost me unless there's something to hide?"

"I don't know, Raz. Maybe he's just busy. Or scared. Or, fuck, I don't know. Why are you even with him if you think he's that bad?"

I look down. My palms are damp. Sticky.

"Because I thought he saw me. The real me. And now I'm not even sure I've seen him."

She stares at me like I've become a character in a Russian novel: yearning, unraveling, already half-buried in the snow.

I open my mouth. My eyes search hers. "Tinsel... it's just so hard for me. People. Holding on to them. It's like they melt when I touch them." A breath. Another.

Her hand touches my back, light as lint. "I know. I do." Her voice is low now. Softer than I expect. "You feel things too much, sweetbum. Like... raw wires. And people can't always get that. That's not your fault."

It almost lands. Almost.

But then she laughs, too quick, too bright, like the silence scared her. "Besides, Wall Street's just another suit, right? You're not gonna marry him. You'll find someone else. Or no one. Who cares? You've always been fine on your own."

And just like that, I'm gone again. Floating outside my body.

My mouth pulls into a smile that doesn't touch my teeth.

"Yeah," I say. "Totally."

She exhales and takes another drag. She doesn't notice the way my spine stiffens. Doesn't feel me curling inward. Doesn't see the distance widen between us like a crack in the pavement.

Because that's the thing:

I don't want someone else.

I wanted *him*.

I wanted her.

I wanted someone to see *everything* and stay anyway.

But people always flinch. They see the first face and think it's the last.

The fox wears nine faces. The predator. The lover. The provider. The god. The mask doesn't lie. It just forgets to tell the whole truth.

And Wall Street? He wore a face that kissed my bruises and called me peace.

But at the party he wore something else.

Something too polished. Too clean. Too still.

So now I need to see what's under his skin. I need to know which face is his *final* one. If any.

Maybe there's nothing under there. Maybe he's hollow, a porcelain mask filled with teeth and spreadsheets. Maybe I'll dig into his chest and find nothing but smooth, cold glass.

But I have to look.

I *have* to.

Because I can't let another mask seduce me.

I can't love a lie.

And if he bleeds when I peel him open, then I'll know he was real.

At least for a moment.

November 12, 2013

It's been 48 hours since I've heard from him.

No text. No call. No ripple in the water.

I've reread our messages, studied the curve of his last punctuation mark like it could reveal a code. I haven't eaten. Except for the thought of him.

I keep picturing his face, soft with sleep, that little dimple that only shows when he's lying.

And I need to cut it off.

I need to slide a scalpel beneath the skin of his jaw and peel it away like wet silk.

I need to wear it, not like a trophy, but like a veil. Like a wedding dress stitched from cartilage and truth.

I need to kiss the place where his lips used to be.

Push my tongue into the wet hole where his throat once held his secrets.

I need to fuck the stump of his neck.

Ride his shoulders while his mouthless head stares up at me from the floor, that bloody O where a voice used to live.

I need to moan into that silence. Fill him with all the pieces of myself he didn't ask to see. I need to cum while staring into his open chest cavity, ribs splayed like bridal lace.

I need to pull his lungs out and dry them like flowers.

Chew his heart like it's Valentine chocolate. Swallow him until there's nothing left to ghost me.

God, he's so quiet now. So still. So mine.

I'd carve a ring out of his vertebrae.

Keep it on my finger.

I'd press my clit against his molars and beg him to bite down.

If I slice him just right, he'll never leave again. If I cut deep enough, I'll find the version of him that meant it. The one who said I was peace.

The one who brushed my hair behind my ear and told me I was real.

I'll bottle his spinal fluid. Dab it behind my ears like perfume.

I'll sleep inside the cradle of his pelvis. I'll call it home.

He let them keep touching her.

And now he's gone silent.

But I'm still here.

And silence has a taste.

And I'm starving.

28

I STOPPED SLEEPING. I've been masturbating to 1970s porn videos for hours now. The apartment reeks of raw meat. My clit is so swollen it's gone numb. I've gone numb. I open the window and let cold air flow in. I turn on the bath and run scolding hot water. Fill it with epsom salts and lavender oils. I lower myself in. I scrub. I scrub until my skin is red and raw. I exfoliate my face with a sea kelp scrub. And I just can't turn my brain off. He left. He disappeared. And those girls. If he lied about this, about them, about what he knew, then every kiss was false. Every touch rehearsed. And I don't just need to know who he really is. I need to know what he thinks I am. He brought me into a world where girls are props and pain is ambiance. And he watched me dance in it. So what does that make me? A decoy? An offering? Or just another toy?

I dry myself off. Pull on a black hoodie and yoga leggings. My body still steamed and twitching. I sit in the hammock chair and pull out my phone.

Scrolling.

Plastic smiles.

Bali honeymoons.

Pregnancy reveals.

Lip filler coupons.

And then—

Some smug man slicing toro like slow cooked tongue in a "5 Easy Steps to Perfect Sushi" video.

I watch it.

Then again.

Then again.

This is a skill worth learning.

I pull on my wool trench coat, my Doc Martens. I grab my purse and head out.

I walk to MTC Kitchen, the street too bright, the sidewalk too slick. I buy a Masamoto KS Yanagiba—the blade thin and terrifying, made for slicing fish so clean the muscle barely twitches.

A Shun Pro Deba for cracking through bone.

A Nakiri for vegetables, for precision, for the delicate dissection of beauty.

A copper-lined hangiri for cooling rice.

A Hinoki wood paddle—soft, warm, perfect for mixing without bruising.

Tweezers for bones.

Torch for caramelizing flesh.

All of it on Wall Street's black Amex.

Then to the market. I buy slabs of sushi-grade tuna, salmon belly, ikura, and uni. A fat bag of Tamanishiki rice. Sheets of nori that snap like brittle bones.

Three hours later, the kitchen looks like a surgical theater.

Knives lined up like scalpels. Blood-red tuna glistening under fluorescent light. Rice shaped with wet hands, sticky-like skin. My fingers tremble from the precision. I slice the salmon. Long, single strokes. Like peeling back skin. I torch the belly until the fat bubbles. The smell is orgasmic. I stuff rolls with cucumber and crab stick and sliced avocado that looks like wet spleens. I wipe the blade clean between each cut. I pretend it's his throat I'm practicing on.

Sushi stacks up. Dozens of pieces, untouched. I don't know who this is for. I don't know what I'm feeding. But I can't stop.

I don't eat at the table.

I eat on the floor. Cross-legged. Naked from the waist down. My hoodie hiked up around my ribs, breasts pressed against the cold tile.

The sushi is everywhere. Spread across cutting boards and baking trays and takeout lids. Nigiri like little bodies. Maki sliced into clean cross-sections like spinal cords. The salmon glistens like muscle. The tuna like raw lungs.

I pick up a piece of uni and let it melt on my tongue. It's creamy. Briny. Vile. Tastes like a secret someone died keeping. I chew slowly. Deliberately.

My mouth moves like I'm practicing a spell.

Every bite is a question.

What did you see in me?

What mask was I wearing?

What mask were *you*?

I eat the toro next. A perfect pink rectangle over a pillowy pad of rice. I stare at it. Then bite. It bleeds umami down my throat. It tastes like submission. Like being known. Like a lie I still want to believe. I keep eating.

One by one.

Each piece an altar.

Each swallow an incantation.

I imagine feeding it to him. Piece by piece. Him, tied to a chair, mouth slack. Me, kneeling in front of him, offering his own body carved into perfect bites.

"Open wide, baby," I whisper to no one. "Say ah."

My fingers are sticky with vinegar and fish oil. I suck them clean.

The room hums. The fish starts to sweat, stink. The rice hardens. My stomach turns, but I keep going.

This isn't food.

This is a séance.

I eat until I'm crying, and I don't know why. Until my jaw aches from chewing. Until I'm full but still starving.

Starving for his face.

Starving for his truth.

Starving for proof that what we had wasn't just another con in a better suit.

And then... My phone buzzes.

I freeze.

A piece of salmon slips from my hand and lands wetly on my thigh.

I reach for the phone with shaking fingers.

Wall Street: *Hey baby. Been slammed. Sorry I've been MIA. Can I see you tomorrow?*

Just that.

Casual.

Soft.

As if none of it happened.

As if he didn't vanish.

As if I didn't spend three days in mourning. Binging porn, blacking out, fantasizing about the sound his skull would make when it cracked open like a soft-boiled egg.

My thumbs hover.

I don't reply.

Not yet.

Not until I know which face he's wearing when he says that.

Not until I decide if I'm going to kiss him. Or peel him open and see what lies beneath his surface.

I set the phone down.

Face-up.

Face-down.

Face-up again.

The salmon slice is still on my thigh, curling slightly at the edges like it's trying to get away.

I don't move it. Let it cling there. Let it fester with me.

The screen dims.

I tap it awake.

Then leave it.

Then tap it again.

Forty-five minutes pass like a fever dream. I sit in the middle of the kitchen floor, surrounded by plates and rice smears and the glint of blades. His text glows like a soft blue lie.

My stomach cramps.

My mouth tastes like metal and soy sauce.

My thighs are sticky with salt and vinegar and fish oil.

I imagine him on the other end, waiting. Not sweating. Just... assuming. That I'll be grateful. That I'll come when called. And maybe I will. Eventually, I pick the phone back up.

Type one word.

Jessie: *Sure.*

Then I turn it face-down again. And eat the salmon off my leg like an animal.

29

THE APARTMENT SMELLS LIKE citrus cleaner and Febreze. I cleaned every inch until the grout squeaked. I lit candles. Styled my hair in loose waves framing my face.

I have no idea where Mr. Wall Street and I stand. By the time he does his three little knocks on the door, I've already applied a full face of makeup, my "innocent and a little unstable" look. Big eyes, flushed cheeks, glossed lips parted, like they're begging for you to put something between them. I open the door in one of his favorite looks: silk slip, no bra, floor-length cardigan I know he likes sliding off my shoulders.

He stands there, tall and still, like he's bracing for something.

"Hi," he says. Voice soft. Real.

I don't respond. I just walk backward, leave the door open, let him follow.

Inside, he closes the door gently, like the silence might break.

"You look…"

He trails off. Eyes roaming. "You look ravishing."

I just stare. Searching for a sign. Something that says he's real.

"I've missed you," he says, stepping closer. "It's been—"

"Three days," I interrupt. "Two and a half, if you're counting from when I fell asleep in your arms."

A flicker of something behind his eyes. Guilt? Strategy?

He places his hands on my waist. "I'm sorry. Things got complicated."

"What kind of complicated?" I ask. No flirt, no pout. Just flat. Sharp.

He doesn't answer at first, just brushes a thumb along my jaw. A distraction. A reroute.

"I had to deal with some people. I didn't want to drag you into it."

He says it like a line he's practiced before.

My eyes start to sting. "You left. You didn't even text."

I let him kiss my cheek. My jaw. My mouth. I taste his apology and decide to pretend I believe it.

He pulls back slightly, searching my face. "You okay?"

I nod, slow. "Now, maybe, I am." Then, quieter: "But I think we need a reset."

"A reset?"

I run my fingers along his waist band. "Somewhere else. Away from the noise."

He catches the signal. "Where do you want to go?"

"Carmel," I say. "My hometown. Upstate. You'll love it. It's quiet. Secluded. We can breathe."

"You sure?"

I nod. "I think we need somewhere the masks can come off."

He smiles. "Road trip?"

I nod. "This weekend."

He kisses me. Deeper this time. Hands tighter. Like I'm already his again.

30

THE HIGHWAY UNSPOOLS IN front of us like a vein. Asphalt shimmering in the late-autumn light, trees bare and clawing overhead. The world looks flayed. Honest. Like skin peeled back.

We're halfway to Carmel. I'm curled sideways in the passenger seat, legs folded, fingers absently tracing the seam of my thigh. Mr. Wall Street drives with one hand on the wheel, the other resting loosely on the gearshift. His sunglasses make him unreadable. I hate that.

"You've been quiet," he says.

I shrug. "Just thinking."

He glances over. "Dangerous."

"Sometimes," I smile. "Depends on what I'm thinking."

He chuckles, squeezes my knee. I let him.

The car hums. Our private capsule of curated music and stale air. His playlist, of course, some kind of moody electronica, the kind that sounds like a heartbeat slowed to half-speed.

"You know," I say casually, eyes on the road ahead, "I never really asked you… what you *do* all day."

He raises a brow. "What I *do?*"

"Yeah. You said you're on leave, but… you're always doing *something*. Meetings, calls, running off. You dress like you're still in the game. So, what's the game?"

A pause. Barely perceptible, but I feel it. Like a missed step on a staircase.

"Consulting," he says eventually. "Private equity stuff. Some clients still want my input."

"Ah," I say, dragging it out just a little. "So those guys at the party… they're clients?"

His jaw shifts.

"Some of them."

"The one with the silver tie? What's his deal?"

Another beat.

"He's… old school finance. Big money. Likes to throw his weight around. We've worked together. He's not important."

"I don't know," I say, tilting my head. "He seemed important enough to whisper with in a corner for half the night."

That earns me a look.

"You're sharp today."

I smile sweetly. "Always."

He exhales through his nose, turning his attention back to the road.

"I don't like everything that goes on at those parties," he says finally. "I've told them that."

"But you still go."

"I have to. Sometimes. For appearances."

"Right," I say. "Appearances."

We drive in silence for a minute. I watch a hawk drift overhead, then vanish behind the trees.

"Didn't you think some of those girls looked… young?"

He doesn't answer.

I look at him. "Like, *really* young."

"I didn't ask for IDs," he says flatly.

"Is that supposed to make it better?"

He sighs. "What do you want me to say, Jess? That I run background checks on everyone in the room? I didn't invite them. I didn't touch them. It wasn't *my* party."

"But you watched."

His grip tightens slightly on the steering wheel.

"I told you—I didn't like it."

"You didn't stop it."

His jaw clenches. The sunglasses stay on.

"You're asking a lot of questions."

I smile again. Slow. Gentle. The kind of smile you give right before brushing someone's hair back for a lobotomy.

Then, with a sigh:

"I just worry. I was worried when you disappeared for three days. I was worried when you looked so stressed at the party. We haven't been together very long, but it feels like you're part of me. Like our lives are starting to fuse."

He says nothing. The trees blur past the window. Still no turn of the head. Still staring at the road.

"I know we said no labels or whatever," I continue, my voice softening, "but I feel deeply about you."

A pause. I glance sideways at him. "I just want to know that's okay. That you're... who you seem to be."

The trees get taller. The roads narrow. We're almost there.

He reaches over and takes my hand. Squeezes.

"You can trust me."

I look out the window at the darkening woods.

And I wonder if he says that to all the girls.

We pull up to a dirt road and turn the car off in front of a two-story stone and wood cabin. It looks beautiful, in that haunted, Victorian ghost sort of way. The air smells different here. Older. Like it remembers things you've long forgotten. Parts of you that were buried deep.

"What do you think babe?"

"It's perfect. I love it." I say wrapping my arms around him.

We unload the car in near silence. The gravel crunches underfoot like bones. Inside, the place is warm and rustic, exposed beams, stone fireplace, soft couches in plaid flannel patterns. Mr. Wall Street sets down the bags and immediately moves to uncork the wine.

I trail my fingers along the edge of the mantle, pretending to admire the space, pretending I'm not still trying to peer through his face.

"Where did you find this place?" I ask softly.

"Airbnb," he calls from the kitchen. "I wanted something private. Quiet."

Mission accomplished. The silence here has teeth.

He starts laying out groceries on the counter: jasmine rice, thick yogurt, egg yolks, saffron threads, raw pistachios, frozen berries, slabs of butter wrapped in gold foil.

I hover. "What's all this?"

"I'm cooking something for you."

He smiles wide, boyish, almost bashful.

"Oh?" I laugh. "You *cook*?"

"Not much," he admits. "But it's called *Tah Chin*. My mom used to make it for me and my sister on snow days."

Pause.

Sister.

Another sliver of him I didn't know. A new ghost.

"And I didn't know you had a sister," I say, bumping my hip into his. "Teach me how to make it."

He lifts me by the waist and sets me on the counter. "Sit back and watch the master."

I smile. Because I'm supposed to.

Because this is what is supposed to make me happy: a weekend away, a man cooking dinner, a fire crackling, candles flickering, red wine breathing on the counter.

So why does it feel like I'm living someone else's fantasy?

Why does it feel like *he's* watching me too closely, like he's memorizing how to play me again?

I study him while he washes the rice, soaks the saffron, toasts the nuts. He moves with surprising ease, like he's done this a hundred times. He tells me little things: his sister lives in Chicago, his mother used to wear jasmine oil instead of perfume, he once broke his collarbone snowboarding in Vermont.

Every story feels like a patch sewn onto a coat I'm not allowed to wear.

"I like this version of you," I say.

He doesn't look up. "What version is that?"

"The one that's real."

He finally lifts his eyes, meets mine. "This *is* real."

I believe him.

Or I want to.

Or maybe I just want to believe in the possibility of him.

But something in me flinches, because *if* this is the real him, then the other version, the one who stood silently beside a basement full of drugged girls, *also* has to be real.

And I'm not sure which version wants to marry me.

And I'm not sure which one wants to fuck me.

And I'm terrified that I'll dream of killing them both and not wake up screaming this time.

I'm in my childhood kitchen.

My father is carving a turkey. But every slice bleeds. Thick, arterial spurts painting his cheeks, the cabinets, the white tile.

He keeps smiling. Keeps slicing.

In the corner, my childhood dogs are skinless and fucking, howling like they're in heat or in hell. Maybe both.

My mother rocks in her chair, knitting something long and red. She's whispering, not prayers, not lullabies. Just my name, over and over. Jessie. Jessie. Jessie.

I try to walk out, but my feet won't lift.

They're melting. Flesh bubbling, fusing to the linoleum. The floor drinks me like I'm soup.

Then I'm choking.

Something hard clinks against my tongue.

I spit into my hands: teeth.

My own.

They keep coming, forced out by something deeper. Sliding down my throat, sticking to the soft walls inside like my esophagus is lined with glue.

I look up.

My parents are laughing.

The dogs are laughing.

The turkey's laughing.

I wake up with a jolt.

Mr. Wall Street is in the bathroom, brushing his teeth.

"Morning, sunshine," he mumbles through the foam.

Like nothing ever happened. Like I'm not still choking on teeth.

I sit up slowly, still tasting enamel and blood. My skin feels too tight. The sheets are tangled between my legs like restraints.

Mr. Wall Street leans in the bathroom doorway, toothbrush in hand, watching me through the mirror.

"You looked like you were fighting off demons," he says with a soft laugh. "You okay?"

I run a hand through my hair. "Just a dream."

"Want to talk about it?"

"No," I say, maybe too fast. Then softer: "I don't even think I could."

He nods like he understands. But how could he? He doesn't know what it's like to wake up choking on your own teeth.

He spits into the sink and rinses. "Come on. I made coffee. Thought we could hike a little. Air might do us good."

Us.

I stare at the way the sunlight hits the hardwood, slicing the room into pieces. I feel like I should say something. Ask him again what he does, where he goes when he disappears, but the words get stuck. Still clotted with teeth.

Instead, I nod. "Yeah. A hike sounds good."

He tosses me his sweatshirt. It smells like him, like cedar, like skin, like the memory of safety.

I pull it over my head.

And for a moment, I pretend I'm just a girl in the woods with a boy and no reason to be afraid.

The trail winds through the trees like something half-remembered. It's familiar and wrong all at once. Dry leaves crackle underfoot. Branches arch overhead like bones, the sun cutting through in long, golden spears.

Mr. Wall Street walks ahead, carrying a thermos of coffee and granola bars. I let him lead. Let him feel in charge.

He talks as we move. Something about a hike in college. Bears. Bad weed. A girl named Lauren who cried when the tent collapsed. I nod when I'm supposed to. Laugh once or twice. But his voice barely reaches me. It hovers on the edge of my hearing, muffled and far away, like I'm behind glass.

I watch the way his back moves. The easy confidence of it. Like he's always belonged out here. Like he knows he won't be followed, or caught, or punished. He's checking his trail app. Before we left, he downloaded the offline map.

My hands twitch inside my sleeves.

"How far are we going?" I ask.

"Just a mile or two," he says, turning to flash a smile. "There's a stream I want you to see. Looks like something out of a painting."

I nod. "Peaceful," I recite, though the word tastes like rot.

Peace is a lie men tell you when they want you pliable.

We reach a clearing. Light spills across it like melted gold. In the distance, the stream gurgles faintly, just as he said it would. He drops the thermos on a rock and turns to me, arms wide, like a magician unveiling his trick.

"Well?" he asks. "Was I right?"

"It's beautiful," I say. And it is.

But all I can think about is how quiet it is. How easy it would be. One push. One rock. One scream swallowed by the trees. The thought comes fast and uninvited.

I press my lips together.

He sits on the rock, opens the thermos, pours two cups. Hands me one. His fingers brush mine and linger. Warm. Familiar. But I flinch anyway.

He doesn't react. Just sips his coffee and stares out at the stream.

"I'm really glad we came," he says.

I study the sharp line of his jaw. The slope of his nose.

I imagine slicing it open. Peeling back the skin like citrus. Would it be soft beneath? Or armored?

His eyes flick to mine.

"What?"

"Nothing," I lie, smiling. "I'm just... glad too."

He nods. "You seem quieter today. Calmer."

I sip my coffee and taste lavender and bile. "Maybe I am."

But the calm is a mask. A borrowed face. One I've learned to wear.

Underneath, the noise is still screaming. And I think—I think—I'm ready to listen to it.

As we make our way back down the trail, the woods begin to shift. The trees lean closer. Their branches twitch. Chipmunks with infant skulls blink at me from the canopy. Squirrels sport long witch noses and lipless grins. The skinless dogs from last night's dream skitter just beyond the corner of my vision, humping and howling with wet, meaty sounds.

266

There's a low static hum behind my eyes. A warm trickle starts in my nose, blood or brain fluid, I can't tell. I breathe in the forest air like it's medicine. Tell myself this will pass. That it always does. That it has to.

"That was fun," I say brightly as I kick off my boots by the door. "Freezing, but fun. Let's not go anywhere else the rest of the weekend. Just get drunk, get naked, keep the fire going."

He grins and grabs my hips, pulling me against him. "How do you always have the best ideas?"

His hands slide up my sides—cold, steady—and then something's wrong. His fingers feel longer than they should. Stretching. Wrapping. Restraining. Like wire.

I gasp. Pull back. The breath sticks in my throat like a scream.

He tilts his head at me, amused. Maybe concerned. Or maybe recalibrating.

"I'll make us some New York Sours," he says, already walking toward the kitchen.

I force a laugh. "Perfect."

And I follow, smiling like I didn't just feel his fingers morph into grotesque tentacles.

In the kitchen, he's calm. Measured. He reaches for the bottle of bourbon, uncorks it, pours with practiced ease. His hands are steady. Too steady.

"Egg white," he mutters to himself. "Bit of lemon. That's the trick."

I lean against the counter, studying his profile like I'm waiting for it to glitch.

"You're good at this," I say, tone light.

He smiles. "What, cocktails?"

"No," I say. "Being domestic."

He laughs. Just a quick exhale through his nose. Then keeps mixing. I don't laugh.

"I used to hear this story," I go on, voice softer now, curling like smoke. "From a friend's mom, growing up. About how the woods, the really old ones? They peel your skin back. Not literally, though sometimes that too. But spiritually. Psychologically. She said the trees remember who you were before you learned how to lie."

He glances at me now, one brow raised. "Sounds spooky."

"She said people who come upstate think they're getting away from the city. From their stress. But really…" I trail my finger along the counter. "The trees are watching. Waiting. And when it's quiet enough, they make you show your *real* face."

He finishes shaking the cocktail, pours it over ice. The foam is perfect. He adds a red wine float with a flourish.

"Good thing I'm not hiding anything," he says, handing me the glass.

The color is gorgeous, deep red swirling into gold. A drink that looks like blood mixing with sunset.

I take it. Sip. The foam tickles the roof of my mouth. The bourbon burns.

I stare at him over the rim.

"Of course not."

He looks back. Smile still in place. But his knuckles are pale on the shaker.

The fire crackles in the other room.

He lifts his own glass. "To us," he says.

I clink mine against his.

"To what's underneath," I reply.

We drink.

And I wait to see what the trees will bring out of him.

The living room is warm now, heavy with woodsmoke and citrus and bourbon. Mr. Wall Street hands me the fourth cocktail, garnished with a lemon twist, grinning like the wolf who just ate Red.

"To cabin weekends," he says, raising his glass. "And the gorgeous woman who makes every moment an adventure."

I clink my glass against his. Sip. Sweet. Sharp. The red wine floats on top like a blood clot.

We move to the couch. He pulls me onto his lap. The fire flickers against the glass of the windows, our reflections shifting like smoke behind us. I straddle him, drink still in hand.

"You really do look incredible tonight," he murmurs, fingers tracing the hem of my silk slip. "So soft. So feminine. Women don't make time for that anymore."

I blink. "What?"

He laughs, shrugs. "I mean, not in a bad way. Just, it's nice. I miss when women weren't so obsessed with being… men, you know?"

My body goes still. The back of my throat tastes like ash.

He keeps going. "I like the dynamic we have. You're a throwback, babe. A real woman. Soft. Intuitive. Wild under control."

I stare at him. The words land wet and heavy, like raw meat slapped on tile.

He takes another sip, drunker now, smirking. "Don't look at me like that. You're special. You know how to play your role."

My pulse skitters. The shadows on the ceiling twist. The fire seems to crack open. The beams of the cabin bow inward, the house breathing like a lung full of rot.

My drink slips from my hand and lands on the rug with a muffled thud. Red bleeds into the wool.

He doesn't notice. He's talking about women again. Exes. Coworkers. The girl in HR who "cried assault because I complimented her dress."

The room swims. His face flickers to flesh melting into latex, his jaw elongating like it did at the party. His eyes stretch wider, glossier, shark-like.

"You okay?" he slurs.

I kiss him to shut him up. Our mouths collide. I pull his shirt off, straddle him harder, push his shoulders back until the couch creaks. He gasps, hard, responsive. Obedient.

But it's not about that anymore. It's about the voice inside me whispering, *"Take him apart. Find the truth. Skin is just a blanket. Remove it, put it back on again. It will be fine. And then you'll know. You'll know. You'll know his truth."*

He tries to pull me closer. His hand slides under my slip.

I see the hand as it is now: gloved in blood, soaked in perfume and liar's sweat.

The room fills with noise. Static, breathing, muffled crying. Somewhere in the walls, something is chewing. Gnawing. Moaning.

I flip us, shove him onto his back. He laughs. "Damn. You're getting wild on me."

I reach for the fire poker near the hearth. Just to steady myself.

He doesn't see it.

His head tilts. "You're not mad, are you?"

I smile down at him. Too wide. Too still.

"Not mad," I whisper. No madder than usual I think. I kiss him hard, biting his lip and release just before tasting blood.

Tap. Tap. Jingle. Jangle. Jingle Jangle.

I look up. Something moves just behind him. In the window.

A figure.

Blink.

Gone.

I freeze.

A girl. Maybe twelve. Maybe seventeen. Pale and slick with sweat. Her hair clings to her face like seaweed. She's standing just outside the window. Watching. Nodding. Mouth open. No sound.

Blink.

Gone.

I grip the edge of the coffee table. Hard. The room swims. The candlelight crackles too loud, too sharp. Copper rises in my throat.

"What's wrong?" he asks, voice sticky-sweet, still lounging like this is any other evening.

Like I haven't been unraveling by the second.

"Nothing," I say, blinking hard.

My throat is tight. My smile returns, brittle, trembling at the edges.

"I just thought I saw…"

I don't finish the sentence.

Because I know what I saw.

Or maybe I don't.

Either way, she's gone.

And he's still here. Still sipping his drink. Still wearing that face.

His eyes scan mine, pupils tight. Pinning me in place.

"What did you see?" he asks again. Sharper. Controlled.

I glance at the window. "Thought I saw a girl. But… it was probably just a shadow."

He sets his glass down. Stands.

"I'll check. I don't need any townies fucking with my car."

He's halfway to the door before I can move.

My legs don't feel like legs. Just bone straws shoved into meat.

I walk to the kitchen.

Open the drawer.

The Masamoto knife. The one for filleting skin from fish.

The one I packed, just in case we wanted to make sushi.

He disappears around the corner.

Silence.

Then:

Footsteps.

Jingle. Jangle. Jingle. Jangle.

What is that sound?

My breath stalls. That sound again. The one from…No. *Keys? Bells? Bone?*

The static behind my eyes flares. I catch my reflection in the dark microwave glass.

But it's not me. Not anymore. It's something ancient. Hungry. Wearing my skin. I see the fur. The fangs trying to break through. My nose elongates into a snout—just for a second—then snaps back. Human again. Almost.

The door creaks open.

He steps back in, brushing snow from his sleeves, muttering something about branches.

Then he sees me.

Knife in hand. Barefoot on the tile.

His smile flickers.

"Babe?"

I don't answer.

I don't blink.

I take one step forward as he takes one step in.

And he walks into my knife.

At first, it's like he doesn't even register it. Just a widening of the eyes. A small, startled gasp, like he stubbed his toe.

Then his mouth twists. Not in pain. In *betrayal*.

"You" he croaks.

I step back. The blade still inside him. His hands press against the wound, wet and red and bubbling. For a moment, we just stare at each other. His pupils blown wide. His lips moving like he's trying to say *my name*.

Then something changes. The fear drains. His face hardens. He lunges.

We crash to the floor, and suddenly I'm flat on my back, wind knocked from my lungs, his full weight crushing down on top of me. The knife handle juts grotesquely from his abdomen, glinting in the firelight like a Christmas ornament.

"You fucking—" he snarls, smashing the side of my head against the wood floor. Stars explode behind my eyes. He does it again. My ears ring. My vision whites out at the edges.

His hands wrap around my throat. Thick. Tight. No hesitation now. No mask.

Just the predator.

I claw at him, fingers slipping in blood. I buck my hips, scratch his cheek, slam my knee into his balls. Nothing works.

His grip tightens. My brain starts to buzz. A high, glassy sound fills my skull.

This is how girls die. With their heads next to fireplaces and men's names still in their mouths.

But not me. I live.

My hand flails, finds the hilt.

And with everything I have left, I *pull* the knife from his gut. Hot blood sprays across my face like a blessing. And then I jam it *up*.

Right under his chin.

The blade slides through soft palate, through tongue, through bone, until it hits brain.

His eyes roll back. His mouth opens in a final gurgle of metal and spit and meat.

And then he goes slack.

His body slumps onto mine, warm and steaming.

We stay like that for a moment.

A lover's embrace.

His blood pools beneath us, soaking the rug. My fingers twitch. My throat burns. My mouth tastes like pencil lead and something else, something *alive*.

I turn my head and whisper: "Now I see you."

My head falls back. My eyes close. Memory slams into me like a strong salty wave. Emma on the stage, her curls soaked in blood. LAX-ative in the penthouse, laughing as he passed me the champagne. Tinsel, sweet, sticky Tinsel, hugging me like she could keep me whole. Like I was hers. My eyes open. The world is still. I breathe. Slow. Heavy. Sweet with copper. I push up from the floor, dragging myself out from beneath his slack, still-warm weight. I flip him over, careful. Reverent. The cabin is silent. No whisper in the walls. No movement beyond the glass. Just me and him. How it was always meant to be. Nothing can interrupt us now.

I lift his arm first.

It's heavy. Limp. Already cooling. I kiss his wrist, trace the vein with my tongue. Then I take the knife and open him again, deeper this time. Not to kill, no, that part's done. This is about revealing him. About creating, carving, an honest and true relationship. This is how we will be together forever. In complete harmony.

His shirt's already soaked, so I slice through it without care. Peel it back from his skin like wet wallpaper. His torso gleams—blood-slick, muscle twitching in post-mortem pulses.

"Let's see what you were hiding," I murmur, parting the wound I left behind like an invitation.

I slide both hands inside him—slow, gentle—tearing upward through his belly like I'm unwrapping a gift meant only for me. The heat of him wraps around my wrists, thick and wet. His insides suck at my fingers as I move through the slick, red pulp of him.

He's so much softer than the ground beef I used to knead one-hand-ed, my vibrator buzzing between my thighs like a trapped bee.

But this? This is real. This is warm.

Now I have you, I think, pressing deeper into the muscle and meat. I'll never need that silly little rabbit again.

I feel my pussy getting wet. His stomach is like a warm feather-down pillow. I lay my face on it just for a moment before finally arriving at his chest.

I cut with the Japanese sushi knife ever so gently. I don't want to make this hurt more than it has to. The skin is thinner than I expected. It peels off like an orange rind.

The ribs crack apart, soft and wet, like crab legs. The heart is right there. Still faintly quivering. I scoop it out and hold it to my cheek. Warm. Beating for me, still.

"I knew it," I whisper. "You *did* love me."

I slide his heart between my legs and press down, grinding against it slowly. My thighs shiver. My eyes flutter shut. *This is what it means to be known.*

Then I make my way lower. His cock is half-hard in death. Waiting. Ready for me. So sweet. I stroke it once, like saying goodbye. Then I slit it open from tip to root making two neat halves. It radiates in my palm like a disobedient tongue. I fill it with stones from the windowsill plant. Smooth river rocks.

"Let me make you *perfect*," I whisper, as I stuff each one into the carved-open shaft.

Plop. Plop. Plop.

I take the stapler from the kitchen draw. It's white, clean, cool metal. Sterile. I kneel beside him, fold the skin back, and staple it shut.

Once.

Twice.

Five times.

There. Now you'll always be hard. Always ready. Always waiting for me.

I climb back on top of him. Blood smears across my skin like perfume. I grind against him, panting, riding his dead body with slow, holy thrusts.

His organs slosh under me. His body opens like a mouth. My climax breaks over me in waves. Sharp and endless and high-pitched, like screaming into a teacup.

I bite his neck, hard. I want to wear him like a coat. My hands shake. My face aches from smiling. I roll off for a moment. Touch his face gently and kiss his lips.

"Oh, baby. You were so good. That was just heavenly."

I splash water on my face before making my way to the garage.

Like every house in upstate New York, the garage is filled with rusted tools and inherited violence. I load the wheelbarrow like I'm preparing for garden club with the ladies.

I go back inside to begin the process.

His stomach opens like a curtain. Guts spill onto the floor in a rush of warmth. I scoop them up, kiss them, rearrange them like ribbons on a gift. His intestines I loop around my shoulders like a boa. The liver I press to my lips like a wine glass before taking a deep, reverent bite. I barely chew, letting the slick organ slide down my throat like it *wants* to be devoured. The lungs I lay side by side, gently, like slippers waiting by a bed.

He's beautiful.

His arms are next. I dislocate them at the shoulders, slice through tendon and joint. One pops free with a wet sound. I cradle it, kiss each fingertip, suck one into my mouth like a lollipop.

Then the legs. I saw through the thigh, the femur cracking beneath me like a snapped branch. I let out a long, low moan. It sounds almost animal. I don't recognize it at first.

The face is last.

I take the knife and trace a soft circle around his scalp. The skin pulls away in my hands, delicate and greasy. I lift it like a mask and press it against my own. It sticks, warm and wet.

I stare into his eyes. They've gone gray.

"To see what was ever real," I whisper, echoing the voice inside me.

I take his face in both hands and kiss it. Long. Deep. Tongue slipping between his slack lips.

And then I slide the knife into his mouth and carve upward, through the palate, through the nose, until I reach the forehead. His skull opens with a crunch, like splitting a melon. I scoop out the brain in handfuls and smear them across my chest like lotion.

I don't know if I'm laughing or sobbing.

I reach down between my legs and finger myself with one bloody hand.

"I love you," I gasp. "I love you so fucking much."

The moonlight streams through the window. I swear I can see Tinsel's silhouette out there, watching. Approving. Her smile soft and wide, like she finally understands me.

And I do this for her.

For love.

For the girl who never said my name like she meant it.

I lie back in the blood. Spread my limbs wide. Let his heart rest on my belly like a baby bird. I am soaked, shivering, radiant.

There's no music. No sirens. No voices in the walls.

Just silence.

And finally, I am full.

31

COFFEE TASTES BETTER WITH blood under your fingernails. I sit at the little pine table in the cabin, naked except for the intestines looped around my neck like pearls.

Outside, birds chirp in chaotic harmony. They know. They saw. And they sing for me.

The world has never made more sense. Sunlight dapples across the kitchen tiles. The breeze smells like rust and rot and pine needles. I feel clean.

He lies in the tub now, or parts of him do. I washed his face. Brushed his teeth. Arranged what was left of his body into a pose that says "peaceful" or maybe "finally."

I even lit a candle on the windowsill and whispered his name three times.

That part felt important. Like a rite. I'm not pretending anymore.

No more makeup.

No more nice voice.

No more smiles that stretch too wide.

No more pretending to be the kind of girl who doesn't think about skinning someone while folding their laundry.

This is who I am. This is what I'm for.

I finally got what I want. Now he'll always be a part of me. He can never lie. Never leave.

The voice in the wall agrees with me now. It hums like a cello string beneath the drywall. I hum back.

"You look radiant," Tinsel says, swinging her legs from the countertop.

She's wearing the striped pajama set she borrowed from me last fall, the one I said she could keep. Capri Sun in hand. Strawberry Kiwi. Her hair is wet. I think she just took a bath with him. I smell rose and vanilla. They must've used my bubble bath.

I don't mind. Sharing is caring. It can be fun.

"You're late," I tell her, sipping my coffee.

She grins, fox-like. "Traffic."

I laugh. I laugh so hard I cry.

Then I get up. I have things to do. Preparation is everything. I need to get back to the city. Change my bed sheets. Cook us dinner. Her room has to be ready.

I promised her, didn't I? I told her she'd always have a home with me. And I meant it. I want everything perfect for her. Candles lit. The house smelling like caramelized onion and garlic. Floral bouquets arranged just so. I pluck a kidney from the fridge and press it to my cheek like a rosebud. Tonight will be beautiful.

Tinsel giggles and claps. "She's gonna be so happy."

"She has no idea," I whisper. She really doesn't.

The drive back to the city is soft and surreal, like sliding into a warm dream.

Tinsel rides shotgun. Legs tucked under her, sipping from a 99-cent can of Arizona iced tea. She's wearing sunglasses even though it's overcast.

"We should've brought the cat," she says. "She would've loved this road trip."

"I didn't want her near the cooler," I say.

She nods. Understands.

The red and white Igloo rattles in the trunk with every turn. Packed neatly with ice and what matters most—his heart, his lungs, his tongue, his liver, his kidneys, and of course, his skull.

The rest I left in bed. Tucked in. Cozy and warm in the rented cabin. No more spreadsheets, no more deadlines, no more finance stress. He can rest now.

I checked out properly. Took out the trash. Left the key on the counter. Folded the extra blanket and draped it over the back of the couch. Wrote a thank-you note to the Airbnb host in my neatest handwriting.

The trees blur into white ice and brown spikes. They're reaching, clawing. But for what? I don't know.

Tinsel sings along to a song that isn't playing. Her voice sounds like radio static. I smile. My hands are sticky on the steering wheel.

We pass a state trooper. He doesn't even glance at us. Tinsel blows him a kiss.

The highway purrs beneath us, endless and twisted. My mind drifts.

We're back in the dorms. September air seeps through the cracked window. I'm on the twin bed, legs dangling off the side, watching her paint her lips with stolen Chanel.

"You look like candy," I whisper.

She doesn't respond. She's humming. Light, airy, detached, until she turns, and her face has no eyes. Just two sockets pouring glitter and blood. Her smile stretches ear to ear.

"Will you help me kill him?" she asks.

Her voice isn't hers. It's the voice of the divine.

"Of course," I say. "You're the reason I exist."

I reach for the knife on the desk. It's already wet. It was always wet. It's been waiting for this moment since the beginning of time.

Copper floods my mouth. My saliva thickens, clings.

My bare feet work the pedals as the skyline begins to rise in the distance. Everything feels different. Slower. Prettier. The filth sparkles under the streetlights.

My building doesn't recognize me. The doorman watches like I'm someone new. Maybe I am. I nod, blood crusted behind my ears.

Upstairs, the apartment is quiet. My little empire. I run my hands across the kitchen counters. I whisper to the walls. "She's coming," I tell them. "We have to be ready."

I refill Pochemu's food and water. She rubs against my leg, purring, sweet, trusting.

I take out my phone and text Tinsel.

Jessie: *Hey lover. Just got back. Cooking dinner. Come over. Wine is flowing.*

Tinsel: *OMG Raz. You saved me. I'm starving!*

Jessie: *Give me two hours?*

Tinsel: *I'm there*

I smile. She always was easy to feed.

I empty the cooler, laying out my ingredients.

For the kidneys, I'll need flour, butter, onions, tomato paste, mustard, Worcestershire. Served over toasted French baguette. Something rustic. Something warm.

The lungs will be light—olive oil and oregano. Nothing fancy. Just honest.

The liver I'll do Italian-style: seared with garlic, thyme, and heavy cream. A rich, fatty bite.

The heart gets its own course. I'll soak it in Veuve Clicquot, then sauté it gently in butter and finish with a drizzle of dark cacao.

That one's for dessert.

I want her to taste him.

I want her to love him the way I did.

To take him in. Swallow him down.

To feel him settle inside her like a secret.

Then—maybe then—she'll finally understand me.

I finish cooking. Plate everything just so. I keep it warm in the oven while I shower.

I take the sugar scrub to my skin until it's raw, pink, and sensitive to touch. I brush my teeth until my gums bleed, spitting into the sink, watching the pink foam swirl down the drain.

I blow out my hair.

I don't bother with makeup. I want her to see me. All of me.

I wear a dark pink dress with an A-line skirt and a black cardigan with pearl buttons. Simple black stockings.

The dogs followed me from Carmel. Still skinless. Still rutting and writhing in the corners of rooms. Always at the edge of my vision. When I try to look for them, they vanish.

I take my time. She'll be late. She always is.

Love is accepting people. Not trying to change them. Keeping them exactly how they are, *forever*.

I hear a knock at the door.

The *jingle-jangle* of keys. Maybe the neighbors.

She's here.

It took a while, but love is patient.

I open it to a cloud of perfume and excuses. Her lip gloss is thick. Her dress is wrinkled. But she looks spectacular.

"Raz! This smells *insane*. Is that garlic?"

I nod. I don't look at the phone in her hand. Or the bags under her eyes. I pull out her chair. Pour the wine.

She sits. Sips. Scrolls. Laughs.

"Babe, when did you start eating meat? I thought you were like, fish-vegetarian or whatever?"

"I'm still pescatarian, mostly," I say. "But these were very special cuts. I wanted to try them. And share them. With someone special."

"Oh my god. You're *adorable*. I love it."

I watch as she puts bite after bite into her mouth. The juices from the organs ooze between her teeth. In, out, swallow.

Chills go up my spine.

I eat, too. It's delectable. With every bite, my brain floods with serration. I've never tasted anything so rich. So succulent. It melts on my tongue. I lick my lips. I'm thirsty for more.

I bring out the dessert course. A delicate medallion with strawberries on the side.

"Wow. Babes. What is *this*?" Tinsel asks, eyes wide.

"Oh, it's his heart," I say, sitting down and taking my first bite. I chase it with a berry.

She laughs, a little too loud. "Wait—what? I thought you said…"

"Yeah. It's Mr. Wall Street's heart. This whole meal's been farm to table. I procured and butchered everything myself. Thought it might be hard, but, no. Surprisingly easy."

She stares at me. The smile hasn't left her face, but it's starting to crack.

"What? You're kidding. What is it, Raz? Sheep? Pork?"

I look her in the eyes.

"It's him."

The shift is instant. Her face twists.

"You're *not* funny. This whole queen-of-darkness bit is getting *old*."

"It's not a joke."

I reach over and lift his skull from the hammock chair.

"This is his skull."

She jumps to her feet.

"What—the—FUCK?!"

Her hand trembles toward her phone. "I'm calling someone. I'm serious. Razor, I'm not fucking around."

"You said you'd never leave me," my voice cracks "You said you loved me."

"Jesus Christ, I was *joking!* We were *teenagers!*"

"You weren't joking. You just didn't think I was real. But I am. I want to show you."

She makes it halfway to the door before the wine hits. Her knees buckle. She grabs the wall.

"What did you…what the fuck did you put in the wine?"

"Just something to help you…help you stay. Be still."

"You're insane. You need *help*. You need…" She stumbles again. Her words slur.

"You always run when it gets real," I growl. "Even now. When I made it *perfect*."

"No! No, go away"

I catch her as she collapses. Her head slumps against my shoulder. I brush her hair back.

"Shhh. You just need to lie down, my love."

Her eyes roll. Her body folds. I carry her to the bed like a bride.

"There," I whisper. "Now you'll never leave me again."

I brush the hair from her face. She's still breathing. Heart pounding like a trapped animal.

"It's just enough to quiet the noise," I murmur. "You'll feel better soon."

I had crushed a bit, well, quite a bit, of Ambien into the wine. I need Tinsel to be still. Still enough to be preserved. She told me this is what she wanted. She said we'd be best friends forever.

This will be good. It's what's best for both of us.

I undress her gently. Wash her limbs. Slip her into the white nightgown I picked out special.

I lay out the tools. The towels. The mallet. The sterilized ice pick.

She moans softly. Eyes flutter.

"This will help you learn. To grow. To understand love," I whisper.

"I know staying still can be hard for you. But this…this will make it easier."

She doesn't answer. That's okay. Stillness is a form of consent.

I kiss her forehead.

Then I press the tip of the pick to the corner of her eye.

32

THE SURGERY WAS A success.

There was a moment, brief, violent, when her back arched, her eyes shot open, and her mouth let out a sound like boiling water. She seized once. Twice. Then stilled.

She breathes now in soft, even rhythms. Her pupils don't respond to light. She hasn't spoken in days.

But her body listens.

When I touch her, she shifts. A soft twitch. A subtle hum through the hips. When I whisper what I need into the hollow of her ear, I swear I hear her beg.

The skinless dogs come and go. They chase their tails, snarl at the walls, fuck each other senseless in the corners. Sometimes, when their panting gets loud enough, I see her smile.

I feed her slowly, spoon by spoon. Wipe her mouth. Hum her favorite songs.

She's so peaceful this way. So still. So close.

I cut her hair on Tuesdays. Just a few locks at a time. I braid them into bracelets, into rings, into little keepsakes I wear with pride.

Sometimes I slice small pieces of skin from her thighs or back, nothing she'll miss, and sear them in butter with rosemary. I chew slowly, reverently, swallowing her love into my body. Then I clean the wound. Apply ointment. Bandage her gently.

I dress her in silk slips and vintage perfume. Pose her in her favorite chair by the window. At night I tuck her into bed and curl beside her, my head on her shoulder, listening to the whisper of her breath.

People always said Tinsel wore a thousand masks. I don't have to peel any of them off. I know them all. And I love every single one.

She's exactly as I remember.

Exactly as she was meant to be.

Forever.

November 28, 2013

Tinsel stopped eating.

Her skin has gone waxy and slack, greying at the edges like an old peach. The sweet, sick smell thickens every day. Cloying, fermented, ripe. Her fingers have curled in on themselves like petals at dusk, black at the tips. Something writhes beneath her belly. Fat, pale maggots burrowing through what's left of her softness.

They're hungry, too.

I don't mind sharing.

This morning, I kissed her lips and one came away with mine. It stuck to my mouth like a communion wafer. I let it dissolve on my tongue.

She hasn't spoken in days. Not even in dreams.

But I carry her voice in my chest now. I know what she would say.

"Make me beautiful."

So I have.

I roasted her ribs with honey and sage. The marrow steamed through the cracks like candle wax. I served them beside mashed sweet potato and buttered corn, garnished with her fingernails, shaved into slivers like truffle.

I carved her thighs into medallions, pan-seared in duck fat with wild thyme. Her calves I confited in garlic and bay leaf, slow-cooked until the tendons melted.

Her scalp I flayed carefully. Laid it flat on parchment. Crisped it in the oven until it curled like autumn leaves. The smell was heavenly.

I set the table with our best dishes. Candles. A glass bowl of cranberry sauce. Her necklace made of teeth gleams beside the silver. I replaced the centerpiece with her head, nestled in rosemary and anise stars. Her smile is still there, frozen, bright. The skin tugged a little when I moved her jaw, but I fixed it with glue and a whisper. I feel so blessed to be spending Thanksgiving with her.

Now she'll live forever.

Inside me. Around me.

The life we always wanted. At last, fully ours.

Happy Thanksgiving, baby.

You're home.

EPILOGUE

THEY FOUND HER THREE days after Christmas.

The neighbors had complained about the smell. They said it was like a dead raccoon roasting in a light fixture. The building super knocked a few times, but no one answered. Eventually, he used the emergency key and let the cops in.

Inside, they found the walls painted with old blood. A bucket in the tub full of bones and skin. A table still set for two. Bowls, forks, wine glasses. Plates licked clean. A roasted hand half-wrapped in foil.

In the living room, a woman dressed in pink was curled beside her malnourished cat. The smell coming off her was enough to make the responding officer vomit into the stairwell. Her teeth were red. Her skin, sticky, stained with blood, bile, and whatever else had soaked into her.

On the table sat a human skull, later matched to the remains found by an Airbnb host in Carmel, New York.

They said they needed more hazmat suits than they used for Dahmer.

She didn't speak.

She just smiled.

And hummed.

ACKNOWLEDGEMENTS

First and foremost, I want to thank my husband, Nael, for his unflinching support and belief in me. His endless patience and his moral, financial, and emotional support made it possible for me to lock myself away for months at a time with only my laptop and too much coffee. This book would not exist without him.

To my editors: Joseph Nassise, who helped me shape the initial structure, and Ariell Cacciola, whose sharp eye and impossibly detailed notes pushed this novel to the next level—I am deeply grateful. Your guidance turned chaos into story.

To Christian Storm, thank you for giving *Hysterical* its beautiful skin, inside and out. Your cover and interior design captured the spirit of this book in ways I couldn't have dreamed.

And finally, to Amy, who kept my house from collapsing while I was barricaded in my writing cave, and to my cats, who patiently listened to every deranged plot debate.

I owe you all more than you know.

ABOUT THE AUTHOR

AMBER DEAN is originally from New York. She now lives in Abu Dhabi with her family and rescue animals. *Hysterical* is her first novel; her second is in progress.